THE COUNTERFEIT COURIER

THE COUNTERFEIT COURIER

JAMES C. SHEERS

CUTTING EDGE

ISBN-13: 978-1-962896-16-0

Published by
Cutting Edge Books
PO Box 8212
Calabasas, CA 91372
www.cuttingedgebooks.com

CHAPTER ONE

avid Black, Senior Attaché at the United States Embassy in
Paris, put his manicured hands into the pockets of his beautifully cut serge trousers, rocked back on the heels of his gleam-
ing black shoes, and said, "Good morning, Van Horn."

The man in the shabby topcoat nodded and said nothing.

It was nine o'clock on an autumn Tuesday morning. The two
men were standing in the high-ceilinged, stiffly furnished, sunlit salon of Black's apartment on the Cours Albert Premier. It
was an elegant room, formal and cold, and neither man made a
move toward sitting in any of its rigid Empire chairs. They stood
and considered one another in silence, like swordsmen in the
moments before combat.

They were wildly dissimilar men.

For someone whose work presumably called for the kind
of build and features that can lose themselves easily in a crowd,
Judson Charles Van Horn was an anomaly. He would have been
conspicuous anywhere except possibly in a gymnasium or a
police line-up. It wasn't so much his being six feet four inches
tall, with thick, square shoulders and a short neck and hands like
catchers' mitts on the ends of arms whose power visibly bulged
their sleeves. It certainly wasn't his clothes, though they had a
pronounced air of charity and hung on him as though he'd run
into them by accident in the dark. Chiefly it was his face that
made him hard to hide. His brow was fairly high under rough
dark hair, and it was a heavy brow, jutting out over his eyes so

1

that he seemed to be looking out at the world from deep inside his own head.

His eyebrows were one uninterrupted straight black line running across the shelf of his brow. The eyes themselves were wide apart, but narrow and green. Hard eyes. The eyes of a professional gambler who suspects every activity on earth except his own estimate of the odds.

What served Van Horn for a nose was a great beak, surprisingly lean and with delicate nostrils, but there was a queer twist in its bridge where it had been broken and badly set. He had shaved only three hours earlier, yet on his cheeks the stubble was already rich and blue. His jaw was wide, square, and sharply cleft at the chin. His mouth was wide, too, but the lips were, like the violated nose, well-modeled and delicate.

He was a noticeable person. As he stood looking calmly back at the man on the other side of the high room, he was an exaggeration of the world's idea of brute menace: powerful, intelligent, and pitiless.

David Black, gray-haired, immaculate, tall and lean, the very model of a modern minor diplomat, looked him up and down with watery blue eyes in a handsome bland face, and must have known better than to believe what he saw.

Black broke the silence, saying, "Hope you had a good trip." He didn't seem to expect a reply and none came. "You don't seem to of changed much," he went on. "It's six years, isn't it, since I saw you in Accra?" The lapse in grammar, like the twanging nasal voice, was shocking from so impeccable a man.

Van Horn shrugged and said nothing.

David Black said, "Let's see. You were recalled to Washington ten days ago. You flew in here this morning. You had time to find out how much trouble you're in. Right?" He looked up inquiringly.

"I know I'm in trouble," Van Horn said. His voice, a grating basso, rumbled through the room. It made Black's reedy Ohio tenor sound almost effeminate.

"Uh-huh. They tell you anything about it in Washington?"

"They asked me some questions. I answered them. That's all."

"Uh-huh. Left it for me to do the job. As usual." Another silence fell. David Black gazed down at his glossy shoe tips.

Van Horn's face took on a set look. Ropes of muscle bunched at the hinges of his jaws. He stared steadily at Black. He had not moved since the older man entered the room, five minutes before.

Outside, the noises of Paris traffic at midmorning were muted and musical.

At last Black raised his head and said in a tone of mild curiosity, "Why do you do this work?"

The muscles in Van Horn's jaws relaxed. He took a squashed pack of Baltos out of his jacket and lighted one with an elaborate Flaminaire lighter like a miniature blowtorch. He took his time. The green eyes were thoughtful as he looked out the tall windows at the sunny autumn garden beyond. Still looking out the windows he said finally, "Because it sometimes accomplishes things I think are important. Because I believe men like me ought to do the work and too few want to. Because I'm fairly good at it. And because I enjoy it generally."

"I see," Black said. "Patriotism, snobbery, inclination and pleasure. All genuine feelings, I suppose." He pronounced the word "gen-u-wine." It went with the voice but not the figure.

Van Horn said nothing.

"You admit," Black went on, "that you behaved very stupidly last month in La Paz in the matter of Anski?"

Van Horn took a deep breath and said, "No, sir. I don't admit it."

The contradiction didn't appear to bother Black. He said, "Anski had sold out. He was using his position as an elder statesman and liberal leader to wreck the government and drive the country into the red camp. He was a traitor and maybe worse. You were sent to help find him and expose him and haul him in to face the law. You found him, all right, and you exposed him right enough. And then treated him so kindly he was able to kill himself. What happened? Did he turn out to be your uncle or something?"

"No," Van Horn said. "He was just a poor, weak, nearsighted, foolish, vain man and I got so it made me sick to look at him."

"Well, then? Any excuse?"

"No. Anski was a great man once. Then he got old and scared and the wrong people duped him and used him. By the time I caught up with him and exposed him, he was no good to anybody for anything any more. He was finished. Washed up. Hauling him in for trial and imprisonment down there could only have been worse than a death sentence for him anyway. I didn't see the necessity for it then, and I don't now."

"Would you behave the way you did there in the same circumstances on another case?"

"Probably."

"I see. Can you think of any reason why we shouldn't get rid of you before you make a mess of something really important?"

"No. It's too late for me to get to be the kind of operator who can't see the trees for the forest."

"That's what I thought," Black said equably. "I've wasted a lot of time talking to Washington about you. Everybody there has their own theory about you. Some of them think you're as tough as you look but can't be trusted. Some of them think you aren't tough at all, but just look the way you do by accident, and are all vanilla ice cream inside."

Van Horn said, with no change in his massive face, "If Washington, in its infinite wisdom, sent me all the way to Paris to be fired, fire me and get it over with. If there's business, let's get on with it. I don't have to take this."

"Oh, yes, you do," Black said. "You have to take it, all right. Take it or quit. You'll take it because you know you rate it. There was also the business of that poor mixed-up scientist in Ankara. You had some scruples about him, too, if I recall it right."

Van Horn sighed. "That was a different matter. Osmin was a fine mind, about as sophisticated politically as a Hottentot. If I'd let the Turks have him, they'd simply have shot him and that's that. He's in Italy now, and doing good work. For our side. It seems to me that's better than fertilizing eighteen square feet of Turkish soil."

Black said, "You understand the Turks were pretty upset when Osmin got away. Several local heads rolled as a result. You understand that?"

"Sure," Van Horn rumbled grimly. "I understand."

Black took a long cigarette out of a flat gold case, then fished in his pocket for a moment, extracted a big kitchen match, broke it into flame with his thumbnail, and set fire to the cigarette. It was impossible to tell whether the cigarette case or the match was affectation, or both.

"Everybody's got their own theory about you," he continued. "But you know what I think? I think they're all wrong. I think you're just a poor boob with a streak of squeamishness, a lot of scruples that don't make any sense, and a lot of what you probably think are 'values' that don't mean anything at all. You're a tough man in a line of work that calls for toughness. But you go all girlish when it's time to be really tough. You could probably think up some reason for going easy with Jack the Ripper. I looked you up. You come from what's called a good family, you had a lot of education. Maybe that's what's wrong with you. You're a useful man, but Washington's got a bellyful. Between you and I, your record is getting a pretty sour look. They think you're nothing but a sheep in wolf's clothing. A couple of people who like you, for some reason, don't. And that's why you're standing here instead of pounding pavements in New York looking for a job as an agent for the S.P.C.A. or some other work you're really suited for. It took all the pull you've got to get you off. As it is, you've got one more go-round."

His conversational air was unchanged. "Make no mistake," he said. "You're very much on the hook. You foul up the works once more and I'll throw you to the wolves. With pleasure. You satisfy me or you hit the street."

"All right," Van Horn said. He shifted position slightly and seemed to relax inside his clothes.

With no alteration in his voice or manner, Black was somehow all business now. "What do you know," he asked, "about a man named Lawrence Trimble?"

"I knew him in the Army," Van Horn replied. His voice was crisper than before. "He's an American, must be about forty-three, forty-four. Lives around Europe. An active member of what used to be called 'The Set' over here. Gets into the papers now and then. Very social and all that. He was in OCS at Camp Ritchie when I was. I was with him in Third Army G-2. I liked him."

"Is that all?" Black sounded disgusted.

Van Horn began to pace the shimmering parquet, taking long drags on the Balto. The floor was polished almost mirror-bright and he put his feet down on it carefully. "About all I can give you on him are reminiscences. I remember him from the Army as a big, quiet, sort of lazy man with a sense of humor and a way of handling himself that people have when they've had real privacy all their lives. He was the kind of soldier whose fingernails always seemed to be clean, regardless of what he'd been doing, and his uniforms fitted better than anyone else's. He wasn't a recruiting-poster type, but he cut a good figure. His French and Italian were first-class. German was pretty weak. That's about all, except that he always seemed to have a supply of fine whisky and he was pretty generous with it. Not ostentatious, just generous. But I'd have liked him anyway, I guess."

Van Horn paused to drink some more smoke from the Balto, then went on pacing and talking, "I got to know him pretty well. He didn't talk much about himself, but I saw him in situations in the war that were revealing enough. Lazy and easy-going, but the kind of man you know has some probably simple but pretty sound code that he operates by. The kind of man who's lazy and easygoing only up to a point but never beyond that point. I haven't seen him in some time, though. He may have changed."

Black dropped his cigarette and ground it into fragments on the floor. It made an ugly mark on the wood. He said, "I was told you knew him pretty well. He's been doing a little work for us in the past few years."

Van Horn stopped pacing and looked at him. "What in hell for?"

"How should I know?" Black said irritably. "He's been passing us little items he's picked up in his social activities. Now and then he's given us something useful. He hasn't sent much lately. Day before yesterday he sent us a kind of SOS. He said he'd gotten onto something big but that he's been spotted and he won't be able to do anything more. He wants to tell us everything and sign off. We've been trying to get to him but he won't play. He's set up a screwy sort of rendezvous—about what you'd expect from an amateur instead of a man with his experience—and he insists on sticking to it. You'd think with the training the Army gave him he'd know better. He may really be onto something important; though if he is, it's the first time. Anyway, we're following his lead."

"Lots of cloak and dagger?"

"Yeah," Black said morosely. "My God, sometimes using these people doesn't seem worth it." He sighed. "He won't go near any U.S. installation, he won't answer our queries, he won't meet anyone except on his terms. He's scared, of course, but what the hell! He's sneaking in a quick trip to France, wants someone to meet him on the train, get his report, and leave him to go about his business."

Van Horn's face was suddenly tight with anger. The black line of eyebrow was drawn down until his eyes were in shadow. He spoke in a rasp. "I suppose I'm elected to meet him?"

"Why, yes," David Black said, smiling faintly.

"Why should I?" Van Horn asked. "I'd like to see Larry again. But I'm not a courier or some damned cookie-pusher."

"Oh, but you are!" Black said, holding up one languid hand. "You're anything I want to make you until you straighten yourself out. Washington wants you chastised, and I'm just the man to do it. Of course, you can always resign." He paused.

"Go on," Van Horn said. "Get it over with."

"Well, you couldn't really expect the people in Washington to just sort of shrug off those carryings-on in La Paz, now could you? You see, they got to wondering just how—uh—*trustworthy* you are. *You* know. In the face of painful duty and all that stuff. So they decided maybe you could do with a spell of discipline. Well? How about it? Take it or leave it?"

Van Horn said nothing.

Black said, "Don't be so hard on yourself. Me, I think you're probably a pretty good man, but I think maybe you're not cut out for exactly the work you've been doing. So I think maybe we'll just find out what it is you're best at. By trying you at a little of everything. Beginning with simple errands like this one." He took out another cigarette and lighted it with another kitchen match.

Van Horn watched him somberly. Then gradually his brow cleared and he laughed shortly.

"Where do I meet him?" he asked.

"Ah! Now that's more like it!—at Modane."

Van Horn expelled the last of the smoke from the Balto and carefully put the stub in an ash tray. "All right," he said.

"He'll be on the express from Turin that gets in at eleven. Tonight. It stops in Modane for half an hour or so. He'll be alone in a first-class compartment. You introduce yourself by asking the time. He'll give it to you wrong by ten minutes. You tell him your watch loses fifteen minutes a day."

Van Horn laughed again. "I suppose all this will be necessary because I'll be wearing a chartreuse wig and he'll be disguised as a *gigot d'agneau.* My God, it's like asking for credentials from your brother."

"He doesn't know you're the one who's meeting him. He probably doesn't even know you're working for us. You'll have no front, no special papers. You'll be yourself. Understand? No monkey business. You'll just be a courier doing an errand. You won't even leave France. You'll bring his report back here in the car that takes you to Modane. You'll pick up the car in Grenoble. Military plane will get you there. I want that report in my hands by tomorrow morning."

"That's all?"

"Yes. But don't forget. If anything goes wrong, on this or any other little chore I give you, and you start tripping over your scruples, I'll fix it so you couldn't get a job with the Sanitation Department."

"You make yourself pretty clear."

"Good. I mean to." Black turned toward the tall double doors behind him. "Come along now. I'll take you over to the office and you can get your travel orders and so on." Van Horn moved to follow him. At the door Black turned suddenly and said, looking straight into Van Horn's face with a slight smile, "I wonder about men like you. Tell me something. Imagine yourself driving fast in a car with bad brakes. A kid runs out in front of you. You turn right, you'll run over an old man. Turn left and you'll run over a young woman. What would you do?"

When Van Horn didn't answer, Black said, "See? You don't know. Like I said, your 'values' don't mean anything. One man's case is as strong as any other's to you."

"What would *you* do?" Van Horn asked.

"Me? Oh, I'd run over the kid. I hate kids, I like women, and I'm getting to be an old man myself." He laughed drily and went with long strides out the door.

CHAPTER TWO

On the draughty C-54 to Grenoble, later that day, Van Horn studied a dossier on Trimble.

Lawrence Peter Trimble was born in 1916, with advantages. After sliding through the usual schools, the usual visits abroad, and the usual excitements of a rich young man in the 'twenties and 'thirties, he'd married an Italian contessa named Serena della Castria. They had one child, a daughter named Flavia, born in 1940.

Trimble was still married to the Contessa, which made him something of a freak in The Set. In the society they moved in, twenty-year marriages were as rare as paid-up taxes.

The Trimbles had lived abroad continuously except for the war years. The Contessa and her daughter held dual nationality. There was a photo of Trimble in the file. It was a studio portrait of a smiling, well-bred man who took good care of himself; tall, heavily built, with regular features and dark hair only a little gray. There was nothing in the dossier to indicate why this man would decide to perform certain unofficial services for his country, free of charge, at some considerable bother, and even apparently some danger, to himself. The entry read simply: *First contact, 12 January, 1947.* Six or eight contacts a year were recorded since then. All of them concerning rather trivial affairs. There was no explanation of what patriotic impulses could have stirred so cushioned a soul to work for his nation's government.

It was cold as charity in Grenoble. A bored staff sergeant met Van Horn at the little airport with a black Citroën 11 and drove him off into the murk of the Hautes Alpes.

Modane is an unhappy agglomeration of habitations crouched in the bottom of a hole in the Alps on the Italian frontier. Beyond its railway station and customs house it has no evident reason for existing. There is one steep little hotel, one gas station, and a café or bistro for every eight inhabitants. In fair weather Modane gets two hours' sunlight a day, the sun popping up over one Alp at about 11:00 a.m. and dropping down behind another Alp at 1:00 p.m. There is fair weather in Modane about a dozen days a year. The shade there is cold, and the darkness is arctic. It was dark when Van Horn got there.

Aside from the station, the only lighted building in the town was the hotel. A dozen or so street lamps gleamed feebly in the crystalline night. There was no train in the station, but it was only ten till eleven.

The sergeant parked the car near the end of the station platform where the first-class cars would stop. Van Horn left him dozing at the wheel and, teeth chattering, choking at every breath of air that seared like fire, he walked to the station.

As he opened the door to the buffet, a blast of light and noise and a mixture of smells exploded out at him. The noise was the raucous high spirits of the groups of skiers who milled about the room. The smells were wet wool, stale beer, tobacco, and the noxious perfume of a potbellied stove that glowed in the middle of the room and seemed to have been stoked with old socks. The temperature in the place was about ninety degrees. A group of sporting brothers was clustered in one corner singing the sort of song in which one shouts "Hey!" or "Ho!" or "Hi!" at the end of each verse. The bar was lined with other robust types. Girls with short-cropped hair, their figures hidden in bulky sweaters and ski pants, moved in and out. The room rocked to the witless good humor that skiers seem to exude like sweat.

In the corner beside the bar a peasant family sat immobile, staring with unamazed bovine eyes at the heartiness all around them.

The choice was simple: freeze outside or stifle inside. Then there was the shriek of a train whistle in the distance and no decision was necessary. Van Horn had no *billet de quai,* but it appeared he didn't need one. Everybody in the station met the train, for no apparent reason—skiers, peasants and railway employees, Van Horn in their midst. Nobody appeared to be getting on the train, but everyone seemed to want to get as close to it as possible, in some impulsive mob greeting, as though they had never seen a train before. Consequently there was a certain amount of footwork required to get Van Horn to the first-class carriages. It was perhaps two minutes after the train came to a halt that he got on. And two more minutes before he found the compartment he was looking for.

A woman was standing in the compartment doorway. A man was visible on the seat beyond her. Van Horn said, "Excuse me," to the woman. She didn't move. He took her arm and steered her a step or two into the compartment. She didn't resist or seem to notice him at all.

The man was in a corner seat, apparently asleep. Van Horn stepped over and nudged his shoulder with one hand, holding the woman with the other. He said, "Excuse me, but do you have the time?"

There was no reply.

Then the man tilted slowly sideways and collapsed on his face on the green plush seat. The lower part of his body stayed where it had been, feet on the floor. An awkward position, comfortable only to a corpse.

His face expressionless, Van Horn bent over the twisted figure. The man had been shot very neatly with a small-caliber weapon just at the back of the neck where the vertebrae join the skull. There was almost no blood.

Van Horn straightened up and looked at the woman whose arm he still held. She was very oddly dressed, in ski pants, boots and woolen mittens, a big floppy hat with a veil, and a handsome, short mink coat. Beneath her veil, which was almost opaque, her gaze shifted from Van Horn to the dead man, and then her mouth opened very wide as she got a look at the neat round hole in the man's neck.

Van Horn lunged for her and clapped his free hand over her mouth just as a high thin noise, that would have been a shriek in another second, began to come out of her. She began to struggle. She was astonishingly strong. She thrashed around for a moment while Van Horn tried to get a purchase on her. Then they stood locked in the doorway, Van Horn with his hand over her mouth, his other arm around her shoulders pinning her arms to her sides.

To anyone passing in the corridor, they might have looked like a couple mesmerized with love. But no one passed.

Finally her clenched muscles relaxed and she went soft against him.

Van Horn put her on the seat across from the dead man and shut the compartment door, pulling the shades down over the windows. His face was shining with sweat and his eyes glittered. Turning from the woman, he pushed the man's body into a sitting position and went through his pockets. Somebody else had searched him not long before and hadn't been doing a very meticulous job. The coat pockets were inside out and the shirt was not tucked into the trousers.

Van Horn worked swiftly and thoroughly. The man hadn't been robbed; his wallet, with money and passport and cards and so on inside, his watch, even the small change in his jacket pocket, were undisturbed. Van Horn put all of it in his own coat pocket and returned his attention to the woman. She was absolutely still on the seat, apparently in shock.

He got her on her feet and tried to make her look as though she were drunk, or very ill. It was no use. No matter how he held her, she looked exactly like a woman either paralyzed, dead drunk, or just dead. At last he picked her up and kicked open the compartment door and carried her out, kicking the door shut behind him.

In first class there was no traffic in the corridor, and the car was stopped past the end of the station. He managed to get her outside without having to explain what he was doing carrying a limp female around in the middle of the night. He found an unattended gate at the end of the platform and carried her through it. This was a very informal station.

The staff sergeant was still dozing in the Citroën when Van Horn came up to it and said, flatly, "You'll find a corpse in the third or fourth compartment of the second carriage. Get him out of there without making it public. Put him in the car. Bring his valise and overcoat to me at the hotel. His hat, too. Move, son!"

The soldier looked at Van Horn and the figure in his arms for a long speculative moment. Then he put the car in gear and drove to the edge of the platform near the gate Van Horn had come through.

Van Horn carried the woman across the street and into the hotel. The lobby smelled of damp and dust. The night porter smelled of sweat and cheap red wine. Van Horn said, "This lady is ill. I want a room for her until the next train departs." He got one hand free and shoved two thousand-franc notes under the porter's nose. "We'll need cognac. Martell."

The porter became suddenly Mein Host. He got a bottle out of some private cuddy, and led the way upstairs to a front room on the second floor, leering heavily at Van Horn and the woman, and hanging about in the room until Van Horn turned so black a frown on him that he reverted to being a night porter and went away.

Van Horn put the woman on the sway-back bed and took off her hat and veil. As the yellowish light of the bed lamp fell on her face, Van Horn—the hat and veil in his hand—stopped dead.

She wasn't a woman at all, but a girl of about nineteen or twenty, and she was a great beauty. She was dark and her head was a small perfection of bones and flesh. At the moment she was paler than the sheets her head rested on.

Her lashes lay on her cheeks and her hair framed her face like something imaginable but never real. She was no conventionally beautiful girl. No magazine would have found her suitable as a model for the ideal symmetrical girl. Her nose was too fine, her jaw too definite and her cheekbones too delicate. She had that strange mouth one sees in portraits of noblewomen of the eighteenth century—a long upper lip, its edge crimson and thin over a full and sensuous lower lip.

Gently Van Horn put the back of his hand against her cheek. It was filmed with moisture and very cold. She was unconscious, in deep shock. He left her as she was and covered her up with a comforter. Then he poured himself a big glass of cognac and drank it swiftly.

There was a knock on the door and the sergeant came in with a handsome calfskin valise, a heavy blue ulster, and a gray Homburg hat. He put them on a chair, turned and saw the girl, and froze in his tracks.

"Jesus!" he said.

"Name-dropper," Van Horn said. "Have a drink." He poured another cognac.

"What about the stiff?" the sergeant asked. He poured himself some cognac and drank without taking his eyes from the girl. They were little brown eyes like raisins and they looked famished.

"I don't know yet," Van Horn said. "Put the car where you can watch it and wait downstairs for me."

"Yeah," the sergeant said, his eyes still nibbling at the girl's face. "You knock the guy off?"

"Sure," Van Horn said disgustedly. "There was no other way to get at the girl."

"You done right," the sergeant said. He grinned at Van Horn and moved to the door. His eyes kept straying back toward the girl. "Some system," he said. "You get this dish, I get a stiff. Some system." He saluted lefthanded and walked out.

Across the street the Turin-Paris Express was pulling out.

CHAPTER THREE

Van Horn had a look into the effects of Lawrence Peter Trimble, deceased. In Trimble's wallet he found eighteen thousand lire, two French ten-thousand-franc notes, and twenty-three Swiss francs, as well as a small sheaf of business cards and a plane ticket from Turin to Milan. The reservation was for Wednesday morning. Tomorrow morning.

There were two photographs in the wallet. Both were of women. One was a snapshot of a tall blonde standing on skis in front of a mountain inn. She was apparently no more than thirty years old. Slim and tanned, she was smiling a sardonic smile into the camera.

The other photo was a reduction of a studio portrait of the girl on the bed. Her marvelous dark eyes gazed off the card calmly and innocently and with a disconcerting directness. Van Horn stared at the picture for a while, and then put it carefully back into the wallet.

Trimble's valise had been searched, too, but again nothing seemed to be missing. It contained everything a well-groomed man would take with him on a business trip of a few days. It also contained a plane ticket for the Wednesday TWA flight from Milan to Geneva.

Trimble's passport told a good deal. A passport is almost a diary for a man who travels widely. Trimble had spent his August holiday in Majorca, and every week since early September he'd flown from Geneva to Milan on Wednesday morning and from Milan back to Geneva on Wednesday evening.

This week, however, he'd altered his itinerary, going from Geneva to Turin by air on Tuesday, apparently intending to go from Turin to Milan on Wednesday morning, where he would resume his usual schedule.

Van Horn went carefully through the sheaf of business cards. There were cards from tailors in London, jewelers in Paris, brokers in Geneva and Paris and New York, antique dealers in Lucerne and Grenoble and Rome, and just plain people in unspecified localities or with unspecified occupations. Van Horn scrutinized every doodle and notation on all of them. Only one of them seemed to say anything. It was a bit larger than the others and it read simply: *Emilio Monselice, 24 Piazza San Carlo, Torino, Italia.* It was engraved in fine copperplate and it had no significance whatever except that it was the only one in the wallet with the word *Torino* on it.

Suddenly, without a sound, the girl rose from the bed. Van Horn moved to help her stand, but she took no notice of him and, weaving dizzily, reeled across the room. Van Horn reached her side just as she collapsed, and he bent and gathered her into his thick arms. Her eyes were closed and her skin was like wax. As he bent lower to get one arm under her knees in order to pick her up, she looked at him blankly for a moment. Then her eyes focused on the forbidding mask from behind which Van Horn confronted the world, and her reaction was instantaneous: Stark terror. With a galvanic wrench she was free of his grasp and running crazily about the room in a frenzy of flight. Van Horn stood where he was and watched her sadly. She twisted desperately at the handle of the room door, whimpering like an animal, then dashed for the windows overlooking the street. They were sealed shut by innumerable coats of cheap paint. At last she fell against a corner of the wall and cowered there, her knees half bent, her hands over her face, sobbing.

Van Horn sighed. "Well," he said, "I usually get a pretty negative response. But I never got anything as graphic as this before."

"Please!" The girl's voice came thin and muffled and pathetic from behind her hands. "Please! Please! Please!"

With the air of a man who cannot restrain himself, Van Horn stepped toward her.

"You mustn't be frightened," he said softly, though his voice still rumbled as usual. "You're perfectly safe."

The girl's body heaved and a strangled sound came from behind her hands. Van Horn moved swiftly to her, put his hands on her shoulders and propelled her through the narrow door to the alcove that contained a basin and a bidet and served as a bathroom. He closed the door behind her and turned back into the room. From the alcove came a muffled moan, then the noise of water running.

Near the window, where the girl had dropped it on the worn and faded carpet, lay a small, square handbag. Van Horn stood staring at it for a moment. Finally he shrugged and picked it up. Undoing the snap, he emptied it onto the bed.

It contained a fantastic collection of trivia—Kleenex, lipstick, a compact, nail polish, small change, two hundred Swiss francs in bills, two combs, one suède glove for the left hand, a cracked mirror, a little wallet that held only stubs of tickets to a football match the previous year and a picture of Trimble, a heavy gold cigarette case, an American passport, and finally a dog-eared brochure from a French country inn. Holding the passport aside, Van Horn put the rest of the jumble of articles carefully back into the handbag.

The passport was made out to Miss Flavia Trimble. The date of issue was three years earlier and the photograph in it must have been taken at the same time. She was dressed in some kind of school uniform, a round white collar over a dark jersey. Her hair had been longer then. But the eyes and their innocence and directness were the same as now.

Looking at the picture, Van Horn smiled. The result was astonishing. The brutality in his face vanished, the menace vanished, and the warmth and gentleness that replaced them changed him in an instant into some other man.

The alcove door opened and the girl tottered into the room. Van Horn hastily closed the passport and raised his eyes to look at her. For a moment he almost seemed embarrassed. Then his face fell back into its usual hardness. The girl, pale and drawn and trembling, frowned at him as though puzzled by what she had glimpsed in his face in the moment before he had resumed control of himself.

He put the passport back into the handbag and held the bag out to her. "I beg your pardon," he rumbled. "It was necessary."

She took the bag from him and looked bewilderedly around the room. Her eyes fell on Trimble's coat and valise. Then they turned darkly on Van Horn. "What have you done with my father?" she asked huskily.

"Nothing," Van Horn said. "He's downstairs in my car."

"He's … he's dead, isn't he?"

"Yes. He's dead. I'm sorry."

"Dead," she murmured. She moved the few steps to the bed as though drawn by wires and lay down on it on her back, so that when she began to weep her tears trickled down her temples onto the pillow instead of down her cheeks. Her arms held stiffly at her sides, she stared straight up at the ceiling and wept, noiselessly but rackingly. Van Horn watched her, his face expressing nothing. After a moment, he moved abruptly to the bed table and poured about two inches of cognac into a clean glass.

"Here, Miss Trimble," he said, holding out the glass. She glanced toward him without moving her head. Her eyes were misty, but they bored straight into his. "Sit up and drink this," he said. "It'll bring you back over on this side of the line."

"He's dead," she murmured again. Then her long sigh filled the room with the sound of mourning.

He put his left arm behind her and lifted her a little. She took the glass quite docilely and sipped at the cognac.

"Knock it back," he said. "It'll prime the pump."

Obediently she drained the glass. When she'd caught her breath she said, "Who are you?"

He said, "I'm a friend of your father's. I knew him during the war. He wrote me and told me to meet him on that train. He said he was in trouble and needed help. I got there too late."

"Too late," she said. "Too late!" She turned her face against the pillow and began her silent weeping again.

She cried like a child, with bottomless misery, her whole face distorted. Van Horn turned away and began to pace restlessly, never looking toward the bed.

"Please," he said. "You must try to pull yourself together. I'm terribly sorry, but we haven't much time. We have to make some decisions and we have to move. Please try to get yourself under control."

She took a long breath and raised her head from the pillow. Then she sat up on the edge of the bed with her feet on the floor and rubbed her eyes. "I'm sorry," she said.

"That's better," he said. "I need your help." He started stuffing Trimble's coat into the valise. For a moment he seemed undecided about the Homburg; then he put it on. It fitted fairly well. He smacked the cork into the cognac bottle and put it in the valise too.

"You're leaving?" she asked. Her voice was stronger now.

"We both are," he said.

"Where?" She sounded alarmed.

"Just to Turin. We can talk on the way."

She gripped the bedspread in both hands and said, alarm growing in her voice, "Who are you? Are you some kind of policeman, or ... a gangster or what?"

"Well, neither of those things, really," he said lightly. "And maybe a little of both. But I'm harmless. You mustn't be afraid of me." He smiled at her, and again the miraculous change came over his face and she stared at him in astonishment.

"No," she said slowly, shaking her head. "I won't go with you. I want to stay here. You can't make me go with you."

"I need your help," he said, the smile disappearing. "And I think you need mine."

"No," she said. She said it flatly, a child's refusal. "I won't."

"The gangster side of me could always force you," he said conversationally.

Her eyes widened. "You wouldn't dare," she said. "You couldn't just kidnap me in the middle of—"

"On the other hand, the policeman side of me could arrest you."

"Arrest me!"

"Sure. Why not?"

"But I didn't—"

"I know you didn't. But there are lots of other excuses. I'll think of something. Let's see. How about the Stavisky affair? That happened before you were born, but how do I know you weren't precocious?"

She rubbed her forehead with one hand. "Please go away," she said. "Please leave me alone. I don't feel like joking."

"Then don't make me be serious," he said heavily.

"I won't go with you," she said.

He sighed. "All right," he said. "Then I'll have to be tough. You go with me, like a good girl, or we both go pay a call on the local cops. I'm sure they'd be interested in knowing what you were doing in that compartment."

She looked at him, frowning. "Could you do that?"

"Oh, yes. Could and will, if we don't cut out the nonsense. Now come along." He turned and picked up the valise, and added, "My name, incidentally, is Van Horn." Across the street, the local for Turin was pulling into the station with a great clatter.

"Let's go," Van Horn said. "That's our train."

Without another word she got to her feet and together they went out of the room and down the stairs to the lobby. She did not look at him again.

The staff sergeant was sitting by the front window of the lobby, dozing as usual. His eyes glued to the girl, he roused himself and joined them by the door. The girl withdrew a pace or two as Van Horn spoke to him.

"Go back to your headquarters in Grenoble," Van Horn said. "Get in touch with your G-2. Tell them I want the body sent to Dave Black in Paris. They're to tell Black I want him kept on ice for as long as possible. I'm going on to Turin. My mission, as you military types say, isn't accomplished. I want the body gone over with a fine-tooth comb."

"Dave Black, huh?" he said. "Never heard of him. What about the broad?" His little eyes had never stopped nibbling at her.

"She goes with me." Van Horn winked at him. "Important business."

"Some guys," the sergeant said thoughtfully, "got it made." He shoved his hands into his jacket pockets and went out the door, brushing unnecessarily against the girl as he did so.

CHAPTER FOUR

The girl stood docilely beside Van Horn while he bought their tickets, and as docilely followed him onto the platform. Van Horn found an empty compartment at the extreme end of the last car of the little local train and they settled in. Throughout the train skiers were going strong, milling raucously about, hunting room for their exuberance. Some of them boiled back as far as the last car, one of them laughing the kind of high, whinnying, penetrating laugh that is the special ability and one of the dubious charms of members of the British upper middle classes. It grated on the air like fingernails scraped down a slate.

Three or four rosy sportsmen appeared at the compartment door with their gear hanging from them like Christmas tree ornaments. Van Horn planted himself in the doorway and looked at them coldly. They started to jolly their way past him. Van Horn didn't move. One of them began to protest. Then he found himself gazing into Van Horn's eyes at close range and his protest died. Muttering to himself, he turned and led the others away. They all went clattering off to find places elsewhere, shouting rude remarks about Van Horn in a variety of languages. Van Horn went back and sat down and the train wheezed into motion. Once it got up speed, it racketed along as though it were trying to tear itself apart. There was little likelihood of being overheard in the compartment.

A conductor entered and Van Horn showed him their tickets and he left. Not a word from the girl. She sat bolt upright, cutting the middle distance with cool dark eyes. Outside the lights of Modane fell behind.

The train entered an Alp and on came the Customs people, bored and sleepy and underpaid. Van Horn and the girl showed their passports and offered the usual assurance that they were not secreting anybody's crown jewels among their belongings. The Customs men flashed their teeth at the girl and left.

Van Horn watched the girl's fine profile for a few minutes. She went on staring straight ahead. Finally Van Horn shrugged and said, "I don't mind admitting I'm a little out of my depth. Contrary to popular belief, you know, beautiful, well-bred young ladies are not often encountered in my line of work. I work on what is called the action level. A man I know by the name of Black ought to be here instead of me. He's a lot more present-able than I am. He speaks English like a furrow-hopper from Duodenum, Iowa, but he works on the policy level. He's a kind of diplomat. He'd know how to win your confidence and pretty soon you'd be relying on him like your kindly old uncle. Later, of course, if it seemed the thing to do, he might shoot you, or disgrace you, or get you thrown into prison. And he'd never lose a second's sleep because of it. Anyway, by then he'd have won you over so completely that you'd blame everyone else on the earth but him for what happened to you.

"Me, I have to play by ear. I have to appeal to you directly. I have to tell you again that I need your help, that I really was a friend of your father, and I think you need my help."

He stopped. There was no change in the girl.

He said, "You forced me to get tough back there. Do you want me to go on being tough, or can we leave the jungle behind us?"

She didn't answer.

Van Horn sighed and got up and took the cognac out of Trimble's valise. He didn't offer it to her, but drank a long drink himself, straight from the bottle.

"I take my courage where I find it," he said. He sat down again.

"Listen, Miss Trimble," he went on, rather hopelessly, "I went to meet your father, who was once a friend of mine, to get something from him. At his request I arrived at the rendezvous he set up. I found him killed. I found you in the compartment with him. Now your father, in addition to the distinction of having known me, was also working for the same people I work for."

He got a reaction. She said nothing, but her head turned slowly and she gazed at him. The coolness had vanished. She was simply surprised. Her hands began twisting the woolen mittens that lay in her lap.

"It's true," Van Horn said. "He wasn't on the payroll or anything, but he did an occasional bit of work for us, as a consultant, in a way. I was supposed to have got his last piece of information from him on that train. Afterward he was not going to work for us, according to him. I have gone over what I found in that compartment. I found no report, nor sign of any. Maybe whoever killed him stole it. Maybe your father didn't carry it in writing. Maybe he had it in his head. But all his other reports were at least partly in writing and my guess is part of this one was too, and somebody swiped it. Did you swipe it, Flavia?"

"No," she said softly, shaking her head. She looked completely bewildered. "No, I didn't even know he—"

"Well, I believe you," Van Horn said, "innocent that I am." He had another go at the cognac. "A drink to my glittering innocence," he said. Then he went on, "Naturally, I was upset. I get paid for results and somebody got between me and my results. So I whipped out my trusty reading lens and had a long look at your father's belongings." Van Horn's drinking seemed to have no effect on him except to lighten his tone a little. He said, "I found out some odd things about your father, Flavia. And they raised some odd questions I've got to find answers to." He paused. Her hands were working hard on the mittens. "Will you help me find those answers, Flavia?"

She shook her head. "I ... I can't help you," she said.

He said, "I think you will, whether you think you can or not. They're big questions. For example, your father must have known he was in danger. But if it was danger as a result of his report, he had only to appeal to us for protection and he'd have got loads of it, as he knew perfectly well. So we can assume his danger wasn't connected with the report, but with something he didn't want us to help him with or felt we couldn't help him with. Who was after him? And why? I think you know or could make a pretty shrewd guess.

"In the second place, there's you. My assumption is he asked you to run away with him. He told you to meet him on that train at that place. Why didn't you leave with him in the first place? And why wasn't your mother invited along?"

"My mother!" she said in a tone of furious disgust. Immediately she seemed to regret the outburst and closed her mouth tight. The cold look came back again.

"All right, then," Van Horn said patiently, "your mother is a dirty word and we'll forget her for the moment. But what about the weekly jaunts your father's been taking to Milan? And what about his trip to Turin today? He'd never gone to Turin before, and he had no legitimate business there or in Milan, so far as we know. Which is fairly far."

With much piteous shrieking from senile brakes, the train managed to stop at Bardonecchia. Most of the skiers got off to transfer to buses that would take them the rest of the way to their snowy slopes and broken legs and muscular camaraderie. The girl and Van Horn sat in silence, though there was little chance of their being overheard. Gusts of song and boisterous shouts, both overridden by the whinnying English laugh, swelled and receded on the breeze.

After a few minutes the old train complained its way into motion, and Van Horn went on. "Now," he said, "I want to know what became of that report, if there was any of it in writing. That's all I'm paid to be interested in. But, privately, I'd rather like to know who killed your father and why. Happily, in doing my job, I may find out. I've got a big organization behind me. Sooner or later we'll get all the answers to all the questions. I'd like to do it with your help."

All at once, she turned on him and she was pink with anger. It was the first time there had been any color in her face. "I've told you I can't help you!" she said. Her voice was shaking. Around the mittens, her hands were clenched tight. "I wouldn't help you if I could! I don't know anything about any report. I don't want to know. You can do as you like with me. It doesn't matter now."

Only somebody very artful or very young could have had so intense an air of outrage and disdain. Van Horn looked as satisfied as his face would allow him to.

"All right," he said. "If nothing matters now, then you won't care what kind of a mess we turn up by going into this blind."

"What do you mean?" she demanded. There was no anger in her voice now.

"I mean," he said, "that we are prepared to go all out, using all the resources we can muster. That's a lot of resources. By the time we're through all kinds of private information is going to be sprayed around the landscape. If your father ever had anything to hide—from a parking ticket to grand larceny—we'll know about it and so will a lot of other people. But that won't matter to you, will it?"

"You mean it, don't you?" she said, looking at him as though she'd found him by mischance in a dark damp place. "My father was your friend, you say. But you don't care what damage you do him, or anyone, just so you get your stupid report!"

"That's right. We'll have to trot out all the skeletons."

Now the stiffness appeared to leave her, and she shifted moods with a swiftness that would have been suspicious in a more experienced person. She seemed sad now. "Are you really such a beast?" she asked softly.

He said nothing. His jaw muscles bunched under his ears.

"Please!" she said. She was begging. She had probably done very little begging in her life. "Please don't do it!"

Still he said nothing.

"Please!"

His face was like stone.

"I'm sure there was no report or you'd have found it. And now that Daddy's—Well, don't you see? You'll just make everything rotten and bad if you do as you say you're going to. You'll spoil what little is left."

"Left for whom?" he said harshly. "For you?"

"Yes," she said in a little thin voice. "What's left for me."

"My bosses are still going to want to know about the report," he said. "Oh, there was a report, all right. Maybe it wasn't in writing, but it was something important that your father wanted to tell us. The people I work for are going to want to know what it was if we have to go snuffling through your father's life clear back to the day he was born in order to find it."

"Is there no way I can make you understand?"

"No way at all." He grinned at her evilly, without humor. His teeth were big and very white. "My father was a full-blooded ferret," he said. "Offer me money. I sneer at your gelt. Offer me your beautiful white body. I don't sneer, and somebody has to chain me to the mast, but I keep going." She blushed and looked away. He said more gently, "You must be awfully afraid of what we're going to find out."

"I am," she said softly, staring at the floor.

"Flavia," he said, "maybe you're too young to realize that you can't do anything about the truth. It has a nagging way of enduring no matter how you try to ignore it or pervert it or cover it up.

It's one of the few constants in this vale of tears. And the uglier it is, the more enduring it seems to be. That is hardly an original idea, but few of my convictions are."

She was silent.

"You've got to make up your mind," he went on. He sighed and slumped back in the seat. "I feel old and overweight and unloved and unlovable," he said glumly. "You're young as a morning at seven, and you're as remote from me as the far cold side of the moon. But you've got to listen and you've got to understand."

She closed her eyes. After a moment she opened them and turned them on him. "You can be discreet if ... if I tell you what I can?"

"Whatever I can save I'll save," he said. "I promise. And it's a good promise. The heavyweights back of me will be anxious to keep things as quiet as possible, so long as it doesn't get to be more trouble than it's worth. You can help me to see that it doesn't."

For a long moment she said nothing, but chewed her lovely lower lip thoughtfully. At last she said, "There isn't much I can tell you, really." She began worrying away at the mittens again. "But I'm sure of one thing. What happened to Daddy didn't have anything to do with your report."

"Do you know who killed him, Flavia?" he asked.

A peculiar expression twisted her face. It didn't seem possible for such delicate features to assume an expression of such pure hatred.

"Yes," she said, and the word came with a hiss. "I know." Her voice rose over the noise of the train. *"My mother killed him!* She didn't actually fire the gun, but she might as well have!"

CHAPTER FIVE

She sank back against the dusty green cushions as though her outburst had taken the last of her energy. Without looking at Van Horn she said, "May I have a cigarette?"

He gave her one of his bent Baltos and lighted it for her.

She took a deep drag and started to talk, smoke coming from her mouth in little gusts. She smoked as a man smokes. It was odd in so feminine a female. She said, "For the past few years Daddy and Serena—my mother—haven't got on together. They used to. There was a time when we had a very good life, when we were a family. Then—it was around Christmas, four or five years ago—something happened. I think it had something to do with me. I don't know. But after that they were very cold with one another."

Van Horn said nothing and tried to look bright and comprehending.

After a little pause, she said, "I was away at boarding school most of the time, so it was easy for me to get used to the kind of armed truce they had between them. Daddy and I were always … " She stopped and took another drag on the cigarette. "We were always very close. I'd never got on with Serena. And she's never been much of a mother, especially lately. She's a vain woman, and she loathes having a grown daughter. Anyway, for the past six or eight months or a year we've had less money. I mean we haven't been living as well as we used to. And Serena isn't easy to live with when she doesn't have all the money she needs."

Some of the hatred came back into her face. But she went on, "Serena isn't so old really. She was only eighteen when I was born. But still..." She paused to examine her cigarette, looking at it as though there were an obscenity written on it instead of the word *Balto*. Presently she drew a big breath and continued, "Then this summer, before we went to Majorca, I came home from school and found a lot of new people coming to the house. Strange people. The old set we'd always known were—oh, pretty useless, I guess, pretty empty and silly. But they'd been fun, charming. These new people were... I don't know. No fun at all. They talked in loud voices and they were sort of... well, *vulgar,* if that isn't a meaningless word nowadays. They were Serena's friends. Daddy played host to them, but I knew he didn't like them. Then they showed up again, or some of them did, while we were in Majorca, and Daddy got mixed up with them."

She broke off and stubbed her cigarette out. Her mouth was set and her eyes were hot. "Then an awful time started," she said. "Serena and Daddy had a kind of running battle. It was... terrible! They were quiet about it, but I could see and overhear enough to know that Daddy was wretched and that he and Serena had some awful thing between them."

She fell silent and Van Horn spoke for the first time since her outburst began. "What do you think was the trouble?" he asked.

"It was because there was something Serena wanted Daddy to do that he didn't want to do. Something to do with the new people."

"Any idea what?"

"Business of some kind. She wanted him to work for them or with them, and he finally did. She forced him somehow. It was because of the money, of course. That's how she got to him. I think it tortured Daddy that he wasn't giving us the kind of life we were used to. Anyway, in September, when we came back, they stopped fighting and he began going to Milan every week."

"How did things change after that?" Van Horn asked.

"Well, the people, most of them, stopped coming around. And I saw less and less of Daddy, though I was through going to school. And, oh, yes, we had more money. But it didn't seem to improve things between Daddy and Serena. It was worse, if anything, and I was the cause of the trouble again. Though Lord! I don't know how."

"You never learned what it was your father was doing?"

"No, except that it—it wasn't honest." She looked at Van Horn miserably. "I could tell by his manner. He'd never talk about what he was doing. And he seemed uneasy whenever I mentioned it."

"Tell me about the 'new people.' Who were they?"

"Well, there was a disgusting fat man they called Cherubino, and his wife. Her name was Teresa and she used to sing at La Scala under the name of Nardiello before she married. She talked about it all the time. And a thin, nervous man called Zerho. He was the one who had a fight with Nigel Brush on our terrace."

"Who's Brush?"

"Oh, a neighbor of ours. He's English. He moved into a villa near ours sometime in June and he and Serena used to play gin rummy together. I don't know what the fight was about, but he laid this Mr. Zerho out and it was quite something. That was two weeks ago. I never saw them again afterward."

"Uh-huh," Van Horn said. "Any more names?"

"Oh, there were so many," she said dully. She sounded tired. "They came and went all summer. It was an awful summer."

"What did your father tell you about his plans?"

She seemed to have shot her bolt with all she had said up till now. Under the mink, her shoulders sagged, and her eyes were half closed. Van Horn lighted her another cigarette and gave her time to take one of her deep, masculine drags on it.

Finally she said, "Not very much. Last week he was gone longer than usual. When he came back he was very tense and he came and talked to me in my room." She closed her eyes altogether now. She had the air of a person enduring a dull incessant ache; patience on a monument, but with no smiles for grief. "He said he was in a bad situation and that our life there in Geneva had ended. He said my schooling was finished. He said he thought I had no further real need for a mother or a settled family life. Would I go away with him, just the two of us, so that we could start our lives over again somewhere else. In America or some place new? I grew quite excited at the idea. I was sick of our existence there. That's all it was, just an existence. And I'd been wanting him to leave Serena almost from the moment I grew up."

Van Horn said, "Did you ever hear of a man named Emilio Monselice?"

Her eyes opened for a moment and she looked puzzled. "No," she said. "Why?"

"Your father went to Turin this morning—yesterday morning, now. He'd never gone there before so far as we know. Do you know why?"

"No," she said. She frowned slightly and began to work over the mittens again, her slender hands wrenching them until they stretched to about twice their real length.

"Where was your father going to take you after you'd joined forces?"

And suddenly he seemed to have hit a nerve. She went tense. He had lost her again. He sighed and said, "What the hell, nobody tells the truth all the time."

She would not look at him as she said, "I'm telling the truth. Really. I don't know. He sent me to Chamonix for the skiing and we arranged to meet on that train tonight. Well..." Her voice broke a little and the tension left her. "Well," she said, "we met."

Van Horn spoke quickly before she could entirely succumb to the tears that filled her eyes. "Why did you say your mother killed him, Flavia?"

The frown came back and she looked at him irritably. "Can't you see?" she demanded. "I didn't mean she actually...*shot* him. But she might as well have." Her voice grew harsh and the look of hate returned to her face. "Can't you see? She forced Daddy to deal with these people. Somehow she made him do dishonest things. Then when he wanted to stop, when he couldn't stand it any more, the people caught him and killed him. I don't know who actually did it, and it doesn't matter. It's Serena's fault. Daddy only wanted to do what was right for us all. He was no crook, he was a fine man. But she got to him somehow, and then he never had a chance. *He never had a chance!*" She dropped the mittens on the floor and buried her face in her hands and that was that. Sobs shook her, and she pressed her hands hard against her face.

Van Horn hesitated a moment, then put his arm around her and held her against him. Presently the shaking diminished and she said, her voice muffled by her hands, "I'm sorry. I can't expect you to care about this." She took a deep breath and lowered her hands. Her face was drenched with her tears. She fished the handkerchief out of her purse and wiped her eyes.

He said, "You'd better try to get some sleep. It's a long way to Turin." He got up and she stretched out on the seat. He wadded up his old Alligator topcoat to give her as a pillow.

She watched him quietly, then blew her nose and said, "Where are you taking me?" He bent to shove the coat under her head.

"Turin. Then Geneva."

"Oh, please!" she said, sitting up. "Don't take me to Geneva!"

Her face was only about three inches from his. "Why not?" he asked.

"I couldn't bear to go back there! With Serena and those others waiting. They'd know I meant to go off with Daddy, and Daddy wouldn't be there. Please! I can't go back there!"

"We'll see," he said amiably. "We'll see." For an instant be paused, looking into her eyes, his hands arrested in the act of putting the coat on the seat. He cleared his throat and laughed with a flat, unamused bark. "You ought to be reported," he said. "You're a threat to young manhood. Now, go to sleep."

Her eyes still on him, puzzled and slightly alarmed, she lay down on the seat and put her head on his coat. He turned off the overhead light and sat down across from her. There was a long silence. She might have been asleep. But then she said something drowsily.

He leaned toward her and said, "What did you say?"

"I said that you're a fraud." There was a note of lightness in her voice that it had not held since they had met.

"Everybody gets my number, sooner or later," he said.

"No," she said. "I mean it. You are a fraud. You're not really a beast at all."

Then she fell asleep.

CHAPTER SIX

an Horn woke the girl as they were pulling into the city. At his touch, she opened her eyes and looked bewilderedly about for an instant. Then her eyes found his face and she smiled palely.

He said, "You slept well. You looked wonderful. We're there."

She rose stiffly and stretched. The train stopped. It was another day.

They walked out through the big bleak Turin station. It was half-past three. The station was a prime example of bombastic architecture, huge and full of waste space. Like most Italian stations except the great Rome terminus, it looked like a gigantic men's room gone wrong. It smelled a little that way, too.

Van Horn took the girl to the Principe in a cab. He told the driver to wait and he and the girl went inside.

The Principe in Turin is Italy's answer to Conrad Hilton. They have tried to create the kind of modern monolith, full of plate glass, chromium and efficiency, that you find in Chicago or Dallas or Los Angeles. And they nearly have succeeded, unfortunately. The bedroom ceilings are low; the bedrooms, no larger than is absolutely necessary, are full of mirrors to deceive the eye; and every room has a tiled bathroom big enough to sublet. The fixtures work. It can be depressing. Van Horn booked such a set-up for the girl from a very sleek desk clerk, and a skinny bellhop led them into a soundproofed elevator.

It rose to the fifth floor at a creep: even the Principe can do nothing about the speed of Continental elevators.

The room was No. 512, and it was as sleek as everything else. Van Horn left Trimble's bag with the girl, told her to lock herself in and go to bed, and went back downstairs, taking the door key with him.

Few towns look like much on a cloudy night at four a.m., but Turin looks like less than most. It's so heavily industrialized that it's lost the grace of a European city without acquiring any of the garish but cheerful modernity of some place like Detroit. It's just cheap, dirty, and a little melancholy.

The Piazza San Carlo proved to be a small square in a prosperous district. It was lined with shops. Number 24 bore a sign reading: *Emilio Monselice, Fine Engraving and Printing.* The lettering was in the same fine copperplate that was on the business card Trimble had carried. The fact that the sign was in English meant it was a snob shop and catered to a snobbish sort of clientele.

Van Horn got out of the cab and went to look through the show window. But a heavy grille had been pulled down over the whole front of the place and he could see nothing, except that the grille was sealed shut with a little metal seal like the ones they put on freight cars in America.

He was looking at this when a policeman tapped him on the shoulder. The police in Italy have a tendency to look like soldiers (the actual soldiers look like nothing else on earth), and while this makes them less unnerving it also makes them less easy to deal with.

This one said, "Looking for something, Signore?"

Van Horn said, "Why is Signor Monselice's shop sealed shut? I hope he has not gone out of business, for I mean to deal with him."

"At this hour, Signore?" Sardonic grin.

"Of course not! I have just arrived from France. I expect to wait for day."

"Signor Monselice has, as you say, gone out of business." Slyly humorous look now.

"Impossible! He was doing well only last week when I spoke to him from Paris on the telephone."

The brown hand shot out: "Your papers, please, Signore."

Van Horn produced his special passport with the entry time stamped in it. The man was dubious, but the passport stalled him. "You could have come here secretly yesterday morning," he said craftily.

"It would be evident in the passport. Do not be an imbecile, man. I am bona fide. What has happened to Signor Monselice?"

"He no longer is in business."

"Bankrupt?"

"No. A guest of the State."

"Impossible! When?"

"Since yesterday morning. Tuesday."

"Why?"

"Ah! How would I know? Perhaps you might read about it in the newspapers. They know everything." Another close look at Van Horn. "You understand, Signore, there is no point in awaiting the opening of the shop. Signor Monselice is indeed out of business."

Van Horn expressed shock and horror at the news, offered the man a cigarette, insisted he take two, shook hands with him, and got back into the cab. He told the driver to take him back near the station. As they wheeled away, the policeman was still standing in front of the shop, the two cigarettes in his hand. He cut a forlorn figure, with the air of someone who is afraid he has missed the point of a story.

The cab left Van Horn at a *trattoria* that was just opening. The morning papers were being dumped in huge bales on street corners. Van Horn bought a spread of them and read while he waited for the *trattoria* proprietor to get up a head of steam in his magnificent espresso machine.

According to the early editions, which of course were not much interested in the previous morning's news, nobody was particularly moved by the fact that one Emilio Monselice had been apprehended by the State Police in regard to a shooting fracas that had taken place in his shop at 24 Piazza San Carlo, Tuesday at about eleven-thirty a.m. An unidentified man had been killed. The alarm had been sent in by an untraced phone call at about eleven forty-five. When the police arrived, they found Monselice attempting to dispose of the body. He surrendered without resistance. There was evidence of a struggle in the shop. The death of the man had been caused by a small-caliber bullet, fired into the back of his neck. No weapon was found on the premises. It was assumed officially that the killer was Monselice. Motive was found in his shop in the form of inflammatory pamphlets. Monselice was known to be an active Communist. He had apparently been doing some of the Party's printing work. Perfectly legal work. But in official Italy membership in the Party is sufficient to explain any violent mishap. Monselice was being held incommunicado. He had apparently refused to talk.

Van Horn asked the proprietor if he had any copies of the previous evening's papers. The man dug around in a cabinet under the cash register and produced two, a tabloid and the local Communist organ. Both of them gave the killing rather elaborate notice. The red paper referred to Monselice as a comrade, cited his services to the underground during the war, and hinted darkly at political reasons for his imprisonment on such flimsy evidence.

The tabloid was a blurry rag, full of grainy pictures that leaned heavily toward half-dressed girls with chests like wetnurses', murky shots of celebrities at play, and murders. There had been only three violent deaths in Northwest Italy on Tuesday. The spread on Monselice was in between a wonderfully gory photo of a man in Alessandria who had been shot twice, in the throat and full in the face, by what seemed to have been a howitzer, and four angles of the twisted wreckage of a Fiat convertible that had lost a dispute with a moving van.

There was a good close-up of the engraver. He was a dark, skinny man with a small narrow head. He looked rather stern, held between the two big policemen, with his eyes half closed and his mouth firmly shut. There was no blood in view, which must have disappointed the paper's layout man. Three other pictures showed views of the interior of the shop. There was the police officer in charge, bending over the body in a stiff, contrived attitude, looking a little as though his underwear was binding him. The fourth picture was a long shot of the whole shop, and this Van Horn studied at some length. But there was nothing of interest visible in it except a small engraver's press on a workbench.

The espresso machine finally had enough pressure and Van Horn had a *cappucino* and a big gooey bun. Afterward he walked to the hotel.

There was no point in waking the girl unnecessarily, so Van Horn, at the door to Room No. 512 a half hour later, was quiet about putting the key in the lock and turning it. The door opened silently about four inches and stopped, held by the chain latch inside. Van Horn cursed softly. He had told the girl to lock herself in.

On the other side of the door there was the sound of movement. Van Horn opened his mouth to call the girl's name when inside the room someone laughed. It was a high, thin, unmusical neigh, vicious and obscene. Men laugh in such a way when watching or engaging in the perverse or evil. It was an ugly sound. Van Horn closed his mouth.

Rearing back, he threw himself at the door. With a crunch, the chain gave a little. There was a sound of quick movement inside the room and then a sort of chunking noise. Something hit the door. It might have killed Van Horn except that the Principe, true to the twentieth century, has double doors on its rooms with a compartment between the panels for dry cleaning. Van Horn stepped back and flung himself at the door again. The chain pintle on the door-jamb gave a little more. Inside the room a door or window slammed. A third time, Van Horn hit the door. The hasp holding the chain burst away from the door-jamb and he went plunging into the room.

Inside nothing moved. One pair of big windows stood opened on the ornate balcony outside. On the bed lay Flavia Trimble, motionless. Van Horn ran to the balcony. The balcony ran all the length of the front of the hotel; it was cut in sections between the rooms by fan-shaped iron grilles about five feet high. They would present no real obstacle to a man who was truly in a hurry. No one was in sight but a casual pedestrian down in the street. A few passing cars. Ordinary morning people.

Van Horn turned back to the room.

The girl was lying on her back on the rumpled bed, wearing only a brassière and little white panties. She was unconscious. Streaks of blood smeared the side of her face and the whiteness of her belly.

There was only her near nakedness to indicate why the intruder had laughed his ugly laugh.

Muttering, "God, God, God!" Van Horn bent over her. His breath was noisy in his nostrils. Moving very swiftly, he got a washcloth from the gigantic, dazzling bathroom and began to swab away the blood. As he did, and the cool cloth touched her, the girl stirred slightly, then once more subsided.

High up on her right side there was a thin crease in the flesh, the mark of a small-caliber bullet. It hadn't much more than broken the skin, but the wound had bled a fair amount. On the side of her head the dark hair was matted over a damp lump where the visitor must have hit her. In the way of scalp wounds, this had bled like a fountain, soaking the bed.

Van Horn rang for the maid and then went back to cleaning up. When the maid rapped on the door he opened it a crack and gave her a list of things he needed, fumbling for a moment over the Italian word for bandage. He tried it in French and finally made himself understood. The maid vanished without the slightest expression of surprise or interest in his order, or in the split wood and dangling chain by the door. They have pretty blasé help at hotels like the Principe.

When the maid returned ten minutes later, bringing bandages and alcohol, and some unidentified salve, Van Horn tipped her a thousand lire. She thanked him, yawned, and turned away as unconcernedly as though she had merely delivered some clean towels.

The girl moaned softly and shifted herself on the bed when the alcohol stung, but otherwise she gave no signs of consciousness. Van Horn's big hands moved slowly and deliberately and gently. But he was still breathing as though he'd been running hard for a long time.

The scalp wound had already started scabbing nicely and no bandaging or haircutting was necessary. He put a small bandage on the bullet wound and covered her up. Then, suddenly, he bent and kissed her mouth. Not waking, she murmured and stirred under his lips.

After a moment he turned away from her. The room had been hastily ransacked. The girl's clothes were piled beside a chair on the floor. Trimble's valise was gaping open and its contents were strewn about. Van Horn paused and looked into his own jacket pocket. All Trimble's papers and tickets were there. Whoever the visitor was he'd got nothing from the valise.

The girl's little handbag was upside down on the bureau, its trivial, scented things scattered over the glass top. The passport, the brochure of the country inn and a lipstick had fallen to the floor. Van Horn sat down heavily in a chair. Outside the bells of some church rang six o'clock. Van Horn phoned the desk and ordered breakfast.

He sat watching the girl until there was a knock at the door and the breakfast appeared. He took the tray at the door. The cognac bottle from the valise was under the bed but intact. He retrieved it and dumped two ounces from it into a cup of coffee and took the cup to the bedside.

For the second time that night he nursed her back to con-sciousness. It took several minutes of coaxing before her eyes opened and she looked at him, and there was fright and horror in her face. He made her drink all the coffee. With the second cup, he made her wash down four aspirin tablets. She managed to sit up, and some of the terror left her.

"I thought it was you," she said.

"Go easy," he said. "Don't rush yourself. You've had a hell of a night."

"It's all right," she said wearily. "I'm not afraid any more. I was so afraid, at first, that I couldn't move."

"Well, if you're determined to tell me about it, start at the beginning."

"I was asleep," she said. "I must have been asleep a long time because it was getting light. There was a knock on the door. I thought it was you. I got up and put my coat on and went and took the chain off the door."

"Didn't you ask who it was?"

She looked ashamed. "No. I know it was stupid. But I was sleepy, and anyway, I'm not used to this kind of thing." She sounded on the verge of tears.

"I know," he said. "I know."

"Anyway, I undid the chain and opened the door and turned to go back to bed. I was just longing to sleep some more, that's all."

"And your visitor obliged you by banging you over the head?"

"Yes. But he didn't do it right. I was only stunned, and when my head cleared I saw him. He was over by the chest of drawers with his back to me, going through my handbag, and the room was in a mess."

"Why did he shoot you? Didn't you play possum?"

She blushed. "Well, you see ... well, I'd taken off my things before I went to bed, and when I fell the coat came open, so ... "

"So naturally, when you came to, your first thought was to cover yourself up." Van Horn laughed and shook his head. "Right?"

"Yes," she said, and would not look at him. "I tried to close the coat and he must have seen me move in the mirror over the chest, and he turned and shot me. I must have fainted then."

"My God!" Van Horn grunted. "Of course you did. Well, modesty breeds distress, my girl."

"Did, uh ... did you find me like this?" she asked timidly, glancing down at the sweetly curved mound her nearly naked body made under the bedclothes.

He said, "I found you lying in your own blood on the bed. You scared me to death. I interrupted your caller. He carries a silenced gun. Everybody does these days. Did you get a good look at him?"

"No," she said. "It was still pretty dark. Anyway, his back was to me, and when he turned all I could see was the gun in his hand."

Van Horn went to the door and opened the inside panel. In the cavity where more usual guests would find their suits, cleaned, pressed and promptly returned by an efficient management, he found a blunted slug from a .25. He put it in his pocket and closed the door.

"Please," the girl said. "What is going on?"

He went and sat on the edge of the bed and took her hand. "I wish I knew, Flavia," he said. "This has gotten pretty complicated in the past few hours."

He got off the bed abruptly and began to repack everything. He talked as he worked. "I hadn't expected you to be in danger," he said. "That was one mistake. And I hadn't realized how close we were to these people, whoever they are. I have a lot of work to do to sort all this out, and the first item for consideration is your safety. I am finally convinced that taking you to Geneva would be fatal. Do you have any baggage at all?"

"No," she said wearily. "I was being dramatic. When the time came to leave Chamonix, I just put on my hat and coat and left. I was going to make a clean break, leave everything behind me except what I stood up in."

"Uh-huh. Well, we can see to getting you some clothes." He went again to the bed and stood looking down at her. "Orders," he said. "We will finish our breakfast. Then I am going to get you out of here and you're going to visit a man I know. His name is Fabry. He's an Italian, formerly an Italian-American. In the thirties he was requested to leave the States by our oversensitive Immigration Service. He'd become embroiled in some unpleasantness involving booze. During the war he was very useful to the right people on the right side, and so now he works for us. You will, with reservation, put yourself in his hands. He's easygoing and not as tough as he thinks he is, but he's fairly sensible. He's rich, too. Took most of his loot with him when they deported him. Also, he's pretty lecherous."

"Why am I going to visit him?"

"Because he'll keep you out of harm's way until we can unravel this rigmarole we've run into."

"All right," she said, and smiled wanly. "You're very tyrannical, aren't you?"

"I'm a hell of a bo," he said. "Your head will ache for a while and that nick you got will make you stiff for a day or so. But you ought to be all right in jig time if you don't push your luck."

"I won't," she said. "I feel too . . . too beaten. Are you going to leave me with Mr. Fabry?"

"Yes, but I'll be in touch with you. Finished your breakfast?" She nodded. "All right. Now get up and get dressed while I look demurely the other way."

CHAPTER SEVEN

At five minutes past seven Van Horn and the girl were at the front door of an ornate villa two miles outside of Turin. The wan autumn dawn gave only a thin light, but still the countryside visible beyond the elaborate gardens was warmly colored with the remains of the Piedmontese summer.

No one answered Van Horn's ringing of the bell. Raising a massive fist, he set up a regular heavy pounding on the incised paneling of the door. Beside him the girl swayed within the circle of his arm.

Half a minute later the door flew open and a short, rotund man in a voluminous lavender dressing-gown stood blinking at them with sleepy dark eyes. In a throaty tenor, he set about cursing them, fat white hands waving broadly.

"Shut up, Fabry," Van Horn said, moving toward him and half carrying the girl as he did so. "Wake up. It's Van Horn."

The Italian's cursing stopped as abruptly as it had started and he peered at Van Horn. Then his gaze shifted to the girl. If he recognized Van Horn or was impressed by the girl, his face did not show it.

He said at last, "Hah! Awright. Come on the hell inside."

He led them through a marble-sheathed foyer into a living room that was swollen with velour-and tapestry-covered furniture. An immense grand piano filled one corner. On it was a Paisley shawl in the folds of which were set two framed photographs. Fringed floor lamps and rococo ash stands and painted ebony coffee tables obstructed traffic in every direction.

"Siddown," Fabry said. "What the hell you come banging on my door for this time a day?" His words came bursting out in sentence groups, as out of a machine.

"Where's your spare room?" Van Horn said sharply, ignoring him. "The girl is hurt."

"Hah!" Fabry said again. He gestured toward the nearest divan. "Put her down there." He turned and trotted quickly out. In a moment they could hear him bellowing at someone.

Van Horn put the girl down on the divan. She sank onto it with a little moan and closed her eyes.

Fabry came back. With him was a plump woman in a nightgown who was trying to put on a flowered silk dressing-gown as she walked. The shag under her arms was jet black. The rigidly waved hair on her head was the color of butter.

"My housekeeper," Fabry said. "She'll look after the girl."

Van Horn bent and picked the girl up. "'Where to?" he asked.

The woman beckoned and Van Horn followed her out and down another marbled corridor. Near the end of it they turned into a big bedroom. The woman moved hurriedly and straightened the rumpled bedclothes. Then Van Horn put the girl down on the flowered satin spread. Carefully he took off her coat. She opened her eyes and said, "Don't leave me."

"It's all right," he said. "This woman will look after you. I'll be in the other room. Try to sleep." He turned to the waiting woman and said, in Italian, "She has been hit on the head and shot. Stay with her, please, and keep her quiet. We are sorry to intrude."

"It is nothing," the woman said. Her voice was surprisingly sweet from so hardened a mien. "I can sleep elsewhere. I will take care of her. She is very beautiful."

"Yes," Van Horn said somberly. "She is the most beautiful woman I have ever seen."

"Ah," said the woman, and smiled. *"La sua bellisima?"*

"Thank you for your help," Van Horn grunted, as though she had not spoken. The woman began skillfully pulling off the girl's sweater, and he left the room.

Back in the living room, Fabry was lighting a spirit lamp under a coffee machine. Van Horn stood over him. "The woman is trustworthy?"

"Natch," Fabry said. "Been here two years. Knows enough to keep her trap shut and put out when I wan' it Good piece. Keeps the overhead down." He threw back his head and laughed loudly.

"You'll have to look after the girl indefinitely," Van Horn said. "She's on the spot. Where's your phone?"

Fabry gestured vaguely, distracted by the sudden bubbling of his coffee. Van Horn finally located a baroque telephone hidden behind the piano. He set about putting in a person-to-person call to David Black at an Elysées number in Paris.

"Dave ain't gonna like it," Fabry said. "Too early. Prolly got some chick with um."

Van Horn came back, having at some length registered the call.

"Awright, kid, what's it all about?" Fabry said. "I ain't seen you since Christ knows when."

"1950," Van Horn said. "In B.A."

"I unnerstan' you got yer ass inna sling."

"Is that what you understand?" Van Horn asked coldly.

"Don't get snotty," Fabry said. "You penny-ante bums run around down them banana republics, think you're hot stuff. Lotta crap. Minute ya come over here an' get mixed up inna big time, you get loused up and gotta come runnin' ta the old pros. It makes me laugh."

"Does it?" Van Horn said in a dead voice.

"Yeah, take you. Big deal in La Paz. Made yourself a softie. Heard all about it. Got your ass inna sling for real." He poured two cups of his viscous looking coffee and offered one to Van Horn. "Have a cuppa coffee," he said condescendingly.

"Enjoy yourself," Van Horn said. He made no move to take the coffee.

"Go on," Fabry said grandly. "Take it. You come to me for help, I'll give it to ya." Fabry turned serious suddenly. The speed of his speech diminished. He set the steaming cup near Van Horn, saying, "You gotta unnastand. It ain't the same over here. The footwork gets pretty fancy. I ain't surprised you got fouled up. It takes some gettin' used to. What's the story?"

"I was sent to pick up a report from a man."

"Errand boy stuff, huh? Well, Black ain't so dumb. You gotta break into it easy. This is the big league, buddy."

"Oh, for Christ's sake," Van Horn rumbled.

"Naw, I mean it," Fabry went on. Then he seemed to think of something and he grinned derisively. "Or was it maybe because a La Paz? Was it maybe you got told off and it was eat crow or pull out? Huh? That was it, huh?"

Van Horn picked up his coffee cup and took a big gulp of the poisonous-looking stuff. "When are you going to stop trying to be Al Capone?" he asked.

"Aw, can it," Fabry said, looking uncomfortable.

Van Horn moved to the piano and looked at the framed photographs. One was a picture of Fabry, taken about twenty-five years earlier. He was dressed in full evening clothes and standing next to him was Mayor James Walker of New York City. The picture was not inscribed. The other photograph showed Fabry and a large group of stiffly posed men in dinner jackets. They were standing under a big floral sign that read, WELCOME HOME RANDY, and they were beaming into the camera. The inscription at the bottom read, *To my pal Mio; Dutch.*

"Still," Van Horn said, "I suppose if you didn't have delusions and gaudy memories you wouldn't work for us."

The phone rang. Both men answered it, Fabry picking up the receiver, Van Horn holding the extra earpiece clapped to the side of his head.

Fabry said, "Pronto."

It was the Paris call. Mr. Black was not available. A Mr. Hendricks was on the line.

Van Horn took the phone from Fabry and said he would talk to Hendricks. After a few explosive moments a sleepy voice said, "*Oui?*"

"Hello, Hendricks," Van Horn said. "Van Horn here."

"Oh. Yes. Van Horn. We got your parcel. It was nice and clean. Nothing. Nothing at all. Did you keep the balance?"

"Yes. And then some. I'm at Fabry's in Turin. I brought our mutual friend's daughter here. She's a little under the weather and very much on the spot. Where is Black?"

"Can't be reached. He left orders for you. You're to go to Geneva."

"I'd planned to."

"Yes. You'll get word from the usual sources there on the rue des Alpes. Jacques Alain to Belisarius. And then somebody'll come and take over from you. You had no business going to Turin."

There was a long pause. Van Horn stared stonily at the wall. Finally, Hendricks's voice said, "Is that all?"

"Yes," Van Horn said. "That's all." Slowly he hung up.

"Well, what'sa pitch?" Fabry asked.

Van Horn turned and went back to the table with the coffee machine on it. He poured himself another cup and drank it swiftly. Then he turned to Fabry.

"Now listen closely," he said. "You better know as much about this as the rest of us." Smoothly and accurately he recounted everything that had happened since his discovery of the girl and Trimble's body in the train at Modane. Fabry listened, frowning. When the account ended Van Horn said, "Ever hear any of the names?"

"Only Zerho. I ran into him one time in Calabria, back when the Christian Democrats was expropriatin' that land from the big landowners. He was workin' for some syndicate in Milan. He's tough, but stupid. A hired guy is all."

Van Horn dug in his pocket and produced the bullet he'd taken out of the hotel door. He explained how he'd found it and said, "Trimble was shot by the same caliber gun or I miss my guess. So was the guy they found dead in the engraver's shop. It's a long shot. But see if you can find out if this matches the other two. Don't give the show away, though."

"Whaddya take me for, a amateur?"

The blond woman came in and said, "The girl wishes to speak with you."

Van Horn once more followed her out and down the corridor. At the bedroom door she left him, closing the door behind him as he entered.

Flavia Trimble was propped up in bed wearing a brilliant red nightgown and a pink maribou bedjacket. Seeing Van Horn's startled look, she smiled and said, "Angela lent them to me. She's terribly sweet, but I do feel a little overwhelmed."

"You're pretty blinding," Van Horn said, "but you look great."

"When will I see you again?"

"You just stay here with Fabry. You say his woman is all right?"

"Oh, yes. She's wonderful. And she got quite friendly after she found I speak Italian." She grinned at Van Horn and he looked confused for an instant, then grinned himself. "Yes," she said. "I heard you."

"Well," he said, "I meant it. You are the most beautiful woman I've ever seen."

"You ought to know. You've seen most of me, I expect."

"You *are* feeling better, aren't you?"

"Yes. But I wish you weren't going." Again she was serious. "Listen, Mr. Van—What should I call you?"

"Anything. Call me Jud."

"Jud, what about Daddy? I mean, what will be done with him?"

"He'll be sent home for burial, Flavia," he said gently. "As soon as it can be arranged."

"You mean as soon as it suits the people you work for."

"Yes."

She sighed. "All right. There isn't anything I can do, I guess."

"Nothing at all except stay out of sight and get back on your feet."

"All right," she said again. "But please don't just leave, don't keep me in the dark."

"We won't."

"What do you mean by 'we'? You mean it won't always be you?" She frowned.

"No, it won't. But the next guy will be a big improvement probably."

"No. I don't think so. It's strange. I feel as though I've known you for years and years. So much has happened. I have so much to think about."

"Yes," he said. He held out his hand. "Good-by."

She took his hand and held it. "Good-by," she said. Then she pulled him closer. "Find out who it was. Please. Find out who did it."

"We'll do our best, Flavia," he said. "We'll do our best. I liked your father, Flavia." For a few seconds they regarded one another gravely. Then he released her hand and straightened up and left her.

He found Fabry in another ornate bedroom, dressing. "I ast ya," the Italian said. "What'sa pitch?"

"I'm taking off," Van Horn said. "If Black calls, or anybody wants me, tell them I'm on my way to Geneva by way of Milan."

"Milan?" Fabry's head came up out of his heavily starched shirt with surprise rounding his eyes. "What the hell you wanna go to Milan for?"

"Trimble would have gone there this morning. He went there every Wednesday. Some of his chums came from there. If there's any connection I want to find out what it is. And I want to look up his friends if I can."

"Awright, if that's how you wannit," Fabry said, knotting his tie.

"You'll have to let me have a gun," Van Horn said.

"Sure," Fabry said. He casually pulled open a drawer in his chiffonier and lifted out of it a .32-caliber American revolver. "It's loaded an' all," he said and gave it to Van Horn.

"Thanks," Van Horn said. He stuffed the pistol into his hip pocket.

"You got a front?" Fabry asked.

"No."

"You crazy? You can't just mooch aroun' without—" He met Van Horn's eyes and shut up.

Van Horn went close to him. "Listen to me, Fabry," he said. "The girl is in danger. Try to remember that. And she has no reason at all to trust us. So keep an eye on her. Somebody's going to take over for me in Geneva. You may not see me again for another five or six years. But I want you to know that if anything happens to that girl while she's in your care, I'll come looking for you. Understand? Working or not, I'll come looking for you, Fabry."

"Awright, awright, don't getcha self inna uproar. I'll take care a her. They taking you offa the case, huh?"

"Yes."

"Geez, maybe they'll send down Parrish. Or Browning. Now there's two guys know their way around. Real hot ones."

"I thought you'd be pleased," Van Horn said. "So long." He turned and went to the door. Then he turned back. "Remember what I said, Fabry," he said. "About the girl."

"Yeah-yeah-yeah," Fabry said. "I remember."

"I'm taking Trimble's stuff with me," Van Horn said. "So long."

He went out.

CHAPTER EIGHT

The plane Trimble would have taken to Milan landed at Mal Pensa aerodrome. There was no difficulty about Van Horn's using Trimble's ticket. It was a domestic flight, and one American businessman is like another to an Italian.

Van Horn went directly to the men's lavatory, took off his coat and shirt and washed himself thoroughly. Then he shaved, using Trimble's beautiful shaving tackle. As he was repacking the suitcase, he took out the single shirt it contained and put it on. It was a snug fit, but it was clean. He folded his soiled shirt, put it in the bag, and reknotted his tie. As an afterthought, closing the bag, he took out Trimble's overcoat and put it on and put his own light coat in the bag. Then, carrying the bag, he walked out to catch a bus to the city. It was bitter cold.

All during the long ride down the roads lined with big billboards and small farms, through the ugly lean suburbs and finally into the chaotic streets of Milan itself, he sat staring at the back of the head of the passenger in front of him, deep in thought.

He checked the suitcase at the air terminal and, moving out into the teeming street, hailed a cab and told the driver to take him to Police Headquarters.

There, after being misdirected, redirected, and finally personally guided by an ancient porter, he found himself in the anteroom of the bureau that concerned itself with the issuing of identity cards. Here, and in offices much like it in similar buildings in cities throughout most of the countries of Europe, bewildered citizenry had its most direct contact with the monumental cancer of bureaucracy. The process varies from nation to nation. In France, for example, photo-machine pictures are acceptable, but they must show the right profile with the subject's right ear fully exposed. The ear is used for basic identification.

Other nations have other peculiar rules. But everywhere notarized stacks of papers attesting to the applicant's present address, former addresses, occupational status and so forth, are relentlessly demanded. After collecting all the papers, after waiting for from three days to two weeks (depending on the size of the city or the efficiency of the individual police force) and after paying a sizable stamp tax, the applicant is presented with his card, which he is supposed to carry with him at all times, which is supposed to be kept up to date continuously, and which most citizens lose within a month of receipt.

At a worn yellowish desk behind a low railing sat a fat, vacant-looking man, idly picking wax out of one ear with a stubby finger, and humming an operatic aria sonorously to himself. There was no one else in the room. Van Horn walked to the railing and waited.

The fat man hummed the entire aria through to a mellifluous close, wiped his finger on the side of his serge trousers, and looked up.

Before he could speak Van Horn said, smiling, *"Traviata."*

The fat man looked blank for an instant, then shrugged. *"Si,"* he said. "Of course."

"You are in good voice."

"You are an artist?" the fat man asked, looking a little less blank.

"No, no. A dilettante only."

"I too," said the man rather sadly. "I love to sing, but I have no real voice." He sighed.

"But there must be those who listen," Van Horn said. "Listen and admire."

"*Si.*" The man brightened considerably. "You are right." He looked closer at Van Horn. He seemed suddenly a bit suspicious. "You are French?"

"No," said Van Horn, putting his passport on the desk. "American."

The man's face cleared and he smiled so that his whole countenance became involved in the effort. "That's good. Your accent ... I thought you were possibly French. And you know," he added, making a wrenching motion with his fist, "these French ... "

A woman came into the room from the corridor, carrying a thick handful of papers with a strip of photographs clipped to the top. The man looked at her inquiringly and she held up the papers. He waved her toward the narrow bench that stood against the side wall and said, "*Aspetta.*"

"Please," Van Horn said. "Take care of her. My business is not pressing."

It took some time to convince the man that this was true, but finally he motioned the woman forward, inspected her papers, stuck a ticket with the number 1 on it under the clip, and motioned her back to the bench. Then he turned back to Van Horn. "What can we do for you?"

"I am looking for someone, a friend of other days. I thought I might find her whereabouts through your office."

The fat man's eyes narrowed. "Why do you seek her?"

"I met her just after the war. We were ... " He smiled conspiratorially. "We were *very* good friends for a short time."

The fat man exploded his smile again, but it had a rather lecherous air to it now. "Ah," he said. "I see. And now you are back in Italy."

"And I would like to see her again. But alas! I am only here for a few hours and and—it. is most embarrassing—I do not remember her present name."

The fat man looked peeved. "Then how do you expect us to—"

"I remember her professional name," Van Horn said quickly. "It was Teresa Nardiello. And she sang at La Scala."

"Ah! At La Scala." He frowned. "I can recall no Teresa Nardiello."

"It is not surprising. She was never a notable artist. But she had ... other talents more memorable."

"You have asked at La Scala? You have tried to find her in the directory?"

Van Horn looked glum. "She is married," he said. "I do not know her married name."

"Soprano? Mezzo? Contralto?"

"Mezzo," Van Horn said, splitting the difference.

The fat man shook his head in irritation. "I do not remember her. Yet I have not missed a performance in seventeen years." He grunted and rose from his chair. "One minute," he said. "Please wait."

He went out through a door at the rear and Van Horn waited. Ten minutes went by. The room began to fill with people. Van Horn took out a cigarette, but a huge sign over the bench read *E VIETATO FUMARE* and he didn't light it.

A pale man in pince-nez spectacles poked his head out of the rear door and bellowed, *"Uno!"* The woman who had followed Van Horn into the room got up hurriedly and rushed past him through the gate in the railing and out through the rear door.

The fat man re-entered in a few more minutes and without looking at Van Horn began calling the people in the room to his desk, passing out numbered tickets to those whose papers were in order, raining sneers and imprecations and loud dismissals on the rest. He took his time with each applicant, pausing at one point to exchange insults with a skinny Neapolitan woman for a full five minutes. It was a wonderful room in which to learn patience and idiomatic Italian.

At last the fat man rose, beckoned to Van Horn, and led him outside into the corridor. The instant he'd closed the door behind them, a formidable black cigarillo and a lighted match blossomed in his hands and Van Horn was treated to a cloud of acrid smoke.

"The *padrone* has asthma," the man complained with a sigh. "Consequently, we must all suffer for his disease. Smoke?" He offered another of his ropes.

Van Horn said, "Thank you, I have no taste for dark tobacco," and lighted his cigarette. For a minute or two he and the fat man smoked in silence. This was Italy. There was no hurry.

Finally the fat man drew a folded card from an inside pocket. He leaned closer to Van Horn and a look of sympathy wrinkled his face. His wet brown eyes looked sad. "I have bad news for you," he said.

"Ah," said Van Horn. "I was afraid you would have no record of her."

"Oh, I found her papers," the fat man said proudly. "She is still alive, inhabiting a villa in the countryside near here."

"So much the better. You are very efficient here."

"She is married, as you know. Her husband is one Antonio Bocarda. He is well known here. Called Cherubino. A big industrialist."

"That is bad. I am not rich."

"Naturally. He is managing director of a paper mill in the city. A big man. But still, that would not be insurmountable for you."

"What is bad, then?"

"Look!" He unfolded the card and shoved it close to Van Horn's face. It was a duplicate of Teresa Bocarda's identity card. It said she was born in Genoa in 1915, gave her description, noted that she had married in 1949. A photo of her was attached. The card had been issued one year previously.

Van Horn stared at the card. There seemed nothing very sad about it. "I don't understand," he said. "What is wrong? Politics?"

"No, no," the man said impatiently, engulfing Van Horn in smoke again. "Nothing like that. Bocarda is a Christian Democrat, and the signora is one of our fashionable Communists. Lives well off the sweat of those she pretends to work with and champion." A sneer wrinkled his face. "All very usual nowadays. No, it isn't that."

"What, then?" Van Horn demanded. "What is the matter? Is she ill?"

The little man sputtered impatiently, "No, no, no, no, no! Can't you see? Look at the picture, man!" Suddenly he became very sympathetic and sad again. "Look at her," he said dolefully. "I know you Americans. I know your tastes in women. Alas, Teresa can no longer be of interest to you. It is too bad, I am so very sorry. It's the *pasta*, you know. The good *pasta* the rich can eat. Look at her." He shook his head. "Tch, tch, tch! Fat as a pig! I am so very sorry for you!"

Van Horn gave him five hundred lire, thanked him, and fled.

The functionary had held him too long. As Van Horn bolted from his taxi and into the air terminal, the bus for the Geneva run of the Cairo—New York TWA flight was already due to have left. He got the valise out of the checkroom and ran across the terminal, fishing for his wallet and passport with his free hand, saying, *"Scusi, scusi,"* as he banged into waiting passengers. He skidded to a stop at the TWA check-in desk. The uniformed clerk looked up and said politely, "Mr. Trimble? We've held the bus for you."

CHAPTER NINE

Van Horn paused. He had used Trimble's ticket on the flight to Milan from Turin, but that had been a domestic trip and be had not had to identify himself thoroughly or pass through any Customs. This was different. On this flight he would be required to exhibit proof of his identity, and he would have to pass through Italian and Swiss border inspections. The clerk was making little impatient motions. With a shrug, Van Horn drew a deep breath, grinned wryly, and said, "Thanks. That's very good of you. I was delayed."

He handed the clerk Trimble's passport and ticket. Hardly glancing at them, the clerk hurriedly banged the necessary stamps on them, recorded the weight of Trimble's suitcase, and handed Van Horn passport, ticket, baggage check and blanks to be filled out for Immigration and Customs at the airport and in Switzerland. Then he flung the suitcase to a waiting porter with a quick command and said to Van Horn, "The bus is right outside, sir."

As Van Horn thanked him and turned away, a second clerk entered from the rear office behind the desk and said in swift Italian, "We can't hold the bus any longer."

"It's all right," the first clerk replied. "Mr. Trimble has just checked in."

Then the second clerk's eyes were on Van Horn and he was saying, "But that's not—!" Van Horn walked with deliberation toward the bus.

The second clerk, after a puzzled stare at Van Horn's retreating back, shook his head and grimaced and went back into his office.

Van Horn went outside and boarded the bus, nodding to its occupants as he showed his ticket to the driver, and saying in English, "Thank you for waiting. I hope I haven't inconvenienced you too much."

There were a dozen other passengers. If any of them, like the second clerk at the check-in desk, was accustomed to seeing Trimble on this flight every Wednesday, Van Horn's masquerade would be exposed before it started. Then there would be police and embarrassing questions—such as how did he come to be in possession of Trimble's passport and ticket and suitcase, and why was he attempting to make an illegal entry into Switzerland?

As he moved back along the narrow aisle to an empty seat in the rear, he had a look at his companions. They were all classifiable types: An Italian-Swiss family going home; two minor American film people; three nuns; two businessmen, one of them large and German, the other small and Italian; and a young American couple loaded with cameras and other honeymoon equipment including severe head-colds. Some of them, notably the Italian-Swiss family, looked at Van Horn disapprovingly. The rest ignored him. With a sigh, he dropped into an empty double seat and relaxed.

During the ride to Mal Pensa, he covertly studied Trimble's passport photograph. Trimble and he were the same general build, both were dark, and Van Horn was wearing Trimble's overcoat and hat. But Trimble had been a handsome man with a good nose and rather large clear eyes. The fact of the matter was that, bad though the photograph was, a myopic child of eight would never have mistaken it for a picture of Van Horn.

"Well," he muttered to himself resignedly, "that's just the way it is."

The lateness of the bus saved him at Mal Pensa. Holding up an intercontinental airline's flight can throw an entire schedule out of phase.

The check-out was less than perfunctory, and in a matter of seconds the dozen passengers were being bundled aboard. Van Horn found a seat toward the rear of the big Constellation next to one of the nuns. She was busy with her breviary and paid no attention to him. Almost as he settled himself awkwardly in the narrow seat, he was asleep.

The flight from Milan to Geneva (or to Zurich, for that matter) is extremely boring; seventeen thousand feet almost straight up, then seventeen thousand feet almost straight down. And there you are in Switzerland. The only relief is an occasional glimpse of Mont Blanc on clear days. This was not a clear day. Van Horn slept soundly.

The Geneva aerodrome is one of the most pleasant in the world. It lies at the edge of a long and lovely valley and the planes swoop toward it, down over the dark mountains, in beautiful slow arcs, looking much more like birds than planes usually do.

Inside the building they have the sort of assembly line for passing through Customs that most international aerodromes have. Only half a dozen passengers got off the flight with Van Horn—the nuns, the honeymoon couple, and the little Italian businessman.

Van Horn took a position between two nuns at the passport control counter. This was the moment of greatest jeopardy for anyone masquerading as he was, but the passport control officer was occupied in a conversation with the guard standing behind him and checked, stamped, and returned the passports of the nuns and Van Horn with a rapidity born of years of going through the same motions for hours every day. It was obvious that, so far as he was concerned, nuns and Americans were equally above suspicion.

Safely inside the barrier, Van Horn moved to the U-shaped inspection counter where passengers wait, for their baggage to catch up with them. When the eight or ten pieces belonging to the seven disembarking passengers were wheeled in on a hand truck, porters immediately heaved the bags and parcels up on the counter at random, contenting themselves only with keeping each passenger's property separate from the others' by checking the baggage tags. Consequently, before Van Horn realized what was happening or could have moved to prevent it, the little Italian businessman was hovering over Trimble's valise, gesturing to a nearby inspector that he was ready.

A moment later the other five people had moved to claim their belongings, and sitting by itself in between the honeymoon couple's shiny new equipment and a nun's wicker hamper was a second calfskin suitcase. It was almost, but not quite, a duplicate of Trimble's.

Grinning faintly, Van Horn moved over and stood by it. Ten feet away a Customs official was by now deep inside Trimble's suitcase, thumbing Van Horn's dirty shirt, poking among the other innocent articles it contained, while the little Italian talked rapidly in very bad French, protesting the thoroughness of the search.

The suitcase in front of Van Horn was of the sort that has straps on the sides as well as across the top. Under cover of the nun's high wicker hamper, Van Horn unbuckled the left-hand side strap. Putting Trimble's passport on the top of the bag with his right hand, he forced his left hand inside the narrow opening.

A paper-wrapped bundle bound with shaggy hempen twine entirely filled the suitcase. Moving his big fingers with difficulty in the confined space he'd given himself, Van Horn tore at the paper.

It was flimsy, fine-grade stuff and several layers of it came away. All he encountered beneath was more paper. Whatever was in the bag, it was formidably wrapped.

His minute was up. A second Customs official was walking toward him. Van Horn stuffed the torn bits of paper into his pocket and rebuckled the strap. The Customs official, having evidently decided Van Horn was more important than either the honeymoon couple or the nuns, planted himself in front of the calfskin bag and picked up Trimble's passport. And the old miracle happened again. The thin green booklet with the gold seal on its face had all the power of a pass to Heaven signed by God Almighty. There are few frontiers in Western Europe that cannot be crossed effortlessly—never a bag opened, never a statement disputed—with one ten-dollar chip off American prestige. The Germans will sometimes be troublesome, and so will the British or Swiss if they are suffering a run of contraband. But otherwise, barring cases of mistaken identity, from Scandinavia to Greece to present a United States Passport is to move unhindered anywhere. It is a result of the dollar supremacy, and most Europeans regard it as just another reason to distrust and detest Americans. It is, after all, a kind of unintentional blackmail, from their point of view. But it has been the way of the world since the war.

"*Rien à declarer?*" The most negative question possible.

"*Rien du tout.*" The easiest answer.

The Customs man returned Van Horn's smile with a tight, infinitesimal grimace, stamped his landing card, chalked the unopened suitcase, and turned away, to rummage through the nuns' innocuous belongings like a pack rat.

A porter seized the suitcase and threw it back on the wheeled cart to be put aboard the bus for the air terminal. Van Horn, his face registering pleasant indifference, made his way to the bus outside. The Italian was already there, talking to the driver. He ignored Van Horn. The other passengers boarded the bus and it pulled out. Half an hour later it would arrive at the downtown terminal, the baggage would be unloaded, each passenger would claim his own belongings with his baggage check, the Italian's bag would be returned to him. Van Horn would retrieve Trimble's suitcase. And he would be a successful, if unwitting, smuggler.

CHAPTER TEN

At the downtown Geneva air terminal Van Horn was the first of the passengers to claim his bag. He took it and moved slowly toward the cigarette and magazine counter. The Italian would have to pass the counter to reach the street. At the magazine rack, a short, red-faced man was leafing through a copy of *Match* under the disgusted regard of the counter girl.

As she turned to look at Van Horn, she said impudently to the red-faced man, *"Les magazines sont* à vendre, *vous savez, Monsieur."* She looked at Van Horn, grimaced, and shook her head. *"Vous voulez faire* un achat, *Monsieur?"* she said pointedly.

Van Horn and the red-faced man spoke simultaneously:

"Courage, ma belle, il me faut le temps—"

"Un paquet de Baltos."

Both men stopped and looked at each other. There was nothing the matter with the short man's pronunciation, yet his accent was heavily English. The British are fine linguists, but for most of them their native intonation—except possibly in German—is ineradicable and pervasive. As a rule only those who have been bilingual since childhood can speak a Latin tongue without the light Anglo-Saxon lilt and drawl.

"Mais vous êtes avant moi, Monsieur," Van Horn said to him.

"Je vous en prie, Monsieur," the red-faced man said, bowing slightly.

The girl had already produced the cigarettes. Now she ignored the short man and looked questioningly at Van Horn. He said, *"Merci, Mademoiselle,"* paid, pocketed his purchase and moved away. Over at the baggage counter, the Italian was still awaiting his suitcase.

Van Horn slowly unwrapped the cigarettes and opened the package. Behind him, the counter girl and the redfaced man were still idly sparring:

"*Un billet de mille! Mais* Match *ne coûte que—*"

"*Sûrement, t'as de la monnaie.*"

"*Ah! Ces Anglais!*" The girl laughed in exasperation.

Suddenly the Italian was beside Van Horn, studying the rack of travel folders. He did not look at Van Horn and his lips did not move. His voice seemed to materialize without human agency. He said in thickly accented English, "Where is it?"

There was a pause. Finally Van Horn rumbled, "I put it in your suitcase."

"Where is Chariot?"

Another pause. "In Turin," Van Horn said at last.

The Italian seemed to accept the information. He turned away without having glanced at Van Horn, and strode swiftly toward the street door. Behind Van Horn, the counter girl was saying, "*Vous êtes très rude, Monsieur. Très, très rude!*"

And the short man was replying, "*Et toi, tu es jouissante.*"

Van Horn gave the Italian ten seconds, then moved to follow him. He was on the sidewalk in time to see his man disappear into the back of a black Mercedes sedan. Before Van Horn could flag a taxi, the Mercedes was deep in the traffic stream, headed out toward the road along the lake. There was no possibility of pursuit.

Bag in hand, Van Horn walked the few blocks to the Hotel des Bergues, near the lake. Out on the water the incredibly tall fountain was playing. Under the gray sky the city, humming with activity, was not beautiful. Geneva is a city meant to be sunlit. Paris on a gray day has a wonderful etched quality, and London cloudiness is also never really unpleasant nor gloomy. But Geneva, like Rome, loses all its attraction when the sun fails to shine. Without the sun it has the melancholy air of an outdoor café that is doing poor business.

He checked in at the Bergues, using his own name and passport. They gave him a pleasant room overlooking the park in front of the hotel. Alone, he took out Trimble's wallet and went over it again. He took it to pieces, once more examining minutely everything it contained. He found nothing he had not found before. Finally he turned his attention still another time to the money. The lire were all leathery old bills with the strange universal perfume of old money. The Swiss currency was small and discreet and equally old. The French money was brand new, flimsy, beautifully engraved stuff. The French put pictures of poets and the Spirit of Plenty and such things on their bills, in the perfectly sound belief that these are handsomer than the Republic's presidents. It makes for distinctive if dubiously valuable money. The two bills Van Horn held in his hand were pristine examples. He looked at them, frowning, for a long time, then shrugged and returned them, with all the other odds and ends, to the wallet and put the wallet in his jacket.

Thoughtfully he riffled through the phone book on the bed table, then picked up the wall telephone and put in a call. Presently a man's voice said, *"Allô, oui?"*

"Voulez-vous me passer Monsieur Trimble, s'il vous plaît?"

"Monsieur Trimble est sorti de Genève, Monsieur."

"Ah. Est-ce que Madame la Comtesse Trimble est chez elle?"

"Qui est à l'appareil?"

"Monsieur Van Horn. J'suis un ami de la famille."

"Quittez pas, Monsieur." The receiver was put down with a thud.

A full minute went by. Then a woman's voice, liquid and deep, said, *"Allô?"*

"Madame la Comtesse?"

"Oui."

"How do you do? This is Jud Van Horn speaking. I don't know if Larry ever spoke of me to you. We were friends in the Army."

"Ah, yes! Of course!" Her English was very nice to listen to, the accent a mixture of influences, mostly French and Italian. It was the English of someone who speaks many languages, and has much the same accent in all of them. "I remember hearing about you."

"It's been a long time."

"Where are you?"

"Here, in Geneva. Just got here, on business. I looked you up in the book. I'm only in town for a short time, and I thought it would be nice to renew old acquaintance."

"Of course. How very nice. Larry has been out of town, but he should be back at any moment. Are you free to come to dinner this evening?"

"Well, that would be fine. What time?"

"Oh, come as early as you can. *Pour le cocktail.* We shall be so glad to see you. I know Larry will be very pleased."

"Say, about five-thirty?"

"Yes. Very good. The address is—"

"I got it from the phone book. I'll take a taxi. Till five-thirty, then."

"Fine. Good-by."

Van Horn hung up and sat on the edge of the bed for a moment, gazing at the wildly flowered wallpaper. The woman's voice, even mechanically distilled by the Geneva telephone company, had been heavy with a kind of powerful sensuality, totally female, full of strength.

Van Horn muttered to himself, "They never look as good as they sound." Then he rose, put on his rumpled Alligator, leaving Trimble's coat and hat hanging in the closet, and went out into the city.

Across the park in front of the hotel under one of the passageways on the rue des Alpes he stopped at a stationery shop. This was the "usual source" Hendricks had spoken of. The proprietress was stamped out of the same mold from which they make concierges: a shapeless, stringy woman, dour and black-clad, with wiry gray hair and an array of moles. A sexless figure of small commerce. Van Horn leafed through her editions of American magazines while he waited for her to get rid of the other two customers in the place.

When they were alone he said to her, "A Monsieur Jacques Alain said he would leave messages for me here."

The woman looked at him for a moment. Then she said, "Your name?"

"Belisarius," Van Horn said. "It could have been worse," be added. "It could have been Fauntleroy. Or Anaximander. Or Charlemagne."

The woman looked at him blankly, then shrugged and went into the back of the shop. In a moment she returned and handed Van Horn an envelope. "This just arrived," she said.

"Thank you," Van Horn said, digging in his pocket. But she held up one hand and shook her head. No money. "You're un-Swiss," Van Horn said. "You'll get into trouble with that attitude." He thanked her again and left.

On his way back to the hotel he stopped at two stores and bought fresh linen and toilet articles. He entered his room at the Bergues less than three-quarters of an hour after he'd left it. But that had been sufficient time evidently. The place had been very thoroughly searched. Looking at the scattered contents of the gaping suitcase, Van Horn laughed aloud. Counting the Swiss *douane*'s search, the unoffending bag had been ransacked five times in twenty-four hours.

Nothing was missing. There was nothing in it to interest anyone. Yet it seemed to draw searchers like a rumor of uranium. Van Horn grinned down at it and scratched his big chin. His beard was already well started and his fingernails rasped against the ironlike whiskers. Taking off his jacket and rolling up his sleeves, he set about reassembling the room. Moving swiftly, he tumbled the scattered clothes and toilet articles into the bag, closed it, and threw it into the closet. He straightened out Trimble's overcoat and hung it up again where it had been.

The bed had been stripped and the drawers were pulled out of the chest; two pictures of Alpine scenes that had hung over the bed lay on the floor, the paper backs ripped off them; the mirror over the chest had been laid face down on the top of the chest and its backing was also torn off; the rug showed evidence of having been rolled back, then kicked flat; the valances over the windows were askew. In five minutes, moving at a quick, regular pace, Van Horn set the place in order. He didn't make the bed, but pulled the rumpled covers up over it and patted them flat. When he was finished, the room had the air of being kept by a clean but disorderly housekeeper.

In the bathroom the top to the toilet tank was lying on the floor. Nothing else had been disturbed. He replaced the top on the tank, saying aloud, "What the hell, they must have a pretty low opinion of me."

Back in the room he sat down on the bed and took the envelope out of his pocket. It was from Black's office in Paris. It reported simply that Trimble's body had given no hint as to why he had been killed. The bullet that killed him was a .25 caliber. The make of the weapon was not yet determined, if in fact it could be determined. Van Horn was to do nothing more. His replacement would contact him later in the day.

Van Horn carefully burned the note and flushed the ashes down the toilet. Then he stripped and turned on the faucets in the tub, let it run to within six inches of the brim, and got in it gingerly. The water, steaming hot, sloshed gently.

For a while he just soaked, turning slowly red where he was submerged, his eyes staring unseeing at the wall opposite. Then he pulled himself up and reached for the soap, cursing softly to himself.

Ten minutes later, he stood naked in front of the basin, lathering his face with shaving cream. He did it with terrific deliberation. It was the second shave of the day and was bound to be painful. Van Horn was a thickly built man, his big body solidly fleshed, the muscle cords smoothly hidden, his back tapering from his wide shoulders to his hips with no indentation at the waist, but with no lard, either. For a man with so heavy a beard, he had relatively little hair on his chest.

He used Trimble's razor again. He had taken one careful stroke with it across his cheek when suddenly he went motionless. From the other room, beyond the half-opened bathroom door, there was silence, then a faint brushing noise. More silence. Then a spring creaked.

Van Horn turned the hot-water tap in the basin full on and carefully set the razor on the edge of the bowl. Turning, be reached out to his trousers, which hung on the bathroom door. From the right hip pocket protruded the butt of the revolver Fabry had given him. His hand was inches away from it when a light voice he had heard before said, "No, no, please, Mr. Van Horn. Go on with your shaving. There's plenty of time, and no sense whatever in being foolish."

Van Horn, making no further attempt to reach the gun, pushed the door open and stepped, just as he was, into the bedroom. In the room's only easy chair, regarding him in the mirror over the chest of drawers, sat the neat little redfaced man Van Horn had seen earlier teasing the girl at the magazine counter in the air terminal.

He had a wonderful face, this man—rugged, even handsome, full of wrinkles and lines that appeared worn there by the weather rather than by age or hard living. He had fine crow's-feet by his eyes, and reddish hair. He was wearing a handsome cheviot suit and no topcoat. He looked about forty-five and in the trim.

At the moment his bright blue eyes were amused under cocked, sandy eyebrows as he gazed at Van Horn who stood in the bathroom doorway, huge and naked, his face two-thirds covered in foam. "Oh, I say," the little man said. "This *is* embarrassing." He turned around and faced Van Horn. In his hands there was no weapon, only Van Horn's papers. But under the left side of his jacket there was a square bulge.

"You the man who took the place apart before?" Van Horn rumbled.

"Afraid so," the man said. He scratched his coarse, curly hair and looked apologetic. "You see, I was come all over curious to know who you were. Sorry to have left you such a mess, but all the room told me was that you were Trimble, and of course I knew you weren't Trimble, so I took rather too long about it and you came back before I had a chance to put things to rights here; and anyway, I was a little peeved at not finding anything. Thought I'd drop in and have a natter with you, don't you know. Straight from the horse's mouth, so to say. But you saved me the trouble, leaving your jacket out here while you went about your whatchamacallums—your ablutions, what?"

"You always talk so much?"

"I talk a good bit, I must confess. Now shall I come in while you finish shaving, hm?"

In one motion, he tossed Van Horn's papers onto the chest and arose from the chair, and somewhere in the course of the motion a large automatic pistol appeared in his hand. Van Horn grunted, and grinned through the mask of drying lather. "Very slick," he said.

The man stepped over and deftly lifted the pistol out of Van Horn's trouser pocket. He put it in his side pocket and then the automatic vanished inside his jacket. "Now then," he said. "We can talk peaceably." He walked past Van Horn into the bathroom and sat down on the edge of the tub. Waving a hand toward the basin where the hot water still gushed, he said, "Please. Do go on."

Van Horn shrugged and returned to the basin and recommenced shaving. The lather had begun to dry out. He washed his face and started all over again.

"I'm really awfully sorry," the little man said, "surprising you in such circumstances. I mean to say, it *is* undignified. And I certainly won't tell anyone. Because, after all, it might not set too well with your superiors, now would it, Mr. Van Horn?"

"Cleanliness is next to godliness," Van Horn said. "Get on with it."

"Well, then, let me present myself. My name is Sean Butler. Spelled S-E-A-N, pronounced Shawn. Have a devil of a time with it, but there you are. Anyway, it's my pleasure to inform you that we have mutual interests. Really a great deal in common, we have. For example, we were both at the air terminal a while ago, and we both have an unusually intense interest in Lawrence Trimble."

"Small world," Van Horn muttered, scraping carefully around his left ear lobe. "Infinitesimal."

"Ummm. And then, of course, we're in the same sort of work, you know. I'm with M.I.6. You've heard of us, I suppose?"

"There's been a lot of talk," Van Horn said.

"Well, so here we are. Two sensible men both pursuing the same dreary quarry. So what say? Shall we throw in together?"

"Why should we?"

"Why shouldn't we? Obviously you've managed to cover a good deal of ground in a short time. I must say you Yanks are always impressive that way. Imagine my surprise! Here I am, patiently gumshoeing along, doing my simple best to keep things from getting out of control, waiting for something to turn up— something such as Mr. Trimble arriving from Milan on the Wednesday midday flight. And whom should I see get off the plane, wearing Trimble's coat and hat and carrying his valise, but a giant of a man who isn't any more Trimble than I'm Winston Churchill! I tell you, it took my breath away!" He paused and began laboriously loading a huge briar pipe with shag tobacco. When he had it nicely boiling, he went on, "Well, I'll be frank with you, Mr. Van Horn. My besetting sin is curiosity. I absolutely *had* to get to the bottom of it. I had to know who you were. So I took the liberty of following you here and ransacking your room. Then I came back to find you in the altogether in the lavatory, with your papers and whatnot conveniently laid out for me. My weakness overcame my scruples, I had an unethical peek and lo, and behold! I find you carry a special passport with some interesting entries. You carry a pistol. You're a colleague! I can't tell you how pleased I am! It makes everything much simpler."

Van Horn by now had finished shaving. He dried himself and led the way into the bedroom, carrying his trousers over his arm and his shoes in his hand. Butler followed him and dropped into the easy chair where Van Horn had first seen him. While Van Horn unwrapped the linen he'd bought, the little man went cheerfully on: "Because you see, of course, working together we can probably unknot this whole wretched business in less than half the time it would take either of us alone. So, once again, how say you? Is it clap hands and a bargain?"

Van Horn, having donned and buttoned his new shorts and his new shirt, had clumsily dropped a cuff link while threading it into the shirt cuff. Now he bent over, very close to the easy chair, reaching to pick it up, saying, "Sing on. I'm open to suggestion."

"An excellent attitude," Butler said. "I'm prepared to go more than half way." He gestured grandly, pipe in hand. "After all, I suppose, it's up to me to—" He stopped and shifted his position slightly, saying, "Incidentally, I wouldn't try to—" But it was too late.

Van Horn's right arm, at the moment when in bending his shoulders were on a level with Butler's, had shot out with snake-like speed and clamped around the little man's chest, pinning his arms to his sides. With a gusty grunt Butler's breath left him as though he'd been hit by a log, and for the first time since Van Horn had seen him he was silent. The big pipe fell on the floor, spilling a few dead ashes.

Crouching beside the chair, Van Horn brought his left arm across and lifted the automatic pistol out of Butler's jacket. He didn't appear to be exerting much pressure with the arm that held Butler, but the little man's breath was coming in gasps and his face had gone quite pale.

With the automatic in his left hand Van Horn stepped back and straightened up. The man in the chair sagged slightly when the pressure left his chest, and closed his eyes for a moment.

"Now who's embarrassed?" Van Horn asked. "Get up and take off your jacket and turn around, and if you make one move I don't think is friendly I'll bang you over the head with your own gun. Come on! Up!"

The little man took a deep breath and got out of the chair. Smoothly he took off his jacket and handed it to Van Horn, and then he turned his back. Van Horn recovered his own gun and all that the jacket held—tobacco pouch, wallet, notepad, pen, pencil, nail-clipper, handkerchief—and then he emptied Butler's trouser pockets of small change, matches, a key ring, a checkbook, a big Swedish steel clasp knife, and another handkerchief. "Drop your pants," he ordered. "It'll tend to limit your activities."

There was a pause. The already ruddy back of Butler's neck grew slowly crimson.

"I beg your pardon?" he said.

Van Horn was grinning wolfishly. "You heard me," he said. "Drop your trousers. Come on! Move!"

"Oh, now, I say!"

"One more word and I raise a lump on you. *Drop your trousers!*"

The little man began to fumble at his belt buckle. Then he stopped and shook his head. "No," he said. "You are free to crack me on the head. It's the less dishonorable way."

Van Horn relaxed and laughed. "All right," he said. "Good. I'd have made the same decision." His face went hard again and his voice grated. "But I don't like being held up in my own quarters, frisked by a joker half my size, particularly while I'm buck naked and lathered up."

"I apologize," Butler said. "And I'd like to give you satisfaction. But I'm a man with skinny, undignified legs. And so we're even. Quite even." The high color in his neck was subsiding. "Shall I sit down while you go through my things? Though I can assure you you'll find nothing of the slightest interest among them."

"Yes. Sit down," Van Horn said. "And for God's sake, shut up!"

The little man sighed and moved to the chair he had been in, retrieved his pipe and sat down. "I must say," he said chattily, "you are very nearly the strongest man I've ever met. And you're certainly the bottest-tempered. I came in here with the worst intentions, I admit, but after I identified myself I thought surely you'd—"

"*Shut up!*" Van Horn roared. Then, more gently, "My God, you talk, a lot!"

"Yes. Another of my many failings, I'm afraid." Butler clamped the pipe in his teeth and looked at Van Horn in mock contrition.

Van Horn sat down on the edge of the bed and swiftly investigated the contents of Butler's pockets, the two pistols near him. But the little man had been right. There was nothing of interest among his things. No identification, very little money, no name printed on the checks in the checkbook, no significant stub entries, all withdrawals being to cash. Nothing. Van Horn tossed the packet of odds and ends onto Butler's lap. The automatic he kept by him.

"You see?" the man said. "Waste of time. And if you have your people call my people, my people'll claim they never heard of me and know nothing about me or any other agent at work here. And I'm sure if my people wanted to know about you they'd get the same response from your people. Eh?"

"Probably," Van Horn admitted.

Butler put his jacket on again without rising from the chair. "Now then," he said. "What about my proposition? You've nothing to lose by it. And a good deal to gain."

Van Horn put on his trousers, shoving his revolver back into his hip pocket, and said nothing.

"I understand your reticence," Butler went on. "Naturally, you want evidence of good faith. Well, then, I'll break the ice. I'll state my case, and then, if you're agreeable to it, we'll work together—and I don't mind telling you I'd welcome an ally as powerful, in every way, as you are. If you aren't agreeable, then I've lost time, and given away something for nothing; but we part friends and that's an end to it. All right? Very well. I am after a man by the name of Nigel Brush. Very unsavory character, Brush. We keep an eye on the likes of him more or less out of habit. He's been fiddling about on the Continent for some years now, got into a couple of scrapes that made him nux vomica in a few countries, and ended up in Switzerland, right here in the dear old land of free currency and expensive hotels. And then he got awfully rich awfully suddenly. We thought it a good scheme to find out how."

Van Horn was fully dressed now. He stood dangling Butler's gun by the trigger guard, and said, "There isn't much point in going on. You're way past me already. We're the two straight lines that cross only once. There wouldn't be any sense in our working together. We're going in different directions altogether."

Butler held up his hand in admonishment.

"Now, now, don't be hasty. Might as well let me spill what beans I will, eh? Free, gratis, for nothing. What's there to lose?"

"All right. But hurry it up. I've got an appointment."

"Yes, of course you do," Butler said comfortably. "Well, you see, ordinarily we'd simply have asked the Swiss police to look into Brush's carryings-on, but well—there's one rather shame-making thing about the man. That is, I'm sorry to say, he once worked for us. Yes," he said, looking abashed, "it's saddening to have to admit that we use what materials we can find. So during the war and for a time afterward friend Brush was a registered British agent. Then he turned a bit too sour even for our rather jaded tastes and we sacked him. But it wouldn't do now to have him involved in anything off-color in a country where he'd once been known to be one of our chaps. Politically embarrassing, don't you know. So I came to have a look-see and investigate his purity, and I found him jolly cozy with a man named Trimble. Ready to reconsider my offer now?" He cocked an eye up at Van Horn.

"Look," Van Horn said heavily, "all you're managing to do is make me feel stupider than I usually do when I'm dealing with you people."

"Oh, come! You're far too modest."

"No," Van Horn said, sighing. "That's why I had to square things with you about catching me in the john that way. We're self-conscious when we're up against you British. You've been in this game so long and you're so well organized, and you seem to breed a special kind of man who's so good at the work and so sure it's the finest life there is, that our gang of college boys and unemployables and misguided patriots, like me, can't help but look pretty sick by comparison. We do all right, I suppose. But we're children at this work. You people practically invented it."

The outright flattery was stated with great sincerity. Only Van Horn's eyes failed to reflect the respectfulness in his voice and manner, his air of grudging admission of inferiority. But Butler appeared convinced. He said, waving a hand deprecatingly, "You're too kind. And after all, what has our reputation earned us? Perfidious Albion. Remember?"

"I'm sorry," Van Horn said. "But you've wasted your time. No dice."

"Why not?" Butler seemed really regretful. "I know it isn't precisely according to the rules for our sort to collaborate, but what the devil, we're only doing a job, and a bloody boring one at that."

"Yes, but it wouldn't be fair to you. I can't do it."

Butler sighed and stood up. "Well," he said, "we part friends and no hard feelings. But I hope—I feel certain—you'll reconsider. I'll be getting in touch with you again. Now, may I have my gun back, please?" He held his hand out.

"Sure," Van Horn said. He handed over the automatic, butt first. Again, with that fluid motion, it vanished into the little man's jacket.

"You'll be going to see Madame la Comtesse, I should imagine," Butler said. It wasn't a question.

Van Horn looked at him blankly.

Butler smiled and all the creases and wrinkles were busy on his rugged face. "Let me put it this way, old chap. If you're thinking of paying a visit to the lady, keep a weather eye peeled. Young men like you form a staple in her diet, I hear."

"You hear?"

"Yes. Never met the lady, I'm downcast to report. But she has the kind of reputation that can only be enhanced, as you might say." The smile deepened and he looked very merry and very wicked. "So, *prends soin de ta fleur, mon brave. Prends soin de ta fleur.*"

"I'll bear it in mind," Van Horn said.

"Bear me in mind, too," the little man said. He went to the room door and opened it, turned and waved. "I'll be seeing you again I expect. Ta-ta." And he went out.

CHAPTER ELEVEN

The valet led Van Horn into the big, airy salon of the Trimble villa, announced him, and withdrew, softly closing the double doors behind him. Serena Trimble advanced toward Van Horn from across the room, her hands outstretched.

She was very much like the photo he'd seen of her when be was going through Trimble's wallet. Tall, very blonde, slim and lightly tanned. A well-kept woman. She was wearing a housecoat that was made of some stiff crimson and black material and fitted her snugly. Her hair was loose down her back like flax. Her skin was luminous, her lips scarlet, her eyes dark, almost black. She moved, under the housecoat, with powerful grace. It wasn't until she was standing close to him, shaking his hand and greeting him, that Van Horn could see that she was closer to forty than to thirty-five, and that she was cockeyed drunk.

"Ah, hello, Mr. Van Horn," she said, the voice that had seemed sensual on the telephone sounding still more so vis-à-vis. There was a great deal of fire in that voice, and—-whatever she had drunk—it had affected her power of speech no more than her ability to move. It was only her eyes and a slight looseness in her mouth that gave her away. "Come and mix us both something to drink and let me welcome you to Geneva!"

She drew him across the room, still holding his hand, and led him to a big wheeled table in the corner where a formidable array of potables was laid out. "I'm so terribly sorry that Larry isn't here," she said. "I cannot imagine what has become of him. He should have been back hours ago." For a fraction of a second her eyes looked worried, even frightened, but then she laughed a deep, liquid laugh and said, *"Mais quand même, pourquoi pleurer? Quand le chat est parti les souris dansent, hein?"*

"I'm glad to be here," Van Horn said. "What'll we have?"

"Well, I have just had a *fine à l'eau.* Perhaps I'd better be consistent."

"Good," he said, and mixed two dark ones, adding, "I feel I know you rather well. Larry talked about you so much during the war."

"I thought men spoke to one another only of their mistresses, never of their wives," she said, smiling at him as she sat on a low settee near a broad bay window. Outside, the mountainside looked cold in the deepening twilight.

"Some wives are worthy of discussion," he said. He handed her a glass and took the other and raised it. "Well, here's to old friends and young ideas."

"How nice!" she said, clinking glasses with him. "I'll drink to that." And she did, a long, deep draught that left the glass a third empty. She sighed. "I wish I could say that Larry had told me all about you. But he didn't. I know very little of his life in the war. Was it very awful?"

"Horrible," Van Horn said, grinning.

"I do not believe it! I am sure you all had a most wonderful time, all you men without your women, playing at war like boys." She smiled at him and drank another inch of her drink. "Tell me, are you married?"

"No, unhappily. I suppose I'm not the husband type."

"You're not. You have *l'air d'une brute,* like Von Stroheim." Her dark eyes inspected him coolly. "There are women who like brutes, though."

"That's encouraging."

"You are in business?"

"Not really. I work for the government. Very small potatoes." He did not appear to notice the look of interest in her eyes as he spoke of the government. "I run errands," he added. "It's a lousy life. Not like this."

"Like this?" she said in surprise, looking about her.

"Of course. An establishment like yours and Larry's—two handsome people, plenty of money, a family, a beautiful home in a beautiful country. What more could a man ask of life?"

It was growing dim in the big salon. Van Horn took a pull at his drink, watching her face.

She frowned and said softly, "I do not know about a man. But a woman could ask a great deal more!" She drained her glass, and he took it from her and went to the liquor supply and mixed them both fresh drinks. A pause developed, and he did nothing to interrupt it, concentrating on mixing the drinks. He made them both as dark as before.

The valet came in and drew the curtains over the windows and lighted a few lamps, and the room became almost cozy. Minutes passed. Still Serena Trimble said nothing, but sat with her fresh drink in her hand and stared bleakly at the carpet. Van Horn sat discreetly on a *bergère* chair six feet away from her, watching her calmly over the rim of his glass. The silence grew and became chilly, full of a confused kind of intimacy. It ended all possibility of further polite, banal conversation.

At last she looked up at him and her eyes were blurred with tears. "Come here," she said.

He rose and went to her and sat carefully beside her.

"Do you know," she said, "that you are the first human being I have spoken to in two days that was not a servant?" She sighed. "No. You would quickly grow bored by this 'establishment,' as you call it."

He said nothing, but fished his Baltos out of his pocket and gave her one and lighted it and lighted one for himself.

"I disconcert you, do I not?" she asked, smiling bitterly. "You have been here what? A quarter of an hour? And I am already becoming terribly personal. And that disconcerts you, doesn't it? People one has just met are not supposed to behave this way. They are not supposed to reveal their troubles or their discontents." She drank a couple of inches of the new drink. "Well, nor are hostesses expected to be tight when they greet guests they have not met. And wives are not supposed to be deserted without notice."

Van Horn frowned. "Deserted?" he said. "I can't believe that!"

She drank again. "Yes, it is true!"

Van Horn was silent.

"Look at me," she said, spreading her arms wide in a gesture so abrupt that part of her drink spilled onto the upholstery of the settee. "Look at me! Am I not ripe? Am I not desirable? Look at me!"

"I am looking at you," Van Horn said heavily.

"Yes," she said bitterly. "All woman, all wasted. And now deserted. If I were old or ugly, yes, perhaps this would be sensible, to be left. But I am not Lea—you know, the woman in that book by Colette—I do not catch sight of myself in my mirror and cry, *'Qu'est-ce que c'est! Qui est cette vieille femme!'* Yet I am lonely, desperately lonely, trapped on this mountainside like an animal. I live in silence. What are men, that they can abandon such as I!"

Van Horn gently took her glass from her hand as she bent her head and wept. He replaced the glass with his handkerchief and waited.

She wept silently for a moment, then wiped her face with the handkerchief and said without looking at him, "But I am high, and you are attractive and sympathetic, and I feel sorry for myself. *Je m'excuse.*"

He stuffed the handkerchief back into his pocket and gave her glass back to her. "You're sure about Larry?" he asked.

Her voice was flat, uninflected. "Yes, he has gone. When he did not come back this afternoon as he should have, I was not alarmed. Then you called, and then he still did not come back, so

I went to his room. I found all his baggage gone, all the clothes and personal belongings he would need for any length of time. I could not believe it at first. I tried to think of some other reason why he would have taken so much with him. There is no other reason possible. So then I came here and began to drink." She stopped and put her cigarette out in an ash tray on the table behind the settee and addressed herself to her glass again.

"Perhaps," Van Horn said gently, "he went to see your daughter at school."

Her head came up from the glass and her eyes were fiery. "That little bitch!" She spat. "They are together, you can be sure. They have met somewhere and are off together like lovers!" There was tremendous venom in her words. Her hand shook so that the ice clinked against the glass. Her whole body was tense as a strung wire. "Yes," she said, "he went to her, but not to visit. And not at her school. My darling Flavia has been out of school for months. No. She went skiing, very conveniently, over the weekend." Suddenly she looked bewildered and her body went slack. She was turned, half facing him, and she slowly fell forward until her head was against his chest. Her voice came brokenly, muffled: "Why? Am I such a virago? Am I so fearsome that they could not speak to me, could not tell me their thoughts of me?"

A change had come over Van Horn's face as he drank. The four ounces or so of cognac he had consumed had at first simply increased his expressionless calm. But now the calmness left, and in its place a kind of grimness tightened his mouth and narrowed his eyes. For a few seconds he gazed down at the top of her flaxen head. Then he set his glass and cigarette on the table behind the settee and very gently began to stroke the back of her neck under her hair. His teeth, exposed by the tightness of his lips, gleamed in the lamplight.

Presently, speaking more strongly, Serena Trimble said, "I had known Larry was a villain. And I knew what he had done to our daughter. I should have expected this, or something like it. I was given every sign." She raised her head and looked into his eyes, their faces nearly touching. "Do you know what it is to live with someone and yet be lonely? Do you know how many months it has been since I have been made love to by my husband? Do you know what a woman loses when she is not loved? She loses all her sense of herself as a female, all her juices dry up, she has no *chien,* no womanness. She becomes merely a hulk in the form of a female."

There was a moment when, after she had stopped speaking, their eyes were locked across the inches that separated them, and the only sound in the room was their quickening breathing. At last with a kind of moan she moved to him and kissed him on the mouth. Seconds went by. Van Horn did not move. Under his jacket the -great muscles tensed. Then, with a movement as though wrenching himself free, his arms went around her and he responded. Her mouth opened under his and she put her arms around him, turning like a big cat as she did so until she lay across his lap. The room was silent except for the sound her hand made moving inside his jacket. It was a long kiss. She was very expert.

They broke apart at last and Van Horn threw his head back and took a deep breath. For a moment he stared out into the room with a look of savage disgust on his face. She lay pressed against him, her eyes closed, the splendid hair fanned out over his arm and the arm of the settee. She said, "Please! Please!" Her voice shook liquidly. He looked down at her. Without opening her eyes, she found his hand and put it on her breast. "Please!" she said once more, urgently.

Van Horn bent again toward her face, his eyes open, glowing like an animal's. His breath hissed through his teeth as his face closed on hers.

Far away, somewhere deep in the house, a bell sounded.

Serena's body went rigid under his hands. She opened her eyes and there was confusion and terror in her face.

Van Horn, with a sigh, straightened up. With a single move-ment Serena swung her feet to the floor and stood up, button-ing her housecoat. Frowning, she looked down at Van Horn suspiciously, started to say something, then turned and walked steadily out of the room through the double doors.

After she was gone Van Horn stood up, shook himself, and barked a laugh that fell dully on the empty room. He found his glass on the table and drained it and lighted a new cigarette. "Close," he said aloud, "but no cigar."

Serena Trimble came back through the double doors and walked over to him. She stood in front of him, frowning the same suspicious frown. Her eyes were furious. "You must be feeling very pleased with yourself," she said viciously. "What a Lothario! Making love to a poor, sex-starved woman while your thoughts were far away. Did you learn whatever it was you wanted to learn, Mr. Van Horn?" She shook her head, her face twisted in revul-sion. "Ah! What a fool I am! I feel filthy."

Van Horn looked at her mildly and said nothing.

"I suppose," she went on, her body bent tautly, her face close to his, "that you know nothing about what I mean. I suppose you came here honestly as a visitor, in town on business. Fa! You are not clever. You are not even very attractive. And you should make better arrangements. After all, there is no telling what might have happened if your colleague had not called when he did."

"My colleague?" Van Horn asked, looking honestly puzzled.

"Oh, please! Spare me your innocence! Your Mr. Parrish is on his way up. So inconvenient for you when you had so nice a chance to combine business with pleasure!"

"Oh," said Van Horn. "I see. Two American Government employees call on you the day your husband seems to have deserted you. Yes. I guess it does look like too much of a good thing."

She turned away from him disdainfully as the valet entered, conducting into the room a tall thin man in a suit of flannel so dark it appeared black. His shirt was starched, his cravat was perfectly tied, and he obviously had left a stick, gloves and a Homburg downstairs. His sallow face was long and equine, with rather large and boyish gray eyes that seemed much too bright for the somberness of the rest of him.

As he advanced, the valet said, "Monsieur Pah-reesh, Madame," and withdrew.

The tall man went smoothly toward Serena Trimble, bowing as he reached her and quickly kissing her hand. "Roger Parrish, Madame Trimble," he said in a mellifluous baritone. "From the American Embassy."

"So your card informed me," Serena said haughtily. "I expect you are acquainted with Mr. Van Horn?"

"Uh, yes," said Parrish, nodding toward Van Horn. "Hello, Jud."

"Hello, Roger," Van Horn said. "It's not very nice to see you."

"Shouldn't think it would be," Parrish said equably.

Serena cut in impatiently, "What can I do for you, Mr. Parrish?"

"Shall we all be seated?" Parrish said with some diffidence. Serena seemed for an instant to be about to refuse, but then she perched herself on the edge of a chair and gestured toward the settee. Parrish sat down on it as though expecting it to shatter under his weight. Van Horn stayed where he was, watching Serena.

"Thank you," Parrish said. "I am terribly sorry to intrude myself this way, Madame, but it is necessary, and, I must add, painful to me that I do so. I am afraid I bring you tragic news, very bad news indeed." Years of living in all sorts of countries while impersonating all sorts of people had given Parrish a tone in English that deprived anything he said of weight or of what could be construed as real sympathy. It had only a sort of mechanical accuracy.

"Yes?" Serena said, and her face was all at once starkly pale, almost gray, under her tan.

Parrish sighed. "I regret that it is my duty to inform you," he said, "that your husband, Lawrence Trimble, is no longer alive."

"What? What did you say? Wha-a-at!" Serena's voice rose loudly. "What do you mean?"

"I mean, Madame," said Parrish, "that your husband is dead. I am most terribly sorry to have to—"

Serena was out of her chair and standing over him, her face distorted with what could have been rage or pain or the last moments of sanity. "How? How dead? Why is he dead? Where is he?" Her voice sawed through the room.

Parrish rose awkwardly as she pressed toward him, and tried to put a hand on her arm. She snatched her arm away and he said, "Please, Madame. He was killed. Shot. Yesterday evening."

"Where? Where?"

"On a train to Paris, Madame. The—uh—body is being held in Paris for investigation. We shall be able to send it to you shortly, I believe. Meanwhile—"

"Why? Why was he killed?"

"We are doing our best to discover that, and so are the French police, I can assure you."

Serena began to wring her hands and rock back and forth where she stood. "The imbecile!" she said. "The *imbecile!*" Her breath was noisy in her throat. Then she said, "And my daughter? Where is my daughter?"

Van Horn's gaze went swiftly to Parrish. But there was no change in the long horse face as the tall man said, "Why, we know nothing of your daughter's whereabouts. I'm sorry."

"Oh, my God!" Serena said in a kind of growl. Then, her voice rising to a hysterical shriek, her eyes staring wildly, she said, "*Dio mio! Sono sola!*" And she collapsed like a toy inside the rustling housecoat.

CHAPTER TWELVE

Van Horn in one big stride was beside her and caught her as she fell. He scooped her up in his arms and looked down at her. Even drained of blood her face seemed young and her skin was fresh. "Poor Serena," Van Horn said. "All alone." He put her on the settee.

Parrish had moved to the door and was calling, "Valet! Valet!" He turned back into the room and said to Van Horn, "This is a break. We can turn her over to the servants and clear out. Wonderful thing, the power to faint."

"The whole family's pretty good at it," Van Horn muttered.

The valet entered in a hurry, Parrish explained matters to him, and he turned on his heels and ran out. In a moment he was back with a fat woman in an apron who took charge of the unconscious woman on the settee with practiced efficiency. Van Horn and Parrish, murmuring sympathetically, left. In the foyer, Parrish found and collected his hat and gloves and stick, saying, "Good-looking woman. She'll make a formidable widow. Ought to have no trouble finding someone. Plenty of scratch, too, I'm told. Well, life goes on, doesn't it?"

Outside, light snow was beginning to fall. The two men got into Parrish's new Frégate, and Parrish wheeled the car swiftly out onto the smooth road along the mountainside.

"Hungry?" he asked Van Horn.

"Yes," Van Horn said. "I was asked to dinner back there and never got it."

"I'm famished myself. They sent me on here so fast from Aleppo that I hadn't time for real preparations. And that airline food is more than I can stomach. There must be a place near here somewhere."

They found one, a touristic chalet tucked into a fold in the mountain. When they had been seated and had ordered, Parrish sat toying with his fork, saying, "Jud, I'm sorry about this. But you know why I've come, don't you?"

"Sure," Van Horn said glumly. "You're taking over."

"Uh-huh. Dave doesn't think you're sufficiently chastised as yet. He's probably digging up some new humiliations for you." Parrish paused and looked as serious as his bright eyes would allow. "Listen, Jud," he said. "I think you ought to know that we're all sorry about this mess you're in. I don't suppose any of us understands it, or understands you, really, but we're all sorry. And we all wish we could help."

"Word does get around, doesn't it?" Van Horn said, smiling. "I suppose there isn't an operator from Washington to Outer Mongolia who doesn't know I'm on the hook. Well, for your sympathy, much thanks."

A waitress brought them their soup and Parrish fell to. Between rather noisy sips he said, "You better bring me up to date. I'll be working this second-hand and I ought to know all you know."

Van Horn sighed. "All right," he said. Swiftly and sparely, he outlined the events of the night before, as far as the moment when he'd interrupted the intruder in Flavia's hotel room. By then, they were halfway through their entrees, and Parrish interrupted for the first time.

"Surmise 'A,' " he said, "two sets of people after Trimble for two different reasons or the same reason. Surmise 'B,' the people who killed Trimble didn't get from him what they were looking for, saw you and the girl leave the train, decided you had it, followed you to find out."

"Or," Van Horn said, "surmise 'C,' Trimble was killed for reasons apart, and his death left a second group without something they wanted. If he was killed because of the report he was supposed to give me, then either his killers failed to find the report on him, or did find the report on him and, by killing him, put some entirely different group of people in a jam."

"Or," said Parrish disgustedly, "the girl killed Trimble because he wouldn't raise her allowance."

"Well, now listen," Van Horn said. "There's more, and more interesting."

He described his trip to Milan, his inadvertent masquerade as Trimble, and his participation in the smuggling.

"Well, well, well!" Parrish said delightedly. "You do get the breaks, don't you? And with no front, no special identity, nothing. Just young Jud Van Horn, playing himself, facing life honestly—It's amazing!"

"It was a break, all right. Though two minutes after I'd gotten into that bus I regretted the whole thing. It was just an unnecessary risk. Later, of course, it seemed like a stroke of genius."

The waitress took away the leftovers of their entrees and began mixing a green salad for them. Parrish watched her work, speaking idly. "Then our friend Trimble was playing it fast and loose and there might have been any number of people who would be either upset or delighted by his demise, depending on their point of view."

"Yes," Van Horn said. "And I've got a kind of an idea who the parties of the second part are, or at any rate what they're up to."

"Do you, now?" Parrish watched the waitress serve the salad, and then attacked it skillfully. "Tell all, Swami. I couldn't possibly guess."

Van Horn took Trimble's wallet out of his jacket and laid it in front of Parrish. "Have a look at this," he said. "It took me two go-rounds in it to see what there is to be seen."

Parrish dutifully put down his fork and began methodically dismantling the wallet and its contents, much as Van Horn himself had done twice earlier. As Van Horn had done, he ended by checking the money for marks. Finally, he gave it up and returned to his salad, saying, "No good. Tells me nothing. Trimble's troubles are still between him, his murderer and his God, so far as I'm concerned."

"Look at the French franc notes," Van Horn said.

"I've looked at them," Parrish said, a bit testily. On one of the leaves of lettuce in his salad, a beautiful little green inchworm was gracefully creeping. Parrish saw it at the same time Van Horn did. Each knew the other had seen it. Neither mentioned it.

Van Horn said, holding up the two big ten-thousand-franc notes, "There are no pinholes in them."

"Shocking news," Parrish said. "But what does it mean? I don't know anything about French money. See little enough of any kind of money, as a matter of fact."

"You've been away too long," Van Horn said. "Inflation in France has got to the point where as soon as a batch of new money arrives at a bank from the mint, the receiving tellers pin the bills together in batches of ten in each denomination. It makes it easier to handle."

Parrish, carefully skirting the lettuce leaf with the worm on it, had eaten two-thirds of his salad. Now he decided it was time to discover the worm, and he sternly called the waitress over. When she arrived, he pointed at the worm and frowned at her. She looked at the worm, looked at him, shook her head hopelessly, took his plate away and began to make a new salad. Parrish turned to Van Horn, triumph in his eyes. "Uh, yes," he said, bringing himself back to the subject. "But after all, if you cashed a big enough check at a bank, they'd have to dig into the fresh currency from the mint in order to pay off and it wouldn't be pinned."

"But Trimble," Van Horn said patiently, "according to his passport, hadn't been in France in months. Swiss and Italian banks don't stock fresh mint French francs. And black market operators try never to handle the stuff. It's too easy to trace or register. Besides, this was all the French money Trimble was carrying. Twenty thousand francs are worth about forty dollars. You don't live very riotously for a very long time on forty bucks. No, I think that maybe all I helped to smuggle in that suitcase this morning was what I found in it. Paper. I think Trimble picked these bills up when he visited Monselice yesterday. I think this is twenty thousand very queer francs."

The waitress banged the second salad in front of Parrish and flounced away. He dug into it happily, saying, "So Trimble was working with a combination smuggling and counterfeiting outfit. All right. Hook it all together for me."

Van Horn gathered up the wallet and its contents and put them back in his jacket. "I'll give the whole works to Black in the morning," he said. "I think it will hold water. Monselice is an engraver. They're useful people in any funny-money game. And Teresa Nardiello's husband, the guy they call Cherubino, is a fat Milanese industrialist who runs a paper mill. Also useful if you want a lot of something pretty special and don't want to call attention to it. Monselice makes the test runs on the plates, Cherubino makes the paper. The printing is done in Switzerland, where it's easy to hide a little plant—or even a big one, for that matter. A *Brigade Politique* man here once told me that whole battalions of men could hide out in corners of this country and never be found if they didn't get careless."

"All right. So why Trimble for the smuggling?"

"Because of his passport. He's an honest American business-man, commuting to Italy every week looking after his interests. They probably changed the receiving agent, or accomplice or what have you, every week. That Italian today was probably given a loose description of Trimble that fitted me too, and a detailed description of the suitcase. Anyway, there's plenty of reason for them to want to use an American."

"But why Trimble? Dave indicated he was doing all right."

Van Horn seemed suddenly angry. "How the hell would I know? All I know is it's too damned bad! I liked Larry Trimble, the little I knew him. He had a lot of style. You don't find much of that these days. Maybe he got pressed for dough for reasons we don't know about. Maybe he did something foolish and was being blackmailed. I don't know. I wouldn't mind so much if he'd been mixed up in something important in the way of crooked- ness, something with some dash or for very high stakes. It would be less degrading. But this! Common smuggling! Nobody makes anything out of it except the boys at the top who organize it and finance it. And Trimble must have been a very small cog—prob- ably didn't even know for sure what was going on. A good man like that, decent and strong and intelligent. And he ends up a small-time crook no better than a pickpocket in a precinct jail. It's too damned bad!"

"Here, now," Parrish said. "You're getting yourself all worked up. Let's have some dessert and you tell me the rest of your adven- tures. Calm down."

Van Horn with an effort brought himself back to the events of the day. He explained his encounter with Butler and the little man's proposal that they work together.

"Wanted to be chums, eh?" Parrish asked. "You think he might be helpful?"

"Not especially," Van Horn said. "And not without letting him know too much about our operation. He's after this Nigel Brush. My guess is that Brush was the joker who engineered the business of getting Trimble into the counterfeiting organization. The girl and Butler both have said he was around the Trimble villa a lot and was friendly with the Countess. But Butler's inter- est in him is strictly on the criminal side."

"M.I.6 interested in crooks?" Parrish looked skeptical. "Well, it's possible, if Brush once worked for them, as Butler told you."

"He might be able to help you find out who killed Trimble and shot at the girl and me and killed the man in Monselice's shop. But I don't think he can help lead you to Trimble's report."

"If there was any report."

An edge came into Van Horn's voice. "And of course, we don't give a damn who did all the killing unless it had something to do with the report, or us, or our work."

Parrish looked up from his *profiterole* with an air of astonishment. "Of course not. What's the matter with you, Jud?"

Van Horn sighed. "Nothing."

Parrish was staring at him. "I begin to see the source of your difficulties with the high brass," he said. "What have we to do with justice?"

"Nothing, of course," Van Horn said. "Nothing at all."

For a moment they ate in silence. Then Parrish said brightly, "At any rate, Butler will lose track of us once you leave. At least until I can find out what happened to that report. Did you learn anything from the Countess?—I mean anything you can talk about." He smiled benignly.

"No, except that the Trimble ménage wasn't the happiest on earth."

"Hope I didn't interrupt anything diverting back there. If I did, deepest apologies and all that."

Van Horn ignored him. "Don't underestimate Butler," he said. "He's a good man, I think. Very tough and able. They're a capable lot, the British. Anyway, I declined his kind offer and we parted company."

"All right. Fine. I'll deal with him if he shows up again." Parrish looked thoughtful. "I don't think I'm going to have an easy time of it. I'm pretty sure there is no report. I think I'll most likely just keep running into these counterfeiters at every turn. They'll go on trying to get at everybody who might have learned about their operation from Trimble and I'll never even get a whiff of the people who killed him. The job will be to try to find out what the report was about, since there isn't much possibility of getting hold of the thing itself now. Trimble never sent us anything very exciting in the past. It's possible he ran onto something big and handled it wrong. But it'll take a good man a long time to cover the same ground and learn what it was Trimble knew. God! What a boring prospect! And I was so happy in Aleppo! Well, there's no help for it. I must simply forge on regardless, like a Grenadier Guard."

"Uh-huh," Van Horn said. Parrish had ordered cognac, and Van Horn toyed with the little *ballon,* his heavy hand holding it lightly, enveloping it. He was scowling blackly at the table top. At last he raised his head and said, "There's one thing, though, I wish you'd do."

"What's that?" Parrish asked idly, but his eyes had gone wary.

"Well, I told the girl, Trimble's daughter, we'd go easy. I mean she knew her father was mixed up in something smelly. And she was pretty fond of him and she's a fine girl. She'd just as soon have him remembered with no blots on the escutcheon. She asked me not to break open the story of his crookedness, and I said we'd do all we could not to. I'd appreciate it if you'd bear that in mind." He looked intently across the table at the bony face of Parrish.

Parrish grinned at him. "You'll never learn, will you?" he said. "Ah, well! I'll do what I can. But you know the rules. If it suits our purposes to smear Trimble in order to flush out the people we want, we'll do it. Nothing I can manage could stop it. You know that."

"Yes," Van Horn said heavily. "I just thought I'd tell you."

"Well, now, cheer up," Parrish said. "I have some odd bits of news. I only just learned most of them. The French have been in touch with the Italians. They've found that the bullet in Trimble is from the same gun that killed the chap in Monselice's shop. Very neat, eh? The body, as you know, was clean. Fabry hasn't been much use, so far, though of course he's been busy with the business about the girl."

Van Horn went instantly tense. His hand closed tightly around the *ballon*. "What about the girl?" he asked softly.

Parrish looked up in surprise. "Didn't you know?" he said. "I suppose Fabry was too upset to tell you. By the by, you certainly put the fear of God into him, somehow."

"*What about the girl?*" Van Horn bellowed. The other diners and the waitress looked up in alarm.

"Why, she flew the coop, old boy." Parrish looked curiously across at Van Horn, who stared back at him uncomprehendingly. "You on my wave-length?" Parrish asked, growing serious. "I said your lady friend flew the coop. Understand? Vanished. Disappeared. Went away like an itch when you scratch it."

The *ballon* in Van Horn's hand shattered under the pressure of his grip, and cognac and blood spattered the tablecloth.

"Oh, my God," he said.

CHAPTER THIRTEEN

"I didn't hear about it until I arrived in Geneva," Parrish said. "I got it from the drop on the rue des Alpes. I'd have mentioned it sooner if I'd known it would mean so much to you."

The waitress by now had angrily cleared away the broken glass and had laid a new tablecloth and had brought Van Horn a new cognac. Van Horn sat looking very grim, his scratched hand wrapped in his handkerchief, drinking the cognac in savage gulps.

"Did the stupid little bastard give any details?" he asked. "Yes. He said the girl slept after you left. She woke up feeling much better, apparently. She got dressed and Fabry's woman started to fix her something to eat. This would have been about the time you were arriving in Milan, I imagine. The girl went over to the front windows for a breath of air or something, and caught sight of somebody outside. She got very upset, claimed she knew who it was, but wouldn't give Fabry any names. Fabry went out to have a look, but whoever it was was gone. If there'd been anybody. Fabry left to go about his shady business downtown. His woman got the girl calmed-down and went to get her breakfast. And while the woman was out in the kitchen, the girl just took off. Put her coat on and left. Just like that."

Van Horn cursed through clenched teeth.

"Oh, come on now, Jud, be reasonable. If the girl wanted to leave, there wasn't anything Fabry could do, short of tying her up. His woman tried to get in touch with him as soon as she found the girl gone, but Fabry was on his way downtown, in morning traffic, by then. It was nearly an hour before she could get word to him. I don't know what you did to him this morning when you were with him, but he was too scared to report the news at first, from the looks of things. Wasted most of the day trying to track her down. Finally, late in the afternoon, he had to admit she'd left Turin, and was out of reach entirely, so he sent word to you in Geneva and it got to me instead."

"Oh, Christ!" Van Horn said miserably.

Parrish let a pause develop, and then said, with surprising gentleness, "Jud, I don't want to tread on your toes. You've made it pretty plain that you've got sort of an unusually strong interest in this girl, but do you think there could be anything crooked about her? I mean, her old man seems to have gone down the garden path, and from all accounts her mother is a man-eater and none too scrupulous. Do you suppose perhaps the girl is mixed up in this too? Maybe knows something she's anxious to hide?"

Van Horn looked at him. "You're a nice guy, Roger," he said. "A very nice guy." He obviously meant it. "But how can I tell about the girl? I knew her pretty intimately for a few hours. She made a big impression on me. She seemed to me to be absolutely straight, a lousy liar, a loyal daughter, decent, beautiful, and generally a damned fine person. But what the hell? I can be fooled. Particularly by somebody who hits me the way she did."

"Uh-huh. Who do you suppose she thought she saw in that street?"

Van Horn shrugged. "Could have been anybody. Could have been somebody who followed us from Modane, for all I know. Could have been the man who broke into the hotel room. Maybe it was the guy who killed Trimble."

"Where do you think she blew to? Geneva?"

Van Horn shook his head. "No. Not Geneva. Anywhere but Geneva."

"She have any money?"

"Only a little. It wouldn't carry her far. But far enough to make it tough to find her, God, I hope she's all right!"

Parrish looked at him sympathetically. "She probably is," he said. "She's likely to be holing up somewhere comfortably until the mess is cleared away. Maybe she'll show up for her father's funeral. Think so?"

"Not if it's in Geneva," Van Horn said.

The waitress brought the bill and put it by Parrish. He pushed it towards Van Horn, saying, "It's all yours, cousin. All I've got are *dinari* and a couple of American dollars I keep for sentimental reasons."

Van Horn looked at the bill. It was for forty-two Swiss francs. A search of his pockets produced seven francs. He had cleaned himself out buying linen and paying for the cab to the Trimble villa. "Damn!" he said. "We're in trouble."

Parrish laughed. "A great pair of operators we are! What'll they do? Put us in a special pokey for tourists?"

"I don't know," Van Horn said. "Let's find out."

"No, wait a minute," Parrish said. "Give me that wallet of Trimble's. We'll put our charm and your theory to the acid test."

Van Horn gave him the wallet and Parrish extracted one of the ten-thousand-franc notes from it. "They'd never take the lire," he said. "And there aren't enough Swiss francs here, even with what you have. So, here we go." He called the waitress over and airily handed her the bill and the banknote, explaining carefully that he and Van Horn were newly arrived tourists and had no other currency. Would the proprietor be so kind as to accept French money?

The girl hesitated, then shrugged and took the money to the cashier's booth near the door.

An interminable parley then took place. It involved the *patron,* the *patronne,* the waitress and, somehow, two diners at nearby tables. At last the *patronne* began a complicated arithmetical calculation on a scratch pad while the *patron* submitted the franc note to a series of rigorous tests. He ground it against a clean sheet of paper with his thumb. He examined the watermark minutely. He read both sides of the bill carefully. And finally he soaked one corner of it in water and tested the fastness of the ink. At last he grunted assent and, drying it on a napkin, folded the bill and tucked it in the cash drawer.

Meanwhile, the *patronne* had figured out its value at something a good deal less than the going legal rate and made change. The waitress brought it to Parrish with a smile.

"A careful people, the Swiss," Parrish said. "Born bankers. If something is genuine to them, then it's genuine. And the hell with your brilliant theory. Counterfeiting may have been Trimble's racket, and probably was. But he didn't carry the queer himself." He handed the change to Van Horn, who was frowning perplexedly. "Here, you bounder," he said. "Your ill-gotten gains. Tch, tch, tch, what a busy day you've had! Smuggling in the morning and crossing frontiers illegally, passing funny money in the evening. Ah, a felon's work is never done!"

Van Horn shook off his frown and grinned at Parrish. "All right. But the game's the same." He left an exaggerated tip for the waitress.

"Agreed," Parrish said. "Although, just between thee and me, colleague, if these counterfeiters aren't idiots they'll have settled on a sounder currency to imitate than French francs. Making phony French dough is a little like stealing first base. You could do it till you died of exhaustion and never make the nut."

"You're probably right. They must have been making Swiss francs, or maybe dollars." Van Horn got up. "You can take me to the hotel now. I'll catch a late plane to Paris."

"Right," said Parrish. "And I don't mind saying I'll miss you, pal. It'd be nice working in harness with you again."

Outside the world had turned white. The snow, one of the first of the season, was light and fine, but steady. The ground was thickly covered. The air was soft. It wasn't really very cold. Van

Horn took a deep breath and said, "I wish I could stay with you. As it is, at least I'll be able to catch up on my sleep."

Parrish turned the Frégate out of the restaurant parking area and onto the highway heading downhill toward Geneva. There had been little traffic through the evening. The snow was barely tracked. Under it, the asphalt was slick, and Parrish went slowly, tooling the car close to the mountainside on their right.

"I'll give Black those bits of paper I swiped, and Trimble's wallet," Van Horn said. "Maybe the laboratory types can make something out of them. Though I don't suppose Dave will be very interested really. He'd only do it to get himself in more solidly with the police."

"You mustn't be bitter about David," Parrish said, peering through the windshield. The road had curved to the right and then left, along the side of a pocket in the mountainside, and the light snow swam in the headlights. Parrish was keeping the right wheels of the car close to the edge of the asphalt. A car coming up behind them, its lights blazing, helped his vision a little, and he went on, "He's only doing his job. And I'll be doing mine. But I'll try my best not to break the Trimble business open, Jud. I really will. If there's any way to avoid it, I'll avoid it." The car behind them pulled out to pass and Parrish brought the Frégate almost to a halt, pulled far over to the right.

"Thanks, Roger," Van Horn said. "I don't see why we should always—"

He never finished the sentence. The other car had pulled abreast of them and now, with a great surge of speed, it shot ahead and cut across the Frégate, skidding, slanted, only about five feet in front of it.

Parrish slammed on the brakes and wrenched the wheel to the right. The Frégate stopped almost immediately, the brakes totally effective at such a low speed. But the right wheels by now were in the ditch beside the road. The car lay for a moment balanced, tilted crazily to the right. Then, slowly, silently and irresistibly, it fell over against the far bank of the ditch on its right side. There was a dull thud as it hit the snow, then nothing. The engine died.

Parrish, cursing, was digging in his clothes for his gun. Van Horn had pulled himself into a kneeling position and was fighting to reach the revolver in his hip pocket. Ahead the other car, looking huge and black and shiny in the Frégate's headlights, had halted and cut its lights. Two men were getting out of it. They were carrying guns. One of them fired twice and the Frégate's lights went out.

Parrish, Van Horn pushing him from behind, forced the left door of the Frégate open. It lifted over his head like a trapdoor. Putting one foot on the steering wheel, Parrish heaved himself up until his torso was through the door, then swung his left leg up. With a lunge he was up and out, dropping into the ditch beneath the car.

Van Horn, gun in hand, started after him. As his head came above the doorsill, a voice in the darkness ahead said in guttural English, "Come with your hands empty. You are covered."

Below Van Horn, Parrish fired twice. There was a grunt from the darkness, then a burst of pistol fire. Van Horn turned and lunged toward the top of the door, away from the road. Swinging himself up, he dropped over the roof of the car and sank deep into a new drift. Holding his revolver clear of the snow, he moved flounderingly to the front of the car. Parrish was firing from the other side. In front of Van Horn a shadow crossed the whiteness of the snow, moving toward the ditch. Van Horn fired at it twice. The shadow fell and a shriek split the air. Van Horn fired once more, then paused. His revolver only held six rounds.

There was a momentary silence. In front of Van Horn nothing visible moved. On the other side of the Frégate, Parrish had ceased firing. Ahead, three more shadows were suddenly visible, two moving out to the edge of the road, the third darting toward the ditch. Still Parrish did not fire.

"Parrish," Van Horn called softly, "get the two on your side before they flank us." There was no answer. Reluctantly, firing from an impossible distance, Van Horn let fly two slugs at the shadows. There was no hope of hitting them. He had one round left. He waited, crouching grimly in the snow, breathing hard through his teeth.

Then behind him there was the hum of a car coming from above, coming fast down the highway. It could be no more than half a mile away. The men in the ditches beside the road heard it and broke for their car, pouring a fusillade at the Frégate. A bullet hit the gas line, there was a dull explosion, and the engine of the Frégate began to burn. Another bullet ricocheted off the car radiator and smacked the ground beside Van Horn. Hopelessly, he fired his last round into the back of the black car. The shadows disappeared into the car and with a grinding roar it pulled out and swept off down the hill in a swirl of snow just as the car approaching from the rear swung around the curve and flooded the scene with light. The driver, apparently not immediately believing the evidence of his own eyes, came nearly abreast of the capsized Frégate before he applied the brakes. The car, an Opel, ground to a halt.

Van Horn, gun in hand, was by then bent over Parrish, who lay crumpled behind the right front wheel of the Frégate. A bullet had hit him exactly between his bright, young-looking eyes. There was very little blood.

Van Horn straightened up. The driver of the Opel, a roughly dressed man of about fifty with the rugged, weathered features of a countryman, was standing in the road, staring in disbelief at the hole in Parrish's forehead. By now the Frégate was burning strongly, and in the firelight Van Horn's face was terrible. The man recoiled at the sight of him and, apparently deciding he was a murderer, backed up and said something incomprehensible.

Van Horn stuffed the revolver into his pocket, bent again and picked up Parrish. Carrying him easily, he put him in the snow by the roadside, a dozen yards away in front of the Frégate. Then he stepped into the highway, to find himself directly in the path of the Opel, which now was in gear and on its way, the terrified driver crouched over the wheel. It was moving at about ten miles an hour and picking up speed by the time it reached Van Horn. The driver obviously had no intention of stopping. Van Horn leaped and grabbed, coming down with a crash on the hood of the car, his face about a foot from the windshield. On the road behind a second car was coming around the curve. Its brakes squealed as its driver was confronted by the burning Frégate.

Spraddled on the Opel's hood, sliding precariously, Van Horn got his revolver out of his pocket, pointed it at the man behind the wheel, and roared "Stop!"

Yawing wildly, the car came to a halt. Van Horn dropped to the ground and opened the left-hand door. The driver cringed before him. "Move over," Van Horn said. *"Bougez!"*

As Van Horn got awkwardly in behind the wheel, the man slid swiftly sideways across the seat and wrenched at the handle of the right-hand door. Van Horn seized his arm with one hand and got the Opel in gear and away with the other. The car took off with such force that the man was thrown back against Van Horn. He abandoned trying to escape and subsided, and Van Horn let go of him. Behind them, the other car had stopped and its driver was out on the road.

Van Horn said in French, "Nothing will happen if you do not do something foolish. I am a policeman. I am commandeering your car to chase some criminals. I will return your car when I have caught up with them." He whirled the Opel around the next curve and the firelit scene behind them disappeared.

The man beside him said nothing.

Following the black car's trail was not difficult, despite the poor visibility. Traveling at high speed, it had cut through the new-fallen snow on the road, leaving a wide black swath. Van

Horn gave the Opel all it had, which turned out to be a good deal for so small a car.

Three or four miles from the scene of the shooting the black car's track suddenly swerved to the right into a secondary road that climbed steeply, in a wide turn, back in the direction from which it had come.

"Where does this road lead?" Van Horn asked, skidding the Opel into the turn without slackening speed.

"I do not know this country," the man said, in the awesome tongue of the Engadine. "These are the Juras. I am from the Zugerburg."

"Ça," Van Horn said, "se voit."

Twenty minutes later they were well up into snow country. Kilometer signs informed them they were approaching the town of St. Cergue, and the black car's tracks vanished in a maze of other fresh tire marks. But there were no signs of any turning off from the direction in which the black car had been traveling and Van Horn did not pause. In another two miles the traffic in both directions increased and he overtook and passed four cars.

Then, half a mile ahead at the end of a short straightaway, the lights of the oncoming traffic illuminated the black car. It was moving at a reasonably high speed but was no longer racing. Its lights vanished around a curve.

Van Horn put the accelerator to the floor. The little Opel whined across the straightaway and wavered around the curve. On the other side there was another straightaway for about a quarter of a mile. At the far end, lumbering cautiously, was a huge truck. A steady stream of cars approached from the direction of St. Cergue. The black car was not in sight.

Two roads led off on the right, one on the left. Van Horn pulled the Opel as close as he could to the right side of the main road, stopped it, and got out, taking its keys with him. The thin air was bitter cold and made him cough. In the lights of the Opel and the oncoming cars, he studied the three side roads. The first on the right had not been traveled since the snowfall began. The second to the right was a maze of tracks. The one on the other side of the road was also heavily traveled, but it was unlikely that the black car could have made a left turn across the approaching traffic stream in the few seconds before Van Horn's arrival.

Van Horn got back into the Opel and started it. Moving slowly, he turned off onto the second road to the right and began tentatively grinding downhill. Under the packed snow the road was unpaved and badly graded. The Opel complained over rocks and potholes. The man from the Engadine muttered glumly to himself.

The road was very narrow. Plowed snow from the whole autumn was piled eight feet high on either side. If Van Horn had made a wrong guess, he would have to back all the way out. There was no room to turn around. He dimmed the headlights.

A mile along the road the descent suddenly increased until the Opel was slipping and skittering through a series of looping curves that laced the side of the mountain. Ten minutes later, inching the Opel around one of these curves, Van Horn saw the black car, stopped, two hundred yards ahead. He put out the Opel's lights and cut the engine.

Ahead, the black car was pulled up before a high wrought-iron gate. It was the first break Van Horn had seen in the snow walls lining the road. Apparently the snow on the right, at this point, was piled against the wall in which the gates were set. Near the gate, out of sight, a dog was roaring. Not barking, roaring. A vast, full-throated, wholly savage roar. Someone was working on the gate. No one appeared to have seen the Opel.

The man beside Van Horn said, "What are you going to do?" He was only barely comprehensible, so thick was his accent.

Van Horn said in German, "I'm going over the wall while the dog is occupied up there. I am going to back up and bring the car close to the wall."

"You will go into the ditch."

Van Horn did not bother to reply but began carefully backing the Opel toward the snow-banked wall. "I will not wait for you," the man said. "I will make a disturbance! You have no right!"

There wasn't time to wheedle the man. Van Horn produced the gun again. Though certainly if the man was as stoically stubborn as most of his kind, he would have preferred being shot full of holes to changing his attitude. In any case, the gun was empty.

Happily, city life had corrupted the man. At the sight of the gun all things became possible for him.

He withdrew into his corner and said nothing while Van Horn backed the car up until it was nearly touching the snowbank.

He put the brake on and got out. The man got out after him and Van Horn said, "Move away from the car." The man did so. He was a pretty frightened Swiss.

Van Horn put on the front seat all the Swiss francs he had left. Then he climbed to the roof of the car. Standing, he could look over the snowbank and the wall behind it and see trees silhouetted against lights. The lights looked inviting, hospitable. The top of the wall looked unprotected. He put the gun back in his trouser pocket.

He crouched, took a deep breath, and leaped up and out, landing heavily with his torso on the wall, his legs dragging in the snow. He gave a great heave and ended lying on his face along the top of the wall. There was no broken glass or barbed wire there.

Down near the gate the dog was still filling the night with his great voice. Van Horn swung his legs over the wall and dropped.

He hit snow almost instantly, another deep drift. He sank into it chest-high. Snow went in his collar and sleeves, up his trouser legs, in his shoes. In half a second he was nearly numbed. On the other side of the wall the Opel started up and roared off as though the Eumenides were in its trunk. Van Horn grinned and began fighting his way out of the snowdrift.

He came out under a tree. The snow there was windswept and only a few inches deep. He struck off toward the lights, trying to shake the snow off himself and out of his clothes as he went. Most of what was inside had turned to ice water by now. He was shivering uncontrollably and his teeth made so much noise he had to keep his jaws clamped shut.

He was moving through a kind of orchard. The trees were low and evenly spaced. He ran in a crouch, but every so often he would bang against a low bough and another shovelful of snow would go down the back of his neck. About halfway to the house the furor from the dog died down and Van Horn put on a burst of speed. It was nearly his last. The black car—a Mercedes—swept up the drive, its headlights sawing through the darkness directly across his path.

He flung himself flat. More snow went down his neck. More ice water melted in his underwear. But the lights swept over his head and passed without pausing.

The house lights were only a few yards away now. He got up and waded on through the snow toward the rear of the house—a postcard type of traditional Swiss chalet, replete with ornate eaves, steep roofs, gables and general gingerbread. The Mercedes was pulled up on the other side and he could hear voices. A door opened and closed. No more voices.

The cellar windows of the house were at ground level and were barred. But there was a little veranda by the back door and Van Horn went up its two steps. Groping, in the icy dark, he seemed to be making a tremendous noise. It seemed impossible that the paranoiac hound would not hear him and come crashing against his back.

The back door was locked. A little four-pane window was set in its upper half. Darkness inside.

Van Horn took out his gun again and wrapped it in his handkerchief. The handkerchief was still moist with the blood he had shed in the restaurant.

His fingers were stiff with the cold, but he managed to get the gun butt wrapped without dropping anything. He held the wrapped gun by the muzzle, like a hammer, near the glass, and waited.

The silence at that moment was the vast, fragile kind of free unbreathing country silence that could be shattered by the click of an eyelid blinking. The gentlest possible crack of a gun butt on a windowpane would sound like the Second Day at Gettysburg.

Several minutes went by. Then the door at the front of the house opened again, and there was a hubbub of several voices; they sounded angry. The engine of the Mercedes was revved, somebody said a rude phrase in German, another voice chimed in loudly and Van Horn banged the gun butt against the lower left-hand windowpane.

He froze and waited. The voices died out. The car was put in gear and drove off. The front door shut and again there was deep silence, broken only by the receding sound of the car.

The whole pane of glass Van Horn had struck had crashed in on the floor. He reached through the hole it left and groped around. He found a bolt, a tumbler lock, and a chain. The people who owned the house had put three different locks on a door with a glass window in it and had apparently considered themselves secure. Van Horn slid the bolt back, turned the tumbler lock, undid the chain, and walked inside.

No one came to welcome him. He risked a light, shielding the cigarette-lighter flame from the door with his body.

He was in a kitchen, a Swiss kitchen obviously, complete with Butagaz stove, refrigerator, and a great deal of porcelain and tile, all immaculate. Two doors led off from it. It was warm there despite the draft from the window he'd broken. He stopped shivering.

He put out the lighter and went to the left-hand door, moving in the darkness by his memory of its position. He got a hand on the knob, turned it, pulled up and in. The door moved without a sound. He was looking down a short hallway. Doors led off it on either side. At the far end a curtain blocked off whatever was beyond. He could hear voices again, rumbling sporadically.

It was possible there was another man-eating hound in there. Van Horn softly closed the door and went to the one on the right.

Darkness greeted him on the other side of it. He waited. No sounds here. He risked another light.

He was at the top of the cellar stairs. He kept the light going and walked down. At the bottom he put the light out and waited. Somebody walked across the floor above his head. Pause. Silence. Pause. Voices rumbled again overhead. He moved a step or two into the blackness and then flicked the lighter on once more.

He was standing in the middle of a well-equipped printing shop.

Immediately before him was a good-sized press in beautiful shape, oiled and ready. It lacked only paper and plates. Near it stood a paper-cutting machine on a table. Supplies of inks in large bottles lined shelves along one wall. Against the opposite wall was a long trestle table. Under it were bundles of paper.

Van Horn moved quickly through the place. The bundles of paper under the table were unmarked. The press was new and had not been used. The whole place was extremely neat, telling little or nothing.

Ferreting through the room, Van Horn didn't notice when the voices upstairs ceased to rumble. He was peering into a cupboard full of binding twine, brushes, and bottles of unidentified liquids, when the ceiling light blazed on.

He started to turn, his gun and the lighter still in his hands. As he did, something hit him on the side of the head. The lighter and the gun flew out of his hands. He fell, and the thing that had hit him hit him again. He was unconscious before he struck the floor.

CHAPTER FOURTEEN

Van Horn opened his eyes a fraction of an inch. He was lying on his left side. A man's foot in a glossy, grained brogan was directly in front of his nose.

He opened his eyes a little wider. The shoe moved. It stuck its toe carefully against his chest and pushed. He rolled over. His head thumped on the floor and, though the rug beneath him had nap almost an inch deep, his eyes glazed again for a moment at the shock.

For a second it appeared he was going to be sick. His skin grew livid and shone with sweat. He took deep breaths through his nose and clenched his jaws.

A light, cultivated voice said in English, "Come, come, my dear! Be a man!"

Very carefully, moving as though made of crystal, Van Horn got himself into a sitting position. He was in a softly lighted, comfortable room with heavy beams crossing the ceiling and whitewashed walls and a dark blue carpet. His coat had been flung into a corner. His gun and papers and Trimble's wallet and papers were lying on a mahogany desk that glowed in the light of a log fire. There were two deep easy chairs drawn near the hearth. In one of them sat a very thin man in a dark suit.

The other man, with whose foot Van Horn had grown to be so intimate, was a squat, black-haired, broken-faced object dressed in a fine gray tweed, a weskit, and those beautiful shoes.

The odor of heliotrope floated on the air of the room.

The cultivated voice spoke again. It, as well as the odor of heliotrope, came from the man in the chair. He said, "That's better. I had begun to think perhaps my man had been overzealous in subduing you."

"He's no slouch," Van Horn said thickly, gingerly touching the lump on his head.

"Now, suppose we get down to cases," the man said. He sat straighter in the chair and gazed at Van Horn calmly. He was gray-haired and very fragile-looking. His hands, folded decorously in front of him, were pale and attenuated, with polished nails. He had a delicate face, with a very narrow nose. His eyes were pale, so pale that they seemed almost white: drugged eyes, or mad eyes, or just eyes that, like a bird's, had no connection with emotion, showed nothing. They were eyes that could look at anything, anything at all, and register nothing, not even interest or boredom. Two lightless gobs of mucus.

He said, "Now, my dear. Please explain yourself." His English was flat and unaccented. Learned English. His "r's" were a bit liquid, and his "s's" sibilant. "Please be cooperative. It will save you a great deal of pain and us a great deal of trouble."

"You first," Van Horn said, leering at him. "You're the cutest."

The big man in tweeds moved quickly toward Van Horn, but the man in the chair said, "No, Yan," and he stopped. The careful voice went on, "You are foolish, Mr. Van Horn. You risk a beating or worse in order to insult me. You must be aware of your peril. You must know that in time, by one means or another, we shall have all we wish from you. What possible profit can you hope to find in recalcitrance and bad manners?"

The man smiled, or appeared to try to smile. It was the merest stretching of his lips, which seemed unnaturally red against his pale face. "So, my dear, why not be a sensible man and speak freely? We hold, you must agree, all the cards."

The man called Yan put his hands in his pockets and looked down at Van Horn. "You had better be sensible," he said in English. His accent was very German, his voice a nasal tenor.

Van Horn sighed and said, "All right. You know who I am. What else do you want?"

"We know you are an American with a special passport. We know your name," the man in the chair said. "That is all we know. For whom are you working?"

"You mean for a living, or tonight?"

"Tonight. And this morning. And yesterday."

"Myself."

"I see. And to earn your living?"

"I'm a junior attaché at the Embassy in Paris."

"You know Mr. Trimble well?"

"I did, yes."

"And where is he now?"

Van Horn snorted. "I was right," he said. "You *are* the cutest." Again Yan started for him, and Van Horn said to him quickly, "Down, Fido. Your boss wants me conscious."

"That will do, Yan," the man in the chair said once more. Again Yan halted. His hands dropped to his sides and he gazed longingly at Van Horn, his big face bright red. "Mr. Van Horn chooses to be facetious," the man in the chair added.

"Sure I do," Van Horn said. "There isn't really any other way to treat you. You're a pretty sad collection of operators. You've missed the boat three times by my count. You missed out in Modane, you missed out in Torino, and you missed out tonight. You're enough to make a man sick with laughter." He paused and looked speculatively at the man in the chair. After a moment he said slowly, "Unless of course you don't know that Trimble is dead."

"Ah," said the man in the chair. "Then it is with you as well as your friend Brush that we must deal."

Van Horn frowned at him. "Brush is no friend of mine," he said finally.

"Then with you alone. Which of course is preferable, from our point of view." The man in the chair placed his fingertips together and smiled his vestigial smile again. "Tell me, Mr. Van Horn," he said. "Just what do you expect to gain from this adventure?"

Van Horn looked at him blankly, then burst out laughing. "Well, I'll be damned!" he said. "So that's how it is!"

Yan scowled and said, "Please, Kirill, let me—"

Van Horn laughed at him. "Shut up, strong boy," he said. "The grown-ups are talking." He turned back to the man in the chair. "I make eight thousand five hundred dollars a year, plus allowances. I'm a man with expensive tastes. I expect to get plenty out of this adventure, as you call it. You might as well resign yourself. This is going to run high."

"You *have* been rather clever," the pale man said thoughtfully. "I am compelled to admit that you have bettered us consistently until this evening. Why, incidentally, did you impersonate Trimble?"

"To get to you, naturally. With Trimble dead, I was nowhere. I had to try to get in touch with the people to deal with—you. That's why I broke into the suitcase and tore the paper. I was afraid that Italian you had running for you might never give you the right idea otherwise. As it was, I had to make myself pretty conspicuous in order to get you to tumble to me."

"Who was the other man with you tonight?"

"Nobody you care about. An Embassy man. He had been breaking the sad news to Mrs. Trimble. You've got a great bunch working for you. If they'd killed me instead of the other man, you'd never get what you want. You better start a refresher course. Or hire pros for a change."

"And why did you break into this house?"

"To see how far along you had gotten, of course. In order to set my price."

"I see."

"We're wasting time," Van Horn went on. "You've got me, but I've got what you want. Let's talk turkey."

Yan had moved behind Van Horn now and the room seemed to have grown quite warm.

"What is your price, my dear?" the man in the chair asked.

"Make me an offer," Van Horn said. "In real money, please."

"Very well. I will tell you exactly what we are prepared to pay. Nothing, Mr. Van Horn. Exactly nothing at all."

"That's a great offer," Van Horn said. "Just great. It leaves it up to Yan, doesn't it?"

As he said the word "Yan," there was the suggestion of movement behind him, and he flung himself to his left, sprawling and rolling away and up onto his feet.

The leather-covered sap in Yan's fist missed him by a foot and Yan was thrown momentarily -off-balance, looking bulky and surprised as his arm arced through empty air. But only for a moment. As Van Horn charged him, he let his over-balance carry him almost into a fall, and when Van Horn's body hit him it found no resistance. The two men crashed to the floor, Van Horn's momentum throwing him on and over the shorter man. The sap swung in another, briefer arc, and Van Horn yelped in pain. When he got his feet under him and stood up his left arm hung limp at his side.

Yan was up, too, circling him, grinning, his bullet head thrust out. "Come," he was saying. "Come to me." He kept just out of Van Horn's reach.

Van Horn said hoarsely through clenched teeth, "I'll make you kill me with that thing." He lunged. It was a clumsy feint, but it worked. As Yan swung to his right, Van Horn pivoted and brought his right fist around in a wide haymaker. It landed beside Yan's left eye, on the temple, with a sound like an ax hitting punky wood. Yan's eyes dimmed and he staggered. Van Horn took another step and hit him again on the same spot. Yan fell to his knees.

"That will do," said the man in the chair.

Van Horn whirled, his eyes wild, and found himself staring into the muzzle of a tiny pistol no more than four inches long. The fragile man was holding it in his delicate hand, braced against the chair arm. Van Horn started for him.

"Stop where you are!" the man ordered. "I am an extremely good marksman. This weapon will not kill, only maim. Think, Mr. Van Horn! Think!" Van Horn hesitated, eyeing the man.

"That's better. I only need you alive, my dear, not necessarily healthy. What would you gain by forcing me to cripple you? In the end it would be the same." His eyes left Van Horn. "Now, Yan," he said brightly, "feeling better?"

Yan was up, shaking his head, his eyes half closed. The upper left side of his face was a darkening purple blotch. He opened his eyes and stared at Van Horn. There was a strangled sound in his throat.

"Pull yourself together, now, Yan," the man in the chair said, as though speaking to a child. As Yan looked uncertainly toward him, he said, "It's all right, my dear. Mr. Van Horn has the use of only one arm, and he knows I shall shoot away his kneecaps and put a bullet in his other shoulder if he makes any trouble. Go behind him and hold him."

Yan moved cautiously around Van Horn, then darted forward and seized his right arm, twisting it high up his back. Van Horn grunted and kicked backward. Yan did something to the arm, and Van Horn cried out with pain and made no further resistance. He was breathing in great gasps and his clothes were drenched with sweat. It had grown terribly hot in the room. Even the man with the little gun looked uncomfortable.

"That's better," the man said. "That's much better."

Van Horn's breath was a metallic rasp. His eyes were narrowed almost shut and his teeth gleamed between his drawn-back lips. He looked at the man in the chair and said nothing.

The man said reproachfully, "How could you make us be so crude, my dear? Torture is for ruffians. Yan was naughty just now, but he was trying to teach you manners. Weren't you, Yan?" He arose smoothly from his chair and put the little gun in his pocket.

"No further violence, Mr. Van Horn. Scientific aids." He went to the desk. Opening a drawer he drew out a flat leather case and laid it on the desk top. Talking pleasantly all the while, he opened the case and exposed a beautifully compact hypodermic kit, complete with cotton, alcohol, and needles sealed in little tubes. "We have found all sorts of new marvels to help us in our work," he said. "Medical science is so impersonal. Who is to be certain where the limitations of the Hippocratic oath are to be found?"

Another odor was beginning to intrude itself under the pervading stink of heliotrope.

The man at the desk expertly filled a syringe with an oily yellow fluid. Van Horn said thickly, "Scopolamine? Or Sodium Pentathol?"

The man glanced up. "Oh, no, my dear," he said. "That is very much out of date. This is something rather unusual." He held the loaded syringe up to the light and squeezed air bubbles out of the needle. "Think of it. To relieve women in childbirth of a part of their agony, science developed a drug. And it was noted that the ladies talked a great deal under its influence, telling their most carefully guarded secrets. Scientists took this drug apart and separated that part of it which had stimulated the ladies to talk." He gestured with the hypo. "This, my dear, is a concentrate of that part of that drug. Oh, we shall know all about you shortly!" He sounded almost glad.

Somewhere outside the house the dog barked a savage challenge, full and deep. The thin man and Yan both tensed, listening.

Silence followed the bark. After what seemed a very long time Yan relaxed and the thin man came on toward Van Horn.

"Put him on the divan," he said to Yan in German.

Yan steered Van Horn across the room to a chaise longue and pushed him down on it on his face. Van Horn made no protest. There was no protest possible.

Yan pulled the jacket sleeve off Van Horn's right arm. He rolled up the shirt sleeve and turned the arm, with a wrench, so that it lay with the inside of the elbow up. Then he closed a big paw around the bicep and squeezed. The vein in the elbow rose obediently. The thin man stepped closer and bent to swab the skin over the vein with a bit of cotton soaked in alcohol.

At close range the odor of heliotrope was very strong and it was apparent that the thin man was wearing light pancake make-up. Under it his complexion looked coarse, pitted. His eyebrows were very pale and he'd outlined them skillfully with a make-up pencil.

Van Horn, as the needle approached his arm, suddenly tensed. The thin man drew back. "Come now," he said. "You are unreasonable. Resistance is futile. You know it is futile. Why must you persist?"

"You wouldn't understand, you tinhorn pansy," Van Horn gasped.

"Hold him, Yan," the thin man said, and Yan bent to grasp both of Van Horn's arms, putting a knee on his back.

Again Van Horn tensed himself as the needle approached his arm. Under Yan's grinding weight, his big body, sinew by sinew, joint by joint, grew rigid for a moment of final violence, final resistance.

The moment never came. The point of the needle was once more hovering over the distended vein, when the room rocked with what sounded like cannon fire. The thin man jerked upright and forward, then fell over sideways in a heap. The syringe landed soundlessly on the carpet ten feet away. Yan's grip on Van Horn slackened. Again the shattering cannonade blasted through the room. Yan let go of Van Horn and knelt slowly on the floor beside the chaise longue. There was a third blast and Yan pitched forward on his face. Nothing was left of the back of his head. It appeared to have been sheared off.

Van Horn lay as he had been left. Ten seconds passed. There was no more noise. Van Horn swung his legs off the chaise longue and sat up. Awkwardly he pulled his left arm around in front of him and put the hand in his lap. Then be looked up.

Across the room, in front of the curtained door near the desk, stood Sean Butler. The cannonading had been simply the firing of the .45 automatic he held in his hand, the explosions magnified in the closed room. The little man was holding the gun loosely. There was no expression of any kind on his ruddy face.

To Van Horn's left the thin man lay on his back on the carpet. Blood was slowly spreading from a wound in his shoulder. He was paler than ever. The eyebrow pencil and lip rouge were grotesque against his skin. He was obviously in pain, but his eyes, fixed on Butler, reflected none of it. They were as they had been—cold, off-white, unconcerned. Not even bored.

Van Horn, his shoulders sagging, looked dopily at the scene. He was drenched with sweat.

Butler said remotely, "Well, laddybuck. Better get a move on."

Van Horn obediently began fumbling with his jacket. Butler, seeing him struggle, put the gun out of sight, stepped over Yan's body as though it were a coffee table or a footstool, and deftly helped Van Horn into his jacket and got him on his feet. "Twisted you up a bit, eh?" he asked casually. "Deadened the nerve, I expect." He kicked Yan's body lightly. "Filthy bastard," he said. He went to pick up Van Horn's topcoat and his eye lit on the syringe, shining in the lamplight. "Aha," he said. "So that was it! I was about to apologize for being so tardy, but perhaps I was a bit previous after all." He grinned as he threaded the topcoat onto Van Horn's arms. "You chaps are always so closemouthed. Might have learnt a thing or two if I'd held off. Well, well, there you are, now, all shipshape. Shall we be going?"

He held Van Horn's right arm and led him toward the door. Then he noticed the thin man glassily eyeing him, and the big gun materialized again and he said, "Hullo, forgot about you. Loose end."

Van Horn spoke for the first time. His voice was little more than a croak. "Leave him," he said. "Let's get out of here."

Butler looked at him. His face had gone expressionless again. "Why?" he asked flatly.

Van Horn said nothing. He looked steadily back into the metallic blue eyes.

After a moment Butler relaxed and pocketed the gun. "Right you are," he said. "Leave him with his thoughts, eh?"

Van Horn retrieved his own and Trimble's belongings from the desk, and they went out.

CHAPTER FIFTEEN

B utler led the way confidently out of the house and across the grounds. It was much lighter outside than it had been. An odd glow illuminated the trees and the driveway. Van Horn muttered something about the dog, but Butler didn't seem worried. He was still talking animatedly: "You Yanks never fail to amaze me," he said. "Absolutely fabulous crew. Now who'd have thought of doing a thing like that but a Yank? Amazing idea! Absolutely amazing!"

"What idea?" Van Horn asked stupidly.

"Why the idea of setting the place on fire, of course. Brilliant thing to do! Can't think how you managed it. Took nerve, too, I should think."

Van Horn stopped and turned and looked back, frowning. The frown changed to a look of blank surprise. The chalet was a torch, its cellar a mass of flames, more flames licking up toward the first-floor windows. It was this that caused the glow they were walking in, this that had caused the odor under the heliotrope and had made the room so warm.

Van Horn said, "Amazing. As you say."

"Haven't time to watch it, more's the pity," Butler said. "Company may be coming. Got to move. Car's just down here. Mind Rover, he's right in the way."

Van Horn stumbled along beside him down the drive. They covered another fifty yards and firelight illuminated the car, an old Wolsey touring sedan, parked just ahead of them. In front of it lay what Butler had meant by "Rover." It was the body of the dog, a gigantic Doberman, its tongue lolling out and its eyes staring. It had been knifed, ripped from throat to groin.

They stepped around it and got into the elegant old car. While Butler started the engine Van Horn got a clear look at the house. It was beginning to go up in earnest now. The second floor was alight and flames had burst out of the first-floor windows and were sweeping up the outside, limning the gingerbread.

The Wolsey rolled downhill toward the gates with the lights off and the engine barely ticking over. "Precautions," Butler said. "Can't ever be too cautious, now, can you, Van Horn?"

The gates by the road were standing open. The Wolsey was about twenty feet from them when the lights of another car flashed across them, coming from the left. Butler slammed on the brakes and pulled over to the left side of the driveway. He whispered, "Just so. Cut it a bit fine, I'm afraid."

The other car slowed as it approached the gates, then turned in, swinging wide. The people in it must have seen the Wolsey and the flaming house behind at about the same instant. Butler, all in one motion, let out the clutch in the Wolsey, put the throttle to the floor, and snapped on the headlights. The heavy old car shot at the gates like a stone from a catapult and, as it bowled past, the other car paused momentarily. Butler sliced his turn a trifle wide, there was a shriek of torn metal, a jolt, then they were free and away, whirling off up the road to the left, the piled snow on either side flashing in the headlights.

Van Horn looked back. There was no sign of pursuit. The fire had probably seemed more urgent than the chase. A curve in the road cut off the view and Van Horn relaxed.

Butler said, "Cigarettes in the dash compartment. Grog in the pocket on the door."

Van Horn got a cigarette going, and found a squat bottle of whisky in the door pocket. He belted down about two inches of it. It was liqueur Scotch. It needed no urging. He winced as his arm began to come to life.

He said, "I'm obliged to you."

Butler said, "My pleasure. Feeling better?"

"Yes. What kept you so long?"

Butler's teeth gleamed in the dashlights as he grinned. "Pretty good timing, eh? Hairbreadth Harry and all that."

"That pansy nearly learned a lot more than a boy my age ought to tell."

"Oh, you'd have been all right," Butler said. "The fire would have given you your out."

"Oh, yes. The fire." Van Horn laughed. "I can't take much credit for that. I was snooping around their cellar with a cigarette lighter when the muscle merchant bashed me on the head. He picked up my gun but I guess he didn't notice the lighter. It must have fallen into their paper supply."

"What'd you find down there?"

"About what I'd expected. A printing shop. Complete and unabridged. Ready to roll."

"Yes," Butler said. He began to load his monstrous bucket of a pipe. He did it very neatly with one hand while the other twirled the car along the twisting road. He never slackened speed. "That must have told you about all you needed to know, I expect," he said.

"It told me a good deal," Van Horn said. "But there are still some things that worry me."

"Try me," Butler said, puffing so furiously that Van Horn opened a window. "Be glad to tell you what little I know."

"What did you expect to get out of following me?" Van Horn asked casually.

Butler glanced toward him, puzzlement and hurt in every one of the two or three thousand lines in his face. "Why, laddy-buck, how can you—" he began in a tone of reproach.

Van Horn grunted. "Spare me," he said. "You followed me to the Trimble place. You must have. And you must have been in the car that came along as I was riding away from that ambush."

Butler sighed. "Yes," he said. "I was. Gives you an idea of my amateur tendencies. I should have been much closer. As it was I caught a glimpse of your circus act on the bonnet of that Opel, and after I'd found your dead friend I took out after you. Pity about your friend."

"He was a good man," Van Horn said flatly.

After a long moment, Butler went on, "Well, anyway, I lost you for a while after you turned off the main highway. But I was fairly sure where you were headed by then, so I went there."

"Where?" Van Horn asked.

"Why to Brush's villa, of course. That's the place you put the torch to. Didn't you know?"

After a moment Van Horn said, "All right. Now, why were you following me in the first place?"

"Well, truth to tell, I had the fatuous notion you might lead me to Brush."

"Everybody seems awfully sure I know where the treasure's buried."

Butler glanced at him quizzically. "Of course," he said.

"You think so too?"

"My dear boy, I'd be the last to know!"

"Sure," said Van Horn, "but I'm caught in the middle anyway, aren't I?"

"Very much so, I'm afraid."

"Then maybe we'd better compare notes as you suggested this afternoon."

Butler let out a long breath. "Ah," he said. "At last!"

"You'll be getting the worst of the bargain," Van Horn said.

"I'll be the best judge of that."

They were out on the main highway to Geneva now, and Butler cut the Wolsey's speed to about twenty miles an hour. Below them in the distance the lights of the city looked like phosphorus on a wave.

Van Horn said, "You knew that Trimble was working for us?"

"No. But we often use the same sort of unofficial agent. Seemed a decent chap, the little I could gather. Pity he fell so far."

"He sent word he had a report to make and was in danger, wanted to report in person and then run for it. I used to know him. So I went to meet him at Modane as per arrangement. Found him dead, shot. I never got his report. The body was clean except for a Turin business card, and a couple of dubious ten-thousand-franc notes. Tickets and his passport told me his weekly itinerary.

"I took his hat and coat and papers and went to Turin and looked up the address on the business card. Monselice was the name. He was an engraver and he was in jail. A man had been shot in his shop the day before. You wouldn't know about that, I suppose?"

"Very little," Butler said.

"You were in Turin Tuesday. You must have been if you were tailing Brush."

"Very well," Butler said. "Yes, I was there. I'd been watching things at the chalet for some time. I'd even followed Trimble once, just for thoroughness' sake. Preparations for printing were about finished. It was time to bring on the last item, which was what I was waiting for. Brush and Trimble had got thick as thieves, to coin a phrase, in the past month or so. So it didn't precisely astonish me when Trimble changed his itinerary Tuesday morning and went to Turin, and Brush arrived there in time to meet the plane. Brush followed Trimble, I followed Brush. They paid no attention to each other. No signals, no clever messages. Nothing. But Brush was very much on the *qui vive* and I had a hell of a time keeping out of the way. He's an experienced devil. Knows all the tricks."

"What happened?" Van Horn asked a bit impatiently.

"Now, now, let me get on with it in my own way," Butler said reprovingly. "Fact is, it wasn't your humble servant that Brush was keeping watch for. It was still another beggar, sent by Trimble's employers to see that nothing went wrong. Oh, we made quite a parade across Turin, the four of us! Trimble in the lead, Brush a good way behind him, me behind Brush, and then all at once this other personage in between Brush and Trimble. We all converged on that piazza like a music hall turn. Brush saw this new chap and let him go ahead into the engraver's place right behind Trimble. Brush hung about outside for a minute or two, then walked into the place, and about half a second later the porridge hit the fan, as you might say. A couple of shots, well muffled, and the door flew open and Trimble came out running like mad with a package in his hand. Then out came Brush at full throttle. He turned the wrong way and ran bang into me. We tangled for a moment, then he got loose and took off. By the time I picked myself up both my birds had flown. You can understand that I'm not terribly proud of my performance."

"Who was the dead man?"

"Fellow called Chariot."

"Yes," said Van Horn. "The Italian at the airport was asking for him."

"Well, so there I was in Turin," Butler went on. "Clueless. Sick-making, you know, for a man of my experience to lose track of things. I rang up the police about the shooting and fiddled about a while. Then I concluded Trimble might have gone on to Milan to go through his usual routine. Went to Milan. Looked in corners. No Trimble. Thought I'd go up to Geneva and have a look about. Only one aerodrome in Geneva. Easier to watch than Milan, which has two. Off I went, and who should drop off the Wednesday p.m. flight but *you!* After our chat, I came to the conclusion that perhaps Brush might be anxious to see you, if he'd had no luck chasing Trimble. So I followed you and you know the rest."

"Brush had lots of luck," Van Horn said. "He shot Trimble in the train between Bardonnechia and Modane about one second after the Customs people had gone through."

Butler sighed. "Then he got the package and I'm no farther than I was."

"No," Van Horn said. "I don't think he did. Trimble had been searched for something fairly large and hard to hide. Late last night," he went on smoothly, "I rented a hotel room in Turin for a few hours, and while I was out of it somebody searched it. It could only have been the person who killed Trimble. Charlot being dead, and Monselice being in the sneezer, no one else could have been at Modane to connect me with Trimble."

"Well, well, well," Butler said. "That *is* interesting. But then who the deuce *does* have that package, after all?"

Van Horn said, "I told you you'd get the worst of the bargain." The nerves in his left arm were coming alive, and he kneaded them with his right hand, wincing.

"Well, never mind," Butler said. "I deserve to be thwarted. Here I am, corpses abounding, that package still at large, and Brush off and running heaven knows where. Even if I nabbed him I'd have no grounds for hauling him in. What's worse, poor Trimble might still be among those present if I hadn't behaved like an ass in Turin. Ah, well, I'm not an ambitious man."

"I'm sorry I'm not more useful," Van Horn said. "But I'd like a couple more answers, if you're willing."

"Shoot," said Butler glumly. "Though whatever I say will likely prove just song and legend."

"What did Brush do for the men in the chalet?"

"Trouble-shooting. It is my murky opinion he was hired to put A and B together to make C. Always was his speciality. He got to the Countess, in my view, and through her to Trimble. Though what he and the Countess used as leverage to move so upright a citizen as Trimble into the paths of unrighteousness I couldn't hazard."

Van Horn yawned prodigiously. "Yes," he said. "That's one of the least reasonable things in this mass of unreasonable things."

"Maybe Trimble was broke," Butler said. "Or maybe it was blackmail. He and Serena were hardly close. And Brush is a slippery item. Witness the present tangled web. He played the bounder, apparently with Trimble's help, sincere or otherwise. Trimble was sent, under guard, to pick up that package and bring it back under cover of his passport to the chalet. Chances are Brush was to appear to steal it from Trimble, probably to use in bargaining for a bigger cut of the swag for both of them. Trimble tried to make it a solo act, from all appearances, and ran to give you information that would smash Brush and hold off the little band of brothers at the chalet, leaving himself with the package and a clear field."

"He might even," Van Horn put in, "have meant to give me both the information and the package. Maybe he only worked with Brush because he knew he couldn't hijack the package without help."

"Frankly, laddybuck, that seems a bit far-fetched, no matter how good a case you can make for Trimble's basic honesty." Butler looked sharply at Van Horn. Then he said slowly, "Do you have any conception of the value of that package?"

Van Horn went on kneading his tingling arm, but his eyes grew wary. "I know what it's already cost in the way of lives and time and trouble," he said.

The Wolsey was moving through streets on the outskirts of Geneva now. Butler pulled it to the curb and stopped, letting the engine idle. He turned in his seat to face Van Horn.

"It's time we cleared the air," he said. In the glow of the dash-lights his face was very serious.

CHAPTER SIXTEEN

"Have you had much experience of counterfeiting?"

"No," Van Horn said. "None."

"Well, there's counterfeit and counterfeit. Some of it is so extraordinarily bad you wonder it passes, but it does. Some of it is so good you wonder its detected, but it is. About ten seconds after somebody invented money, thousands of years ago, somebody else brought out a counterfeit. It's an old art. People have gotten rather good at it."

"All right. What about this package?"

"It contains two steel plates. For French ten-thousand-franc notes. There used to be two others for five-thousand-franc notes, but they got caught. The two sets appeared shortly after the war. No one is sure of their origin, but they were immediately in demand. They changed hands five or six times without ever printing a single bill. To do it right, counterfeiting requires a big organization, capable of a large initial capital outlay for the right paper and inks and plant and so on. About 1947 such an organization got hold of these four plates. Were you in France in late '47 or early '48?"

"Yes."

"You recall then, that the French Government withdrew all five-and ten-thousand-franc notes from circulation, and did it so fast that a good many souls got caught short."

"Yes," Van Horn said. "Afterward, our Embassy used to have to take a couple of suitcases to the Guaranty Trust to pick up the local payroll. The biggest bill in use was one thousand francs."

"Quite."

"Are you trying to say that they recalled those bills because of the counterfeit from these plates?"

"Precisely. Banks along the Côte d'Azur found themselves with bales of funny money so plausible that their tellers were half crackers trying to sort out the real from the unreal. When the stuff began to circulate in Lyon and Paris, the Banque de France threw in the sponge and gave up. The *Surveillance du Territoire* raided a press in Antibes, and came away with the plates for the fives, but nobody found the tens."

"Odd for the *Surveillance du Territoire* to be interested in counterfeit," Van Horn said. "They're anti-spy people. Anyway, fives and tens were reissued in 1950 or '51. What took so long for the outfit to get back to work?"

"Two things," Butler said. "They had to work outside France. And reorganizing so complicated a business, involving so many people one has to trust, takes time. One can't afford to be precipitate. They stored the plates with Monselice and bided their time, building carefully." Butler knocked his pipe empty out the window and reloaded it. He struck a match and held it over the bowl and, puffing, looked across at Van Horn. His eyes were bright and rather cold in the light of the flame. "Well, laddybuck, does that give you some idea of the value of the object all sublime? Hm?"

"Yes," Van Horn said thoughtfully. "But whoever has the plates now can only try to peddle them to an organization that can use them. And I suppose the people at the chalet are the only such organization?"

"Um-hmm," Butler said through a cloud of smoke.

"Who was the pansy with the hypo back there?"

"Oh. Well, I don't know, really. His name's Soloviev. But he's only an underling. There's a devil of a big outfit behind him."

"Think he got out of the fire?"

"Oh, I expect so. Help was at hand, you remember."

"Think they'd deal?" Van Horn was very casual.

"For the plates? Not unless all else failed. They're a patient lot, and quite ruthless. No, whoever has those plates is a poor insurance risk—particularly if he's someone who came by them accidentally and isn't certain of the lay of the land."

"Then he'd be wise to get rid of them, wouldn't he? To someone who does know the lay of the land?"

"Right-o," said Butler. "Though of course he wouldn't get anything like the real value of the merchandise, selling to a middleman. He would, however, go on living till he died. Which is a consideration."

"But even cut-rate, there'd be a lot of money in it."

"True. Enough to turn any man's head."

"Say, how much?"

"What did they offer you back at the chalet?" Butler's eyes were brighter than ever.

"The man said, 'Nothing. Exactly nothing at all,' " Van Horn said. "And then kindly old Yan began braiding my arms."

"You see? They don't have to deal. Nobody else can use the plates. Whoever has them, in the end, will have to go to Soloviev or the people behind Soloviev. And then they will treat him as they treated you."

"Well," Van Horn said, yawning again, "it seems a shame."

Butler took the pipe out of his mouth and looked at Van Horn sadly. "You are telling me that you don't have the plates?"

"Yes. I don't know how I'd act if I did have them, but I don't."

"You ... uh ... have any suggestions about where they might be?" The question was asked almost timidly.

"Sure," Van Horn said. "They're right where Trimble ditched them between Monselice's shop and the train to Modane."

Butler muttered something disgustedly to himself and put the car in gear. They pulled out into the street and continued toward the city. Dawn was breaking, cold and gray.

"But I'm still on the spot," Van Horn went on. "Plates or not. You think I've got them or know where they are. Brush thinks so too, probably. So do the big boys behind the men in the chalet. And there's no way on earth I can prove I don't. Isn't it a shame though!"

"You're wrong," Butler said earnestly. "*I* believe you."

"Thank you, gentle sir," Van Horn said, grinning. "That is small reassurance, considering my position. And the big irony is that not only do I know nothing about the blasted plates, I also don't care a damn about them. All I'm after is Trimble's report, which I am growing to believe never existed on paper. Still, I'm bound to keep hunting for it. It's all my bosses care about. They certainly don't want a criminal case on their hands. And as long as I'm hunting for it I'll be a sitting duck for this platoon of ill-assorted bravos who haven't the shining trust in me that you have. What's even more ironic, while I'm blundering about looking for the report I might just accidentally run across the plates. That would be laughable now, wouldn't it?"

"Hilarious," said Butler gloomily. "We're both in rather a parlous situation, I'd say. You're up against ferocious odds and so am I."

"You have an out though," Van Horn said. "You can always break the thing wide open."

"How d'you mean?" Butler asked skeptically.

"Go to the cops. Connect Brush with the two killings in Turin and Modane. Hang the rap for tonight on the men in the chalet. That fire wasn't enough to melt the press, and baled paper is hard to destroy. Something will be left. The Swiss will get Interpol on it, they'll pick up Brush somewhere or other and remand him to British or Italian custody. The plates will be lost forever, the gang at the chalet will go to ground, and Brush will be safely behind bars."

"That means nabbing him with the right gun in his pocket, or with testimony from me that my people would never allow. No. It's too knotty an affair. But I'll think about it."

They were in downtown Geneva now, and approaching the Bergues.

"Drive past the hotel once," Van Horn said. "I may have callers."

"Yes," Butler said. "Our mutual friends are a subtle group, aren't they?"

There was no one near the hotel, but a small gray Simca was parked across the street from the entrance. In it, a sharp-faced little man was just visible, slumped behind the wheel.

"As I say," said Butler, "subtle."

"Keep going," Van Horn said. "Know him?"

"Too well. Name's Zerho."

"Oh, yes. He's the joker who had the fight with Brush."

Butler gazed at him in astonishment and narrowly missed curbing the big car. "Well," he said, "you *have* covered ground!"

"What was the row about, anyway?"

Butler twirled the car down a side street. "Something to do with hijacking the plates, I suspect. Brush and Zerho had been sidekicks for quite a while. After the fight, Brush sloped off on his own. Zerho hung on with Soloviev. Apparently didn't think Brush's plan was good enough."

"Or the fight was staged so that Brush could cut loose and move freely without throwing suspicion on his partner. And Zerho could stay inside the organization and feed him information."

Butler pulled the car to a stop by an all-night café. His face looked rather grim.

"It's possible," was all he said.

"Well, friend Zerho hadn't better tangle with me," Van Horn said flatly. "Not this morning. I've had a bellyful of being mistreated by hired guns."

Butler looked at him speculatively. Van Horn was an uncivilized apparition in the early light—black-bearded, slit-eyed, rumpled and ominous. "I agree," he said. "Zerho had better try another day." He held out his hand and grinned. "I'm sorry our paths parted so soon, laddybuck. It's been a pleasant association."

Van Horn shook his horny paw and said, "Where can I reach you in case I need you to save my life again?"

"I don't know. Best let me leave messages for you at the Bergues."

Van Horn got heavily out into the morning. Somewhere a clock was striking half past four. He rubbed the back of his head where Yan had hit him.

"I'm obliged," he said again.

"Think nothing of it," Butler said, grinning. Except for a nimbus of ruddy stubble on his jaws, he was exactly as he had been twelve hours earlier. Even his teeth seemed as clean and white and brilliant as they had the day before. Beside him Van Horn looked wrecked. "It was good sport," the little man said. "Glad to've been of service."

He waved, and the Wolsey wheeled away.

CHAPTER SEVENTEEN

It took Van Horn five minutes to walk to the stationery shop near the rue des Alpes, and five more patient minutes to arouse the proprietress from her lair in the rear of the shop, gain admittance, and identify himself. In an expanse of mauve robe, her hair done up in a sort of mobcap and her face smeared with cream, the woman was even more forbidding than she had been in daylight. Van Horn was abjectly apologetic, but it didn't seem necessary. She was stern, exacting about his identification, and very deliberate, but it was plain she would have been all these things at four-thirty of an afternoon. She was obviously accustomed to being disturbed.

Once they were safely inside her back room, with its tightly shuttered and curtained windows, its crowd of heavy furniture and huge, rumpled bed, in a heavy odor of bad breath and perspiration and unaired bedclothes, Van Horn said, "My colleague who visited you earlier this evening was killed later on the road to Montreux. Have you any messages for him?"

From inside her robe she produced another square envelope like the one Van Horn had received earlier. It read: *Fabry has established via Turin police three bullets all from same gun.*

There was no signature. The time stamped on it was one-thirty that morning. The woman had been disturbed twice that night.

Van Horn burned the message and envelope and said, "I will need money."

The woman frowned. "I have very little."

"Let me have all you can spare," he said, and added with some satisfaction, "My superiors will repay you today."

She vanished into the front of the shop and returned holding a neat wad of French and Swiss bills and a big receipt. She counted the money into his hand and he signed the receipt.

"Thank you," he said. "I am very grateful."

"It is nothing," she said. She looked at his beard-darkened face and shapeless clothes. "You need rest," she said, and then she instantly shut her mouth hard, as though the comment had been the worst kind of indiscretion.

Van Horn grinned at her. "Yes. We all do." There was a pause, during which they eyed one another. Van Horn said, "I am wondering why you do this work."

She looked away and shrugged. *"Il faut,"* she said.

"A man asked me the same question not long ago," he said. "I gave the same answer. There ought to be a better reason."

He put the money in his wallet and said, *"Allez, au revoir."* Then, as though on impulse, he bent with great elegance for so big and unlikely a man, and took her hand and brushed it with his lips.

She actually blushed. It was improbable that anyone had ever kissed her hand, and certainly it could not have happened in a long, long time. But she was equal to the occasion. She inclined her head quite regally in response, and instead of the inevitable shopkeepers' *"A la prochaine,"* she said with dignity, *"A très bientôt, Monsieur. Et bonne chance."*

"Thank you," Van Horn said warmly, and she showed him grandly to the door.

The little gray Simca was no longer in front of the hotel. The street was deserted. In the park a lonesome policeman plodded through his shift. The city was quiet.

There were no messages at the mail desk. Van Horn got his key and went upstairs. The corridors were dimly lighted, the sounds of various kinds of slumber filling them with a faint chorus of murmurs. Van Horn moved as though sleep-walking, his eyes heavy with exhaustion. Of the previous forty-five hours, he had slept two.

At his door, he had trouble handling the key into the lock. His reactions were so numbed that when the hard nose of a gun was shoved against the small of his back, he gave no sign of being startled. He merely straightened up slowly, with a stifled groan.

A husky voice said, *"Vas-y. Sans plaisanteries."*

Van Horn finished unlocking the door and stepped inside and turned around.

The little sharp-faced man called Zerho who had been waiting outside the hotel was pushing the door shut. He was an entirely gray little man: hat, clothes, shoes, necktie, hair, eyes, even his skin, all were different shades of gray. The only jarring note was the blue of the revolver in his gloved right hand. The gloves were gray suède.

Van Horn said tiredly, "Oh, for God's sake!"

"Put your hands up," the man said, in creditable gangster English. It sounded as though he had said, "Putcha hanzup."

"No," Van Horn said. He sounded exasperated, almost petulant. "I won't put my hands up. I won't do a damned thing I don't feel like doing. Did you ever eat a revolver?"

"Listen, you don' needa get edgy," Zerho said. "I know ya tough. And I don' wan' no trouble. All I wan' is to make a deal. A nice frien'ly deal. I got what you want. You got what I want."

"Where'd you learn to talk that way?" Van Horn asked. "Warner Brothers has a lot to answer for." He started to take off his coat.

"Go easy," Zerho said. "No funny business."

Van Horn paid no attention to him. The overcoat off, he took off his jacket, moving his injured arm as little as possible.

The man seemed at a loss. When you point a gun at somebody, that somebody is supposed to do as you say. It's a fact of life, a truism, one of the bases of civilization. Zerho kept his revolver pointed at Van Horn and fidgeted uncertainly.

Van Horn unknotted his tie and began unbuttoning his shirt. The pistol in his hip pocket was plainly visible. Zerho apparently decided it was time to assert himself. He strode across the room and jabbed the gun into Van Horn's side.

"Don't gimme no crap," he said thickly. "I'm talkin' turkey. You wanna deal for them plates? Or you wan' I should get rough?"

He jabbed the gun again into Van Horn's side.

The end came.

With a strangled roar, Van Horn turned and hit him on the side of the head with the flat of his right hand. The little man reeled across the room and collapsed over the bed as though he had been poleaxed.

Van Horn went to him and picked him up off the counterpane like so much dry goods. His face registering tight disgust, the end of patience, he struck four times, the flat of his big hand loudly smacking the sides of the little man's head.

Zerho's eyes rolled. He dropped his revolver, his hat flew off, and his carefully combed gray hair began to come apart. When Van Horn at last let go of him, he fell limply across the bed and lay there motionless, his eyes open but very vague, stunned.

Van Horn looked down at him for a moment and then began roughly searching him. There was nothing of interest in the man's pockets except three different *cartes d'identité* and two passports. One of each was made out to Kye Zerho. The rest bore different names, but the same photo and statistics.

Van Horn flipped the man over and prodded him. He found what he was looking for tucked under the little gray man's gray leather belt, next to his skin. It was a flat, leatherbound notebook, an expensive variety of the kind of appointment book that can be bought at any stationery store.

Its pages were crammed with notes in cipher.

Hardly pausing, Van Horn tossed it onto the bed table. Zerho was showing signs of life. Van Horn pulled him upright and said, "Now, suppose we have a talk." Zerho looked at him expressionlessly. Van Horn said, "You understand that I could kill you with the edge of my hand. You know I wouldn't mind doing it. Right?"

Zerho nodded.

"You're no use to me alive unless you talk. And talk the truth. I don't know this whole story, but I know enough to be able to tell if you're lying. And if you lie to me, it'll be the same as not talking. Right?"

Again Zerho nodded and licked his gray lips.

"Right," Van Horn said cheerfully. "Now just for a start, who sent you to me? Hm?"

Muscles bunched in the gray man's lean face and his mouth set itself in a pale line.

Van Horn said easily, "Better answer. It's a long way to the street, even if I break your neck before I throw you out. You ready to die for your boss? Hm?"

Zerho breathed heavily through his nose. Van Horn's cavernous eyes bored into his, and there was a moment's dead silence. Then Zerho spoke. He said, "No."

"Fine. Now, who sent you to me?"

"Soloviev," the little man said. Instantly Van Horn hit him.

"Try again. Who sent you?"

"Brush," the little man croaked.

"He gave you the book?"

Zerho nodded.

"Who do you work for? Soloviev or Brush?"

A pause. Finally, "Both."

"The fight with Brush a while ago was staged?"

Zerho's eyes flickered. "Yeah."

"Why aren't Soloviev's people laying for me here, too?"

A look of something like amusement crossed Zerho's face. He said, "They are. Me, and two other guys watchin' da rear."

"When did Brush give you the book?"

"Little while ago. Out front."

"What did he tell you to do?"

"He told me tuh try'n swap duh book fer duh plates."

Van Horn's hand moved almost too swiftly to see. It struck the side of Zerho's head with an ugly smack and the little man fell over sideways.

"Try that one again," Van Horn said as the little man, one whole side of his face reddened, pushed himself erect.

Zerho sat with his eyes closed for a moment, then said, "He tole me you'd push me aroun'." The eyes came open. "But I di'n' espect nuttin' like *you,* see."

"After I'd pushed you around, what did Brush say I would do?"

"Yuh'd take duh book an' t'row me out'n my ass, an' 'at'd be all."

Van Horn expelled a long breath. "What a sucker you are, little man," he said. "You take some awful risks. You want another clout on the head, or do you want to change what you've just said without any help from me?"

Zerho looked confused for a moment, then disgusted. "Awright," he said. "He told me you'd ast me a lotta questions."

Van Horn's face darkened. "He told you I wouldn't be capable of really getting rough, didn't he? Told you I might bang you around and maybe threaten you, but it wouldn't mean anything?"

Zerho looked embarrassed. "Yeah," he said hesitantly, obviously expecting another blow.

Van Horn grunted. "Word certainly does get around," he said. "What makes you decide Brush is wrong about me?"

Zerho snorted. "I been aroun'," he said. "I know when a guy means it, see." He seemed to draw himself up a little. "I useda be inna ring. In duh States. Bantamweight. I fought good ones, I fought bums. Yuh kin see in duh eyes, see? Yuh kin tell. A guy means it or he don't. You mean it."

Van Horn grinned wolfishly. "Why, thank you, Zerho. You're quite right. The funny thing is that your friend Brush was partly right, too. But never mind. What did he tell you to say when I asked you questions?"

"What I tole yuh before. You got duh plates, we got duh book. We swap. He told me tuh tell yuh I got duh book from Soloviev."

"And after I'd taken the book away from you and thrown you out, what was I supposed to do?"

"He says yuh'd screw off. He says you ain't got duh plates an' duh book's all yuh innarested in."

"Where'd he get that idea?"

Zerho looked at him in surprise. "Hell, he knows who yuh work fer."

"Who else knows?"

"Da dame, Trimble's broad. An me."

"Soloviev?"

"I dunno. I ain't seen him tuh ast him. He don't talk a lot."

"Trimble and Brush worked together on the heist of the plates?"

"Trimble 'n' Brush 'n' *me*."

"Worried about your cut?—Why did Brush have to include Trimble? Why didn't you two pull it off alone?"

"Cou'n't. Trimble hadda do duh right t'ings inna shop or Brush cou'n't make duh haul."

"Why weren't you in on the act?"

"Too risky. Brush needed me fer later, fer when he starteda peddle duh plates, see?"

"I see. Well, this was a nice try, Zerho. And I'm obliged to you for telling a certain amount of the truth. What do you suppose I ought to do with you now?"

Zerho went a shade grayer and grew very tense. "Listen," he said hoarsely, "I—"

"Cheer up," Van Horn said. "Brush told you part of the truth. I have a lot of trouble killing in cold blood." There wasn't time for

Zerho's face to show his relief. Van Horn's big fist, traveling about two feet through the air, hit the side of the little man's chin with a sharp crack, and over Zerho's face there spread a look of dumb bliss as he subsided gently onto the mattress.

Van Horn looked down at him for a moment and his face softened. "You poor little tinhorn," he said.

Fifteen minutes later, shaved and washed and dressed, Trimble's valise packed and the leather notebook in his pocket, Van Horn let himself out of the room. Zerho still lay inert on the bed, exactly where he'd fallen. He was breathing lightly. He showed no signs of recovery from the single blow he had been struck.

Van Horn locked the room and went downstairs and checked out. No one was waiting in the lobby and there were no idling figures anywhere outside in the weak morning light. The lonesome policeman was still plodding his beat in the park. The city was beginning to stir, there was traffic occasionally and a few huddled pedestrians. Van Horn woke the driver of a taxi parked two blocks from the hotel and gave him the address of *Le Journal de Geneve,* the sober Geneva morning paper. There, he spent forty minutes in the morgue at a machine that cast microfilm copies of back issues onto a screen, page by page. He studied all editions for the third and fourth weeks of August, 1944, paying particular attention to those of the nineteenth, twentieth and twenty-first of that month, which were largely filled with news of the liberation of Paris. Then he consulted the card catalogue and selected three issues from April of 1948. They reported, with a kind of editorial disdain, the raid by the French *Surveillance du Territoire* on an illicit printing establishment in Antibes, Alpes Maritimes, which had engaged in printing false five-thousand-and ten-thousand-franc notes. Two men had been captured in the raid, but they were underlings, unable to supply information of the leaders of the ring. They had been remanded for trial. There was nothing to explain the interest of a counterespionage organization in a counterfeiting matter.

From the *Journal* offices, Van Horn took another cab to the offices of *La Tribune de Geneve,* the city's largest newspaper, and there went through the same performance, though the *Tribune*'s morgue was not nearly so well catalogued as that of the *Journal.* Its reportage was also more racy and strewn with bits of sensation wherever possible. It was a quarter to eight in the morning when, his steps heavy with fatigue, he left the *Tribune* and found a cab and told the driver to take him to the Trimble villa. He sank back on the dusty seat with a huge sigh, but, though every line of his face and figure spelled an overwhelming need for sleep, still his eyes now were sharp and hard, he looked satisfied, and he had once more the air of a gambler whose confidence feels equal to his estimate of the odds.

CHAPTER EIGHTEEN

Serena Trimble had apparently had a bad night. She looked her age. Wearing a diaphanous white peignoir over her nightgown, her hair drawn severely back, her face lightly made up, she looked very tired; her eyes were hollow and her hands moved over her breakfast tray uncertainly. Van Horn greeted her distantly and they sat where they had sat the previous afternoon, in the long salon. He refused a cup of coffee and said bluntly, "I came to tell you where you stand."

"I am learning where I stand," she said hoarsely. "It is not pretty to learn."

"You're just feeling sorry for yourself," Van Horn said. He looked at her closely, and then went on, "I can't think you're as totally rotten as the things you've done seem to indicate."

"Thank you," she said bitterly, and sipped her coffee.

"No," Van Horn said, "the funny thing about villains and villainesses is that unless they're insane, psychotic, they never think of what they're doing as villainy. I once pointed out to a lady that something she had done was against the law. She drew herself up and said, and meant it sincerely, 'It can't be illegal. I've been doing it for years!' "

"Please," Serena said. "Spare me this."

"I'll spare you nothing," Van Horn said. "It's time you learned what you should be sorry for other than for yourself. It's time you learned what your selfishness and bitchery and stupidity and cupidity and I don't know what all have cost a lot of decent people, a few crooks, and one or two jerks like me. Was Nigel Brush here last night?"

The sudden question rapped out at her like a thrown object and she winced, and ducked her head.

"Sure he was," Van Horn said. "Come to comfort the bereaved widow. Spent the night, probably, didn't he? *Didn't he?*"

"I fail to see what business it is of yours whom I entertain," she said pathetically, with hopeless hauteur and a shadow of the heat he had seen in her the day before.

"How was he in bed, Serena?" Van Horn asked wolfishly, his eyes hard. "It must have been a new thrill, a great new sensation, being made love to by your husband's murderer."

She gasped and struggled for words and finally flew at him, cursing incoherently in Italian. Van Horn seized her arms and they struggled for a moment, her long carmine nails straining for his flesh. At last she gave up and subsided into a chair, where she lay back with closed eyes as though exhausted. Her breath came hard and the short battle had brought high color into her face. The peignoir had fallen open and under the nearly transparent gauze of the nightgown, her splendid body was exposed as through mist.

"You're a very beautiful woman, Mrs. Trimble," Van Horn said. "Ordinarily, I suppose, I'd get into quite a state dealing with you. But I know too much about you. You can quit trying to sex me. I wouldn't make love to you if I were wearing chain mail and boxing gloves. And I feel pretty bad about the rolling around we did yesterday afternoon. Though things were different then."

"Get out!" she said explosively. "Get out, *get out—GET OUT!*"

Van Horn simply ignored her. "I know far too much about you because I liked your husband and I tried to find out who killed him and why, and then I learned he'd been mixed up with a gang of crooks and I wondered why so good a man went so far wrong. I've found out most of the answers, and most of them come back to you."

She had gone pale again. With a fair rendition of haughty resignation, she drew the peignoir about her and stared away from him out the windows at the morning landscape beyond. But she was listening. There was no way she could have avoided hearing what Van Horn said except by leaving the room. She stayed because she could not bear not to listen.

"Let me bring you up to date," Van Horn said. "Let me tell you what I know. Then you'll answer a few questions for me and I'll be on my way. It all began with your boredom, didn't it? It all began with your frustration at being rich and idle but not quite rich enough nor idle enough. Trimble's income and yours, put together, should have been plenty but they weren't enough for you to move in the kind of world you like. And anyway, twenty years with the same man, perhaps particularly if he's a good and quiet man, can be sort of boring for somebody like you. Maybe Brush wasn't your first lover, I don't know and I don't care. But Brush came along and you met him through your friend Teresa, and Brush was the kind of scoundrel you could find exciting. Right?"

He got no answer but a curse in Italian.

"So Brush was your lover and Trimble took some losses financially and then your life got to seem really bleak and you thought about leaving Trimble. That's a guess, but it would be consistent. Then Brush came up with a bright idea. Want to tell me about it?"

"I see no reason why I should tell you anything," she said.

"All right, I'll tell you. Brush was in business with some people. You'd met a few of them and a glance at them should have told you what sort they were, but then, you weren't of a mind to care. And Brush said he and his partners needed a reliable man with a lot of what they used to call 'presence' back in the old days, and with a green passport. Trimble filled the bill precisely. All he would have to do was travel a little and overlook a few things at the frontier. Nothing at all, really. And for this he would be very handsomely paid, in real money. There was only one hitch. Trimble was an honest man. But you could get around his scruples. You knew him better than anybody on earth knew him, except perhaps young Flavia, and you certainly knew his weaknesses better than she did. So Brush left it up to you. Didn't he?"

There was no answer. She ignored him. Van Horn rose and went to stand in front of her. He took her chin in one hand and forced her head back until she had to look at him.

"That's how it was, wasn't it, Serena? Wasn't it?"

She tried with both hands to free herself from him, but couldn't budge his grip on her. Finally she began to weep and said, "No! No, it wasn't!"

Van Horn let go of her and she sank back.

"How was it then?" he asked.

"I knew of nothing criminal," she said, sobbing. "I swear I didn't!"

"If it's important to you to feel I believe that, all right then, I'll believe it. But the rest is true, isn't it? Brush left the inducements up to you. And he was your lover. Come on, Serena, give up! It's all over now. It's time to tell the truth."

After a moment she said, "Yes, Nigel was my lover, and he still is. He's a *man!*" For an instant she looked at him defiantly. "More of a man than Larry Trimble or you or anyone!" There were tears in her eyes, but she had stopped weeping.

"Sure," said Van Horn equably. "Now let's give you the benefit of the doubt, and say that Brush didn't indicate to you that what he wanted Trimble to do was illegal. Trimble would have known it was crooked the minute you told him about it, and he'd not only have refused, he'd have turned the whole thing over to the cops. Why didn't he? Why did he accept the job and never breathe a word of it to anyone? Why, Serena?"

"Because of the money!" she spat. "Because there was nothing wrong with earning it as Nigel wanted him to."

"Oh, nuts," Van Horn said disgustedly, and sat down. "You can't tell the truth for more than a minute at a stretch. I don't know why I bother with you."

He sighed and went on the attack once more, "What did you have on your husband, Serena? He was a self-respecting man. I worked closely with him for more than three years in all kinds of situations. I never knew a better man. And I never knew a man it would be harder to force into doing something he felt was wrong."

"You make him a god," Serena said venomously. "He was no god. He was cold and self-righteous. And he was a fool!"

"Well, let's get on with the story. Fool or not, for some reason Trimble took the job. He found he was working for counterfeiters, helping them by using his passport to get their supply of special paper into Switzerland from Milan, where your friend Cherubino, the jolly fat man, Teresa's husband, was making it on the side. I wouldn't be surprised if a little research showed that you own a piece of Cherubino's factory." Serena blinked at this, but held her control. Van Horn went on, "See how it fits together? Of course you do! Cherubino's wife knew you and she knew Brush was looking for a good man. Teresa brought you two together and hoped for the best, letting nature take its course."

Serena was looking at him hard now, waiting. She ignored his offer of a Balto, and he put one in his mouth and then hunted momentarily for the lighter he'd lost in the chalet. He finally found a little box of wax vestas on the table near him, got the cigarette going, and went on:

"Some time ago Brush came to your husband with a new offer. Brush was intimate enough with the counterfeiters, through Zerho, to know they hadn't begun printing, didn't even have their plates on hand. He also learned that Trimble was to be sent, under guard of course, to pick up the plates in Turin, where they'd been stored. He made a deal with Trimble. Together, the two of them would get rid of the guard and steal the plates. They would then sell them back to the counterfeiters for a big packet—Am I boring you? Has Brush already told you all this?"

She was obviously interested. All her withdrawal was gone now. She said impatiently, "No, no."

"Good. It's at this point that my ideas and the official ones part company. Because your husband didn't play it straight. He agreed to throw in with Brush when Brush made the proposal, but when they got to Turin your husband slipped away from Brush and lit out on his own. Pretty ungrateful of him, considering Brush'd been obliging enough to kill the guard and make Trimble's getaway possible. I personally think Trimble meant to turn the plates over to the authorities along with the rest of the yam. But I'm an awfully high-minded guy, apt to take a Christian view of human frailty.

"Anyway, Brush is nobody's Patsy, and he managed to catch up with Trimble on the train for France. He found him alone in a compartment. He killed your husband and searched him. But there weren't any plates. None at all. There was just a notebook that your husband meant to turn over to me. Also, he'd planned to leave you and take your daughter with him. So you see, yesterday you were really just as much a woman deserted as you thought you were."

"Yes," she said. "It does not surprise me." And indeed, she did not appear surprised. Simply desperate and very worn. She spoke slowly, hoarse with tension. "You have so high an opinion of my husband, let me educate you. Your opinion of me cannot grow worse. So I will tell you, yes, I *did* know that what Nigel was doing, and also what he wanted my husband to do, was not legal. That was so bad, of course, wasn't it? I am to be damned forever because I helped a man to get another man to break the law. Yes, of course!" There was an edge of hysteria in her tone now, and she spoke more rapidly. "But let me assure you that there is nothing I could do that would be vile enough to equal Lawrence Trimble's vileness! All of vileness I know I learned from him. You say you knew him. Nonsense! He fooled you as he fooled me and everyone."

"I'm willing to reconsider," Van Horn said calmly. "How was Trimble vile? What did he do?" His gambler's eyes never left her face, estimating, waiting.

Under his gaze, she rose and began to pace the floor, the peignoir billowing lightly out around her as she walked.

"I can hardly bring myself to speak of it," she said.

"You brought yourself to speak of it to him, didn't you?" Van Horn inquired without any special emphasis. "Go ahead. I'm hard to shock."

But he nonetheless did appear to be shocked as she said, blurting it out, "He was Flavia's lover! What do you think of that? He seduced his own daughter! Now do you understand me?"

"I don't believe it," Van Horn said flatly. But he looked stunned.

"Oh, Larry denied it when I accused him. He was full of outrage and injured dignity, oh, yes! But then I reminded him that I knew, that I had found them together. And he never said another word!"

"You found them together?" Van Horn asked dully.

"Yes!" Serena hissed. She began once again to pace the room, her hands locked together in front of her, her face hard and cold. "At Christmas time. Four or five years ago. It does not matter. Flavia was fifteen. She went to a ball for young people. That night Larry and I had a great fight. He was such a boor! I left without him for a party we had been invited to. I didn't return until dawn. The servants were not at home. This room was full of the leftovers of the binge he'd been having after I left him. I went upstairs and looked into Flavia's room. Her bed had not been slept in. I went to Larry's room to find out where she was, if he knew and was not too drunk to tell me. And there they were!" Serena stopped pacing and pressed her hands against her eyes and shuddered. "Cuddled up together in his bed like long-standing lovers. She still had on her ball gown. It was ruined, there was no doubt what had happened." Serena groaned. For these past few minutes, whatever else she had been since Van Horn had met her, there was no mistaking her awful sincerity. Van Horn was no longer looking at her. Instead, he stared out the salon windows, his mask of a face expressing nothing.

Serena dropped her hands and stood listlessly for a moment, then went on, "I took her to her room and later we went to see a doctor. She was not a virgin, but there was no other harm. Not physical harm. I never mentioned it to Larry. Not until I had to make him see what I felt for him, and that he had to do what I wanted, not until I saw a way to get us out of this—this emptiness."

As had happened when they first met, a long silence grew between the woman and Van Horn. Neither seemed, this time, to be aware of it, and they could not have seemed more remote from one another.

At last Van Horn sighed and cleared his throat. "All right," he said. "I guess maybe I have to do my thinking all over again." He was silent for a moment, then cursed softly and stood up. Serena turned and looked at him. She seemed spent.

"Yes," she said. "Perhaps now you can understand—" She stopped abruptly at the look on his face. "Why do you look at me that way?" she asked, frowning.

He ignored her question and said, "Listen to me, Serena. It doesn't matter now what you've done or what Trimble may have done. It doesn't matter why the two of you did whatever you did. All that is past. What matters now is saving whatever hasn't been lost yet. And that's Flavia."

"Flavia?" she asked stupidly, frowning.

"I don't care what you think of her, Serena. There must be some maternal feeling for her in you somewhere. And right now Flavia is on the spot. Trimble put her there, although he didn't mean to. She's in terrible danger."

Serena's frown deepened and she said, "Danger?" scornfully.

"Yes. Trimble got rid of the package he took from the engraver in Turin. He ditched it between the time he took it and the time he got on the train for Modane. He must have mailed it to the place where he was going to stay with Flavia. I think Flavia's gone there, alone, not knowing she's come to rest on a bull's eye. I've got to know where that place is."

Serena said, "I do not know what you are saying, what it means. I cannot care where she has gone."

"If I could figure this out," Van Horn went on insistently, "so could Brush, and so could the people your husband was supposed to be working for. You've got to tell me what Brush did here this morning and where he's gone."

"I don't know what you are talking about," Serena said. She seemed to have recovered herself somewhat, and spoke with bland loftiness. "I've told you what you seemed to want to know. Now please leave me."

"All right," Van Horn said. But he didn't move. Instead, he stood looking at her, and slowly shook his head. There came over his face the same look that had puzzled her a few minutes earlier.

"Please go," she said, but his attitude again confused her, and she said once more, "Why do you look at me like that?"

"Because I'm feeling very sorry for you, I suppose," Van Horn said. "Poor Serena!"

"I do not need your sympathy," she said.

"Yes, you do, Serena," Van Horn said. "You need all the sympathy you can get. I think you will get damned little, and you can put up with mine. At least mine is sincere. Because it's always a little sad to see anyone finished."

"Finished?" The loftiness had gone completely, and a kind of apprehension had replaced it.

"Yes. Finished. What have you got left? You drove your husband into a crooked line and he got himself killed following it. Your daughter has run away. I don't think she'll be back. Because she hates you, Serena. And now your lover's gone too. Oh, don't doubt it. He killed Trimble just as sure as sunup, Serena. And he'll hang for it. Wherever he's gone now, he'll never be back. So what's left, Serena? An empty title, a bunch of friends who will drop you like *that* the minute they hear what you've been up to, and they *will* hear sooner or later. As for your crooked acquaintances, they've used you and played on your avarice, and they'll come gunning for you if they think even for a minute that you know too much or are getting in the way. That's all that's left to you now. When the cops catch Brush and nail him, it will all come out, and that'll be the end of your world. Until then, and after that for as long as you live, there'll be the guilt. There'll be knowing, awake or asleep, that it was you who made this mess possible, you who one way or another caused at least three deaths and ruined your daughter's life. Oh, there'll be a lot of guilt, Serena, unless you've grown more depraved than I think you have. That's why I'm feeling sorry for you, Serena. I think you're a very pitiable object."

He had spoken gently and with some feeling, and his words had gradually broken her last shreds of composure. As he turned from her and strode out of the room, her face was crumpled into something very ugly, and her sobs grated through the quiet house.

Van Horn did not leave the villa. Instead, once outside the salon, he moved quickly upstairs. He found what must have been Flavia's bedroom, nearest the top of the stairway. School photographs were tucked under the edge of the dressing-table mirror, and the room seemed unused and a bit airless; it had been unoccupied for a week.

The room next to it was very large and very feminine and had its occupant's personality engraved on it, in the scattered clothing, the great, rumpled bed, the cluttered dressing table, the cheap novels on the chaise longue, and the clothes that filled the closets to bursting. Serena lived here. In an ash tray on the bed table, Van Horn found a little pile of coarse aromatic tobacco, emptied, half-burned, among the carmined cigarette stubs Serena had put there.

Farther down the hall were Trimble's bedroom and dressing room. They too had an airlessness to them, an atmosphere of recent abandonment, and Trimble's closets and drawers and shelves were nearly empty of clothes. Van Horn began systematically searching the place.

He was sorting through the odds and ends left in the top drawers of a wardrobe, when behind him Serena's voice said, "Nigel searched here too."

He turned to find her leaning against the door to the hall. Her face was ravaged and streaked and pale. She was at last a woman without sham.

Van Horn said, "What did he find?"

"Nothing," Serena said. "Only a bit of paper in the wastebasket."

Van Horn went to her quickly. "What was it?"

"I did not see," she said, shaking her head. "It was an advertisement of some sort. Perhaps a travel folder, or a brochure."

Van Horn put his hands on her shoulders and held her hard. "When was this?" he asked. "When did Brush find this piece of paper?"

"This morning," she answered dully. "He was here last evening. He was here while you were here and while your friend Parrish was here. Then he left after you had gone. He came back this morning, very early." She shook her head as though to clear it. "I waked up and he was in my bed. That is how he is. He is swift and very strong, and he can move very quietly. I have no doubt that you speak the truth, that he did kill Larry Trimble. He can be a savage man." She smiled wanly. "Savagery can be an asset in love, you know."

Her smile faded under Van Horn's scowl. He said, urging her, "He questioned you."

"Yes. He asked me about Flavia. He asked me where we had stayed when we went to France or England on visits. I told him, but he was not satisfied. He left me and began to search here and in Flavia's room. He read letters and went through the pockets of the clothing in the closets. I watched him. He did not even know I was with him, I think, he was concentrating so hard. Then he went through the little wastebasket in Larry's dressing room, and he seized the bit of paper and read it. For a while he just held it in his hand and stared at the wall. Then he put it in his pocket and left. He pushed by me as though I were not there and left. By the time I got downstairs, he was driving out of the driveway."

"What time was that?"

"I cannot be sure. Perhaps an hour before you arrived. I had time to make my coffee. The servants are gone off for—"

"What kind of car does he drive?"

"I do not know. It is big and black. But he has also driven a little gray car at times. I do not know. Where has he gone?"

Van Horn took her arm and led her off toward the stairs. "I think he's on his way to France, to the inn where your husband and Flavia were going to go after they met in Modane. Yesterday morning, Brush had a chance to go through Flavia's handbag. I went through it, too, a few hours before he did. In it was a brochure for a country inn, and I think he found another copy of the same thing in that wastebasket. Get me a *Guide Michelin*."

She led him downstairs to a little study near the salon, and together they found a *Guide*. It was several years out of date, but it was unlikely the inn was new. Van Horn looked first at Grasse. Nothing listed in its vicinity seemed to suit him. He turned to other listings in the Basses Alpes and Alpes Maritimes area, and finally found what he was looking for listed under Digne. It was called L'Auberge de l'Empereur. He put the book into his pocket and said, "What cars do you have here?"

"Only Larry's Delahaye. But you are not going to leave me? Please—" She moved toward him.

"Get me the keys, the registration card, and the *triptyque* for it." She started to plead with him again and he said sharply, "Move!"

She recoiled and turned and rummaged in the desk drawers, finally locating a big international travel permit and a registration card. She handed them to him, saying, "The keys are in the car. Must you go?"

"Try to understand, Serena," Van Horn said impatiently, taking the papers from her and moving to the desk. "If your sweet Nigel gets to Flavia, he'll kill her as casually as he killed your husband." As he spoke, he picked up the telephone and dialed.

Ten minutes of repetitive talking to a series of operators elicited the fact that the number given in the *Guide Michelin* for L'Auberge de l'Empereur at Digne was no longer correct. Presently someone found the right number. Five minutes later Van Horn was speaking to a man who described himself as the *aubergiste,* presumably the Emperor's own inn-keeper. He said the inn was empty. He said no one was there but himself and his wife. He said there was no young lady staying there. He did not recall any reservation made by anyone for a M. Trimble, nor for anyone else. He was sorry. He was insistent. He was, finally, abrupt. And then he wasn't on the line any more.

Van Horn hung up and turned to Serena. "Keep calling," he said. "Give my name. Call and call until that silly man gets irritated enough to put Flavia on the line, or until he gives her my name and she answers herself. She went there scared. She's probably nobbled the help to keep her under cover. If and when you speak to her tell her I'm on my way to Digne. Tell her to clear out of that inn and go to the *Préfecture de Police* and simply wait there for me. Tell her to hurry. Got that?"

Serena nodded, and he scribbled the correct number for the inn on a scratch pad on the desk. Then he turned and started for the door.

Serena said tentatively, "One thing."

"Yes?" he said, over his shoulder.

"Please," she said. "I have nothing now. You are right to say I 'am finished. Please. Try to make Flavia understand. Tell her how it is with me. Tell her I would like her—" She stopped and bit her lip. "No," she said at last. "Tell her I have been very evil, that I do not blame her for hating me, but I need her. Ask her to speak to me again."

He nodded. "I'll do all of that," he said. "But you'd better not expect miracles. I can't guarantee a thing. So long, Serena."

"Good-by," she said, and he went out.

CHAPTER NINETEEN

The Delahaye had an electric gearshift and tremendous power, and Van Horn very nearly wrecked it at the outset, taking it out of the Trimbles' garage. But by the time he had safely passed the Customs barrier outside the city he had mastered the thing, and he settled down to a racing clip, not reckless but steady, the speed seldom falling below a hundred kilometers an hour except when he passed through towns. The great car fled over the highway, the kilometer posts snapped past, and it was mid-afternoon when he reached the outskirts of Digne, Basses Alpes, 5,804 inhabitants.

He didn't enter the town, but, following the instructions in the *Guide Michelin,* turned off the Route Napoléon and made his way uphill over a dirt road so narrow that the Delahaye brushed the shrubbery on both sides. L'Auberge de l'Empereur was a half mile from the highway, and consisted of four buildings: the inn proper, a garage, a small stable, and a house for the staff. Van Horn slowed down at the sight of it. Then as he drew closer the grounds came more fully into view. In the driveway, ten yards short of the garage, stood a familiar little gray Simca. The door on the driver's side hung open. There was a dark stain visible on the gray upholstery of the seat and the glass in the windshield had been shattered. The left front tire of the car was flat. Two windows on the second floor of the inn were broken. Standing in the inn doorway, his arms folded, a brown cigarette in his lips, was a middle-aged gendarme. The flap on his holster was open. He stared at the Delahaye attentively.

Van Horn gently accelerated the car and drove on. It took him some time to find his way back to the highway without passing the inn again, but once back on the concrete, he opened the car up and roared down into the little town.

The Digne *Préfecture de Police* was not in the middle of town, and not on the principal route through the town, as is usual in such places since it allows the local law to maintain the payroll at the expense of speeders on their way to the Côte d'Azur, without moving more than a few steps from their front door. Instead, in Digne, the prefecture is tucked away on a thoroughfare called the Boulevard Soustre, on the southeast edge of the town. Before its door, when Van Horn drove past, an antique Black Maria was parked and several dozen townspeople were standing about looking ill-assorted, ill-at-ease, and ill-informed.

Van Horn drove past, turned a corner, and parked in a street called the rue Mère de Dieu. Then he walked back and joined the group in front of the door to the prefecture. There were no gendarmes in sight, which was out of the ordinary and seemed to signal the occurrence of Great Happenings.

Like most people who have been near an event of moment without hearing it clearly, and without seeing it all, the crowd in front of the prefecture was busy telling itself exaggerations and distortions, everyone trying very hard to establish himself in some relationship with what had taken place.

The interested auditor, such as Van Horn, could hear about what must have been a small war, a prolonged and bloody engagement apparently unlike anything seen in these parts since The Hundred Days. Everyone agreed that the noise of the shooting and the cries of the wounded had been better than the 14th of July. But, beyond that, no one agreed with anyone about anything.

Van Horn listened to this for a few colorful minutes, then selected a solid-looking elderly gentleman, wearing pince-nez, who had not opened his mouth since Van Horn had joined the group, and asked him, "What is transpiring?"

The gentleman shrugged. "Our heroic police returned from Armageddon and went inside without explaining anything." He looked as wonderfully disgusted as only a Frenchman can look. "Thus we are all free to hazard. Isn't it marvelous? How much creativity lurks in the minds of people one might ordinarily consider to lack any trace of imagination!"

"Where are the wounded and dying?" Van Horn asked.

"Our stalwarts in uniform brought back three prisoners and a corpse. And one officer was wounded. In the name of God, this is a day from which this town will never recover! It's insupportable to consider. For the rest of our lives the wild variations of today's events will wag the tongues of these people. Today will become folkloric, like Norse sagas or the Trojan wars. Aaaagh! *Quelle histoire!*" He looked really distressed at the prospect, and stomped off.

Gently prodding his way through the press of people, Van Horn reached the high double doors of the prefecture. He tried the knob. It was locked. Without hesitation he raised one fist and began to pound on the door. He had struck half a dozen blows and the crowd, in astonishment, had partially hushed its babble, when suddenly the door flew open and a belligerent little gendarme with finely tapered mustachios glared out and started to speak. Then he found he was glaring at the middle of Van Horn's chest and he closed his mouth and raised his head to look into Van Horn's face.

Van Horn said quickly, "I am from the Embassy of the United States. I demand to speak to the Prefect." He walked in, and the little gendarme, reacting to the voice and figure of authority, gave way before him and stepped aside.

Van Horn strode directly to the raised desk that dominated the room, ignored the two gendarmes who rushed to stop him, and thundered to the sergeant behind the desk, "Call the Prefect

at once. I have come here on a matter of diplomatic importance."
The sergeant scowled and started to reply, but Van Horn cut him
off. "Immediately. I have no time for arguments. Hurry, man,
hurry!"

The sergeant paused, thought a moment, and shrugged.
Van Horn took another step toward him and tossed his
special passport on the desk. "My credentials," he said.
"*Bougez!*"

The sergeant budged. Taking the passport with him, he disappeared into the back of the building.

Van Horn lighted a Balto grandly and said to the man who
had let him in, "I understand one of your comrades is wounded.
My condolences. He will recover, I hope?"

"Yes," said the gendarme. "It is not grave."

The sergeant came back almost running. He was followed
by a squat individual who seemed to be bursting redly out of his
clothes. His eyes were pouched in fat, and all that was visible of
his skin which, considering he was totally bald, was quite a bit,
glowed a delicate puce. He was a monument to his own cellar
and cuisine. He handed Van Horn the passport and bowed vesti-
gially, as much as his physique allowed.

"We are honored, M. Van Horn," he said. "But we are at present rather involved in a matter of some complications. I am the
Prefect. What can I do for you?"

"I am here," Van Horn rumbled, "to find a young lady named
Flavia Trimble. The Auberge de l'Empereur, where I was told I
could find her, is under guard and the people outside inform me
that a great battle has taken place there today. Please reassure me.
You have the girl?"

"*Oui, Monsieur.*"

Van Horn lost some of his poise. He said, "She is well? She
has suffered no harm?"

"None at all, none at all," the Prefect said hastily. "She is at
this moment making a deposition. It is all most regrettable."

"Perhaps," Van Horn said, "you would be so good as to tell me what has transpired. The people outside are quite confused about the details of the day's happenings."

"Come into my office," the Prefect said, and escorted Van Horn into a dim and crowded cubicle that contained chiefly a heavily loaded neo-Gothic desk. It loomed like a cathedral in the little room. The Prefect retired behind it, seemed to acquire some confidence from this situation, and asked bluntly, "You will tell me now why you have come to seek the girl?"

"As I said," Van Horn repeated, blowing smoke at the incised ceiling and settling himself in a chair, "it is a matter of diplomatic importance. Furthermore *c'est une affaire du coeur.*" He smiled with great condescension at the Prefect. "You understand. You are a man of the world. The girl's family is very highly placed. The girl has suffered certain emotional reverses. She fled her home, telling no one where she was going. Her family insist on the greatest discretion. They learned that she had hidden at the Auberge to elude her suitors and her family equally. They asked me to come and, with all possible discretion, return her to her home. I went to the Auberge, and the rest you know. Now, please, what has happened today?"

The Prefect asked, "Her family is rich?"

"Extremely," said Van Horn. "And *old* rich, furthermore. Old and powerful rich, the kind who will have no publicity of any kind under any circumstances, if you understand me."

"Perfectly," said the Prefect and a look of enormous satisfaction spread over his mauve countenance. His eyes nearly disappeared under the squint of fat. "It is as I thought. The fact of her richness explains everything. Tell me, who were her suitors? They were worthy men?"

"Oh, eminently," Van Horn said righteously. "But she spurned them. And they were distraught. Which is comprehensible. You have seen the young lady."

The Prefect sighed. "Yes, I have seen. She is delicious, truly delicious. Worth some anguish." He pulled himself together. "Her suitors' respectability makes the case all the clearer. The young lady is an American heiress. She came to our quiet little city to seek privacy. She enlisted the aid of the *aubergiste* to keep her presence unknown. He foolishly agreed."

"It's understandable," Van Horn said with avuncular tolerance.

"But of course. In any case, he had no other clients. There were only himself and his wife at the inn." This seemed a slur on the area's attraction, and the Prefect hastened to add, "This is the off-season, you understand, Monsieur. In season, Digne is a veritable touristic Mecca."

"Certainly," said Van Horn.

"At all events, Mademoiselle Trimble passed several days at the Auberge, and she was not disturbed. Then today, this morning, she received numerous telephone calls from Geneva."

"Yes," said Van Horn. "That was her family, attempting to reach her. The faithful *aubergiste* denied any knowledge of her."

"True, true," the Prefect said. "Then, sometime after the hour of lunch,"—this was obviously an hour of real importance to him among the day's twenty-four—"a man came to the Auberge in a large black foreign car. He entered the building without being seen by either the *aubergiste* or his wife. He went to the girl's room and forced an entrance." Warming to his subject, the Prefect began to act out his account, waving his stubby arms, scowling with enormous menace or looking demure or terrified as the scene warranted. Van Horn looked on, transfixed. "The young lady cried out in terror. The *aubergiste* rushed to her aid, only to be confronted by the intruder and knocked senseless. The *aubergiste*'s wife sagely fled the inn and ran to a neighboring house to telephone us here and ask for aid. But that took many minutes. During her absence a second car arrived at the inn, a gray Simca, and it was followed by another large foreign machine. In these there were many men, heavily armed. As they ran to the inn, the man in the young lady's room opened fire on them. The newcomers returned his fire. The man driving the gray Simca was slain. Great damage was done to the inn by small-arms fire. Ah! It was frightful! By the time our men arrived on the scene, the attackers were preparing to rush the building. The intruder, the *aubergiste,* and the young lady would most certainly have been killed. In the event, the attackers found themselves attacked by our men. They turned to defend themselves. The girl's captor made his getaway. The attackers equally made their retreat, but not before we had let them feel the force of our arms!"

The Prefect subsided, apparently played out from the strain of re-enacting the engagement. He mopped his lofty brow with a crumpled handkerchief.

Van Horn said heavily, "No prisoners?"

The Prefect looked wounded. *"Hélas,* no," he admitted. Then he brightened and looked pleased with himself as he had earlier in the interview. "But, in any case, I know who these criminals were."

Van Horn looked honestly astounded. "You do?"

"But of course," the Prefect said, rocking back in his chair and putting the tips of his stubby red fingers together over his chest. "They could have been but one thing—*des gangsters Américains!*"

"Oh," said Van Horn with careful seriousness. "I see."

"In France," the Prefect went on, pedagogically, "we have, of course, our criminals—thieves, murderers, brutes of all the ordinary kinds. But there are certain refinements of crime that have never—how shall I put it?—have never *appealed* to the French criminal mind, one might say. And your American gangsters have perfected some of these outrages in a high degree. Kidnaping for ransom is the chief of these. We in France are seldom confronted by this. There is something…*extreme* about it that appears to repel our felons."

"Uh-huh," Van Horn said. Then he managed to rise to the moment and said, "You are most probably perfectly correct. It was surely the work of rival gangs this afternoon. Now that you have pointed this out, it seems quite evident."

The Prefect glowed an even ruddier hue under the flattery. "I have only to turn over the entire story, and the depositions of the principals, to the *Sûreté*," he said, "and they will find these monsters with dispatch."

"I hope there is no necessity to keep the young lady here," Van Horn put in firmly. "You can understand that her family is distraught. She herself must be terribly upset by her experience and most anxious to go home."

The Prefect arose ponderously. "Oh, certainly, certainly. With her deposition, and with you to vouch for her availability to the *Sûreté* if they have need for her, we have no cause to detain her. Come, she should have finished telling her story now."

Van Horn right behind him, the Prefect led the way out of the office, through the outer room, and through the rear door into the interrogation room. It was a dim and musty chamber containing two clerical-looking gendarmes, two tables, several resilient chairs and a massive, deafening, antediluvian typewriter. One of the gendarmes was tentatively bashing at this as Van Horn and the Prefect walked in. The other gendarme was reading over his shoulder. And seated in front of the typist was Flavia Trimble, wearing a clinging knitted dress, stockings and shoes. The mink jacket was thrown over the back of her chair.

She looked haggard as she raised her eyes. Then she saw Van Horn and recognized him and a look of overwhelming relief came over her delicate face and she smiled palely. "Hello, Jud," she said.

"Hello, Flavia," he said warmly. "You all right?"

"Yes," she said. "I'm all right now." She added in French to the Prefect, "May I go now with my friend?"

"But of course," said the Prefect grandly, "if you have told us everything."

The typist said, *"C'est fini. Mademoiselle parle un français magnifique. Je vous remercie, mademoiselle."*

He wound the deposition out of the machine, bowed, and gave her the paper to read and sign. There followed elaborate and warm farewells, assurances and reassurances. It was evident that it would be quite a while before the police force of the town of Digne would forget Flavia Trimble. She was the most admired deponent in their experience.

"Is there a rear exit to this building?" Van Horn asked the Prefect. "I do not wish to expose the lady to the stares of the curious."

"Yes, of course," the Prefect said. "I will show you."

"I will bring the car around," Van Horn said to Flavia.

She said in English, "Do you think we should leave, Jud? It seems so ... *safe* here, with all these uniforms. I'm so tired of running! Maybe if we explained what is really wrong ... " She looked at him pleadingly.

He shook his head. "Our host here would go wild if he knew how juicy a mess this really is, and we'd never get loose. We're sitting ducks here. We've got to run for it. There's no second way. We can send for your things later on."

"All right," she said rather hopelessly.

He grinned at her. "The official view here is that your visitors were trying to kidnap you for ransom. Don't shatter their illusions."

He left her then and followed the Prefect to the rear door of the prefecture. It opened into an alley which was empty. On his way back to the Street of the Mother of God and the Delahaye, he made several stops, doing a kind of shopping that is peculiarly French:

In a dusty hardware store he bought two kilos of roofing nails. Two doors away, at a bakery, he bought two *baguettes*, long, thin breadloaves, very fresh. Farther down the street he entered a butter-eggs-and-cheese shop and bought three kinds of cheese, gruyère, roblochons, and some local goat. In the Street of the Mother of God he found a little sporting-goods store where he bought a box of .32 caliber revolver shells. On his way back to the car he stopped in a *charcuterie* and bought a pound and a half of cold cuts. Almost back to the car, he went into a branch of the Nicolas wineshop chain and bought two bottles of a 1949 Chateauneuf du Pape. At last, juggling the collection of packages, he returned to the car and climbed into it, stowing his purchases in the tonneau. The French believe in specialization.

Three minutes later he drove into the alley behind the prefecture. The girl slipped out of the door and into the car, they waved casually to the Prefect, and Van Horn, careful to seem unhurried, eased the car out of the alley.

"Why, this is Daddy's car!" the girl said amazedly.

"I had to borrow it," he said. "It's a wonderful machine, and right now it's about our biggest asset." He turned left at the mouth of the alley and began threading his way through the town's narrow back streets, heading generally south, parallel to the highway. He told her briefly how Brush, and he himself, had tracked her down. "Brush got careless in his haste, I guess," he said. "Anyway, Zerho and the people your father used to work for were able to follow him. And I came galumphing after, miles behind."

They passed the southern limits of Digne and he kept on, headed into the country, pressing the car as hard as was safe over the bumpy back roads.

"Where are we going?" the girl asked.

"Away from here," he said. "Away from Brush and Soloviev and their ilk. I have a place in mind."

"Away," she said thoughtfully. "I thought I had got away when I came here. Now I realize I should have stayed where you left me. I should have trusted you."

"I know. It's all right." He paused, then said gently, "Flavia, this is likely to be a rough trip. I'm fairly certain both Brush and the other outfit are sitting somewhere out of town, waiting to pick up your trail. They may even have had somebody in the crowd there by the prefecture keeping an eye on both of us."

"Oh, Lord," she said despondently. "What can we do?"

"Well, we're not completely helpless, you know. We've got a superb car and lots of gas, a little money, a gun, some food, and all the roads of France to get lost in. Who knows? We might even enjoy the trip." He patted her knee. "Cheer up," he said.

Van Horn, driving without lights, kept eyeing the car's rear-view mirror as they rumbled along, but it was growing dusk now, and little was visible behind them. No headlights. There was no way to know if they were being followed.

Twenty minutes' hard driving brought them to a little road labeled N207. Van Horn turned right on it, headed toward the west and the Route Napoléon. When route N207 reached the Route Napoléon but while they were still some distance away, he pulled the car to a stop. There was a good deal of traffic on the highway for that time of year. They had to wait three or four minutes before the wide road was empty as far as the eye could see in both directions. Then Van Horn gave the car all the acceleration it would take, and they rushed down the last few yards of N207, shot across the main road, and rumbled at top speed into the continuation of N207 on the other side, which a marker indicated led to Durance and Manoque. Van Horn switched on the headlights. For ten minutes they drove in silence. Then abruptly a pair of headlights appeared in the rear-view mirror. Perhaps half a mile behind them, they were high and wide-spaced headlights, white instead of the amber required in French lamps. They were coming on fast.

Van Horn put the accelerator pedal down to the floor and said, "Company coming. Weather clear, track fast. Hang on to your hat."

There was no question now of safe maximum speed, but only of maximum speed. The car leaped along the rough-crowned road, swaying and pounding. The girl clung to the seat, her lips compressed, trembling but silent and in control of herself. The lights in the rear-view mirror receded slightly.

Van Horn said pleasantly, "This is nice country through here. Pity we have to see the world at night."

A farm truck approached them, moving slowly, their own terrific speed making it seem to swim with dreamy swiftness out of the growing darkness. Van Horn edged the Delahaye to the right edge of the road and the car's outriggerlike wheels kept it upright as they rocketed by. The girl's sigh of relief was audible.

Van Horn's voice was still pleasant as he said, "If you'll dig in the pile of purchases I dumped in the back, you'll find a bag of nails. I'll try not to bang you around too much."

Without a word the girl turned and knelt on the seat and in a moment she turned back and sat again, the bag in her hands.

"I'm psychic," Van Horn said.

Half a mile farther the road bent sharply in a right turn. Van Horn wheeled the Delahaye around it and pulled to a stop. Taking the bag from the girl, he got swiftly out of the car, ran back fifty feet to about the point where a following car, coming into the straightaway out of the curve, would be reaching top acceleration. There he spread half the roofing nails in a thick band across the asphalt. Their points gleamed wickedly in the light of the Delahaye's tail-lamps.

"If all that's behind us," he said, getting back into the car and stowing the nail bag behind the seat, "is a peaceable farmer rich enough to own a foreign car, I'll be very sorry. But it wouldn't pay to take chances." He put the car in gear. "Now," he said, "you had better talk to me." Once more they roared off over the old road.

"You're an amazing person," the girl said.

"That won't do at all," he said. "I said talk, not flattery. While you're developing your material, dig around again back there and fix us some supper."

Once again the girl twisted around to search in the tonneau.

Van Horn glanced over to her. "You've done some shopping, haven't you?" he asked. "Do you realize this is the first time I've seen you properly dressed? You looked great in those ski-pants, but for all I knew you were pure Bechstein from the knees down, with claw-and-ball feet. It's a great relief to learn the truth."

"Oh," she said, smiling for the first time since their drive had started, "these clothes were there when I arrived. My dramatic idea of leaving everything behind didn't work out." She grew serious again. "Daddy had most of my things sent on with his."

"What did he send—of yours and his?"

She looked at him curiously. "Just clothes and a few books he was fond of. Why?" Her lap was full of parcels of food and bottles.

He took his big knife from his pocket and handed it to her. "Nothing else?"

"No."

"Did he mail anything?"

"No. You're thinking about what Nigel Brush was looking for, aren't you? You're looking for it, too. What is it? Please! I don't care what it proves about Daddy, I just can't stand not knowing what this is all about."

"Tell me first about Brush's visit."

She shivered. "He came so suddenly I didn't have time to do anything. I heard someone on the stairs, and a second later my door flew open and there he was, grinning at me. I screamed, and he waved his pistol at me and told me to shut up or he'd hurt me. But I went on screaming. He started for me, and then the inn-keeper came in, and he was caught too. Brush said if I made any more trouble he'd kill the inn-keeper, so I kept quiet. He walked over then and just hit the inn-keeper with his gun ... just *hit* him, the most casual way. I couldn't believe he'd really done it. But the poor inn-keeper fell down in a heap. It was awful."

"Poor Flavia!" Van Horn said softly. "What a time you've had!"

After a moment, she went on, "He started tearing everything apart then, searching. I stood and watched him. I was just paralyzed, I guess." She began slicing the bread lengthwise and packing the slices with meat and cheese.

"He wasn't very careful, was he?" Van Horn said. "He wasn't looking for anything very small. Ripped the backs off things and so on, huh?"

She looked at him. "Yes. He kicked in the sides of all the boxes and suitcases and Daddy's footlocker. And he broke the backgammon board, too. That made me angry finally, and I almost went at him. But then he heard a car pulling up in front of the inn and he ran to look. Lord, he moves quickly, like an animal. He doesn't seem to have to think, he simply *acts*, the way a wild animal will do. Anyway, he suddenly ducked and a shot was fired and the window broke and then he started firing and I . . . I lay down on the floor." She laughed ruefully.

"Very wise move," Van Horn said. "All soldiers are taught that the better part of valor consists of keeping one's bottom down. What then?"

"Well, then there was a whole lot more shooting from outside, and I supposed it was the police. Brush ran off and down the stairs. Then there was even more shooting, until it sounded the way war must sound. And finally I heard two cars going away very fast and then the police came in. I told them the broken things had got damaged when the inn-keeper and I were struggling with Brush. I didn't tell them I knew who Brush was."

"Good enough. Otherwise they'd have kept you there till doomsday."

"That's what I thought. And all I wanted was to get to an American Consulate and give up, give up, give up!" She groaned.

Then she looked at Van Horn and said, "What was Brush looking for?"

"For two metal plates. Plates for printing ten-thousand-franc French banknotes."

There was a brief pause before she asked, "Daddy stole them?"

"He seems to have," Van Horn said mildly.

Flavia sighed. "These plates … they must be very special." She handed him a sandwich and began opening a bottle of wine with the corkscrew on his knife.

"I've only just begun to realize how special," he said, taking a big bite.

They rode in silence then for a long time. Van Horn concentrated on getting the maximum speed out of the car over the narrow, twisting, two-lane road. They crossed the Durance and went through Manosque to Apt, from Apt to Cavaillon. At Cavaillon, they turned north on an even smaller road, N538 to Carpentras. There was no sign now of their being followed, but still Van Horn pressed the pace. The streets of Carpentras were deserted. It was mealtime in these parts. The world outside was invisible from the interior of the softly lighted car. They were in an intimate little room, filled with the rich smells of bread and cheese and wine. Van Horn, steering easily with one hand, stretched himself in the seat, rubbed the back of his neck and sighed.

Flavia passed the wine bottle to him and said, "How much sleep have you had since I saw you in Turin?"

"Almost none," he said. "I'm the new Tom Edison."

"I can drive, you know."

He looked over at her and grinned. "I'm all right, little mother," he said. He took a long swig of the wine.

At Brange they finally reached National Route No. 7, the great highway that connects Paris with the Côte d'Azur, and Van Horn was able to push the car to its limits. Near Fontainebleau, at nearly three in the morning, he swung the Delahaye off No. 7

onto a dirt road that led west, and forty minutes later they pulled up at the Auberge de la Moutière in Montfort-l'Amaury.

The night porter let them in, grumbled at their having no reservation, seemed little cheered by the huge tip Van Horn gave him, made no comment on their lack of baggage, told Van Horn he could register the next day, and led them to what amounted to a little independent house attached to the inn proper by a covered passageway. The house consisted of two bedrooms on opposite sides of a sitting room, and two bathrooms. There was a fire laid in the sitting-room fireplace. The air was sweet with the smell of old wood and the furnishings were somehow both simple and luxurious. It was a beautiful little retreat. The porter started the fire, mumbled a good night, and left.

Van Horn said, "What a place! A man I know came here once to spend a weekend with his lawfully wedded wife, who happened to be six months pregnant at the time, and they damn near threw him out."

"It's a lovely place," the girl said, looking at the titles on the leather-bound books in the bookcase. "There are even things here it might be nice to read."

"I doubt much reading gets done here," Van Horn said. He started to unknot his tie, and then paused, noting the girl's uneasiness. He smiled at her and said, "Pick your bedroom, milady. But be quick, or I'll fall asleep on my feet."

"Oh," she said. "It doesn't matter." She moved to the nearest door. "I'll take this one."

There was a pause. They looked at each other. Then the girl said, "Thank you, Jud, for everything." He started to reply something disparaging, but she went on, "No, I mean I am really grateful. Not just for all you've done, because you might have done those things anyway as a part of your job. I'm grateful to you for being a man. Except for Daddy, I've never known many real men. The strong ones were usually brutal, and the gentle ones were usually weak. You're—well, you're an amazing person, and I'm very glad I'm with you."

She spoke with a great maturity and obvious sincerity, and Van Horn seemed to find himself with nothing to say. At last he muttered, "Good night, Flavia," and turned abruptly and went into the other bedroom.

He stripped to his shorts and climbed heavily into the bed, moving as though in a dream, his eyes half closed with fatigue. Then he was asleep.

For five hours he lay as though dead, in a slumber so deep it was like a coma. Yet the instant the girl walked into his room, he came awake, sitting up tensely, his eyes squinting in the thin autumn dawn sunlight that streamed through the window.

The girl was standing in the doorway watching him. She had thrown the mink over her shoulders as a dressing gown. Under it, she was wearing a slip, and her legs and feet were bare. "I'm sorry," she said, as he shook his head sharply and rubbed his eyes. "I didn't mean to wake you. I woke up a few minutes ago and it was so still I was afraid you'd gone."

"Gone?" he said. "I wouldn't leave you. Not again." He was wide awake now, sitting in the bed with the sheet up to his waist. "I wouldn't leave you, Flavia."

Then neither of them spoke. The girl gazed into his eyes with great calm. She seemed completely serene. It was as though, having accidentally awakened him, she had no doubt whatever of the outcome. She neither spoke nor moved. When at last he swung himself out of the bed and walked to her, looking very grave, almost menacing, she kept her eyes on his and did not move. Apparently she had decided to accept whatever happened.

Van Horn stood before her for a moment and then gathered her into his arms, gently at first and then, as she responded and her arms went around his big back, more strongly, but still with a kind of trembling restraint. He kissed her, also with restraint at first, then with increasing violence. Bending over her, the muscles along his back stood out like cables.

When, after a long while, he drew back and looked at her, there was color in her face and her breath was fast, but still she wore the look of serenity. Slowly and rather deliberately, he pushed the mink jacket off her smooth shoulders. It fell to the floor with a gentle thud. Then he picked her up and carried her lightly to bed.

CHAPTER TWENTY

Now and then the girl kissed him with great delicacy on the edge of his mouth. It was chilly in the room, but they were blazing hot wherever they touched.

The girl whispered something. He said, "What did you say?"

"I said, so that's what it's really like." She sighed. "Love, I mean."

"Yes," he said. "I didn't know it either."

She drew her head back and looked at him with a little frown. She said, "I didn't mean...I wasn't trying to pose or anything." She blushed. Since she was naked except for the little bandage on her side, it was a very extensive blush. She said, "I wasn't a virgin. I didn't mean to pretend I was."

Van Horn said nothing, but he had grown suddenly tense.

Flavia said, smiling suddenly, "There was another time. But it wasn't like this."

"Don't," Van Horn said. He looked a little pale. "The hell with any other time."

"But I want to tell you about it. I want you to know all there is to know about me."

"Listen, Flavia," he said harshly, "there's no need for this."

"I *want* to," she said gravely. "I want you to hear. It's important. Anyway, you'd think about it. And it's educational, too. It's typical of how girls like me learn the facts of life."

Van Horn closed his eyes and said again, "The hell with it! It doesn't matter."

But she went on, "I was fifteen. I didn't know anything. Think of it! For two years I'd been old enough to have babies, and no one had ever explained a thing to me! It was during Christmas vacation. I remember I had a new ball gown that had lots of ruffles and things in front because I didn't have much chest. Oh, God, how I used to worry about my chest!" She laughed. "Anyway, I had a date with a boy named Pietro. I don't remember his other names but he had a lot of them. He was sixteen, the son of one of Serena's friends, one of her Italian nobility friends. He was quite glamorous and tall and suave or at least I thought he was. Though I remember he was absolutely stupefied when he came to get me and walked in on one of the worst of Serena's tempers. She cut him dead, poor kid. Daddy was pretty tight, but he made up for it as best he could and saw us off."

The girl was staring off into a far corner of the room, her eyes bright with remembrance. Van Horn, tense and pale, made no further effort to stop her.

She said, "It was a funny scene, Daddy and Pietro being men-of-the-world, with Serena raging and cursing in the background. Anyway, Pietro had his father's car and chauffeur and we went to the ball, somewhere near Montreux, I think, though it doesn't matter. Pietro tried to kiss me in the car, but I wouldn't let him though I'd been kissed before. We went to the ball and danced and they had punch and a *souper* and we played silly games. It was like any other ball. It was terribly hot in the ballroom after a while, and I told Pietro I needed a breath of air." She stopped and laughed softly. "No," she said. "That isn't true. I just wanted him to take me out on the balcony and kiss me. I was ready to be kissed by then, I guess.

"He took me outside and there were several other couples already there. It was terribly cold, but we didn't mind, and he kissed me. He was really very good at kissing for sixteen, but then of course he was an Italian, and nobility to boot."

Van Horn, frowning, opened his eyes and looked at her. She was still staring into the corner, but now her eyes had gentle amusement in them.

For a moment she paused. Still not looking at Van Horn, she began to stroke his chest.

She said, "He suggested we take a walk and I agreed and he went to get my wrap and I went off into the gardens. The gardens were all covered with snow, and it was very bright in the moonlight. Beautiful. I think I probably knew that this was going to be an important night in my life. I know I felt unbelievably grown up."

"Ah, God, Flavia," Van Horn said weakly. He kissed her throat.

"Now don't interrupt," she said. She went on stroking his chest. She said, "I was standing looking off into the mountains when he came up behind me and put the cloak over my shoulders. But he didn't stop at that. He slid his hands around onto my stomach and bent and kissed the back of my neck. Nobody'd ever been like that with me before, and I don't know, I just lost all feeling of anything real. His hands were so ... so *broad* on me. I leaned back against him and he kissed my hair and kept on kissing me and then he began to move his hands. I knew he was going to put them on my breasts and I got awfully tense wondering if he was going to be disappointed. But I guess there were so many ruffles around there he couldn't tell what I had!" She laughed aloud. It made a lovely sound. Van Horn grinned.

"This is all very cockeyed," he said. "You're making me jealous of a sixteen-year-old boy I'll never meet. Cut it out."

"I could feel him—you know—against me," she went on, ignoring him. "And I was shocked, but I was excited too. When he led me away, I just went with him. He took me to the parking lot and we found his father's car and he got into the back of it with me. We lay on the floor and it was a big car, but Lord! it wasn't big enough! I didn't know what he wanted, and I *certainly* didn't know what *I* wanted, and I'd never had any brothers so the sight of him threw me rather badly, and he didn't know what to do about my clothes—all that tulle and catches and snaps and elastic and things. Oh, it must have nearly driven him to tears! I just lay there, too scared to do anything for fear it would be the wrong thing. Then, when he finally got around to it, it was all over before I had any idea what had happened. He lay there, blowing like a porpoise, and I was still all worked up and I remember I thought, 'Well, this is no fun!'

"Of course, he was very awkward about everything afterward. We didn't go back to the ball. I was too much of a mess and he was probably pretty frightened. I think it must have been the first time for him, too. He went and called the chauffeur from the house and we went straight back to my house. He kissed me very gingerly at the door and then practically *ran* off! I went in the house and I remember I took a long time going upstairs. There was no one waiting up for me, though it wasn't much past midnight. I was calming down by then, but I was full of curiosity. I knew all about the biological business, the way they teach it at polite girls' schools, but my Lord! this was something else. I decided to talk to Daddy about it."

Once again Van Horn went tense and closed his eyes. "All right," he said. "Get it over with."

She didn't seem to hear him. There was a note of sadness in her voice. "Daddy was in bed," she said, "but I woke him up and sat on the bed and I thought he was just terribly sleepy, but afterward I realized he must have been drunk as a lord. I found out later his fight with Serena had ended with Serena going out alone and Daddy going to bed with a bottle. I tried to tell him what had happened to me and finally he seemed to understand. And he looked shocked. I told him I hadn't minded it, that I was all right, but I didn't understand it. I asked him all kinds of questions, but all he kept saying was, 'Poor little baby, poor little baby! You'll be all right.' And at last he fell asleep. I started to leave, but he woke up and wouldn't let me. He said he needed me with him, so I stayed there with him all night. I thought and thought about what had happened to me, but I couldn't make sense out of it, and toward morning I fell asleep too."

Van Horn took a deep breath and let it out slowly. He let his muscles relax a little. But she was not finished; there was more.

"Serena got back about six in the morning," she said, "and she came in and woke us up and raised Cain. I was sent off to my own room and I guess Daddy must have told her what I'd told him, though she'd have found out anyway with one glance at my dress. It was ruined. The same day I was packed off to a doctor, and sure enough, I wasn't a virgin any more. But it turned out I wasn't going to have a baby, so it was all right. Serena never said a word to me about it and I'm glad she didn't. She'd have turned the whole thing into something bad and rotten. Anyway she was busy making life hell for Daddy after that."

Flavia turned and looked at him then, saying, "So that's my true confession. That's the only other time. Oh, I've kissed boys and let them do a lot of things. I guess that's the foolishness of growing up. But you're my first lover. I'm glad I'm not your first mistress." She laughed delightedly. "Mistress! That's what I am, I'm your mistress. How nice!" She turned her head and kissed him.

After a while Van Horn drew away and said, "I've got a confession to make, too."

Flavia said, "I know! Your first love was a sheep. According to that nosy American doctor, it's quite—"

"Listen to me," he said, and the seriousness of his tone sobered her. She looked into his eyes in her peculiar intense way.

"Jud," she said, "are you going to tell me you went to bed with Serena?" She sounded perfectly calm, almost amused.

He looked at her in astonishment. "No," he said, a bit hoarsely, reddening. "But I nearly did. Which doesn't exactly make me proud of myself."

She kissed his shoulder. "Darling," she said, "I wouldn't mind if you had. I know what she is. I know how she works."

"My God!" he said. "You *are* something!"

"Serena's sort of pathetic, really," she was saying. "Sex is her one big weapon or key or whatever you want to call it. And she knows that in ten years or so it won't be much use to her any more. She was unfaithful to Daddy often. I knew that years ago, once I was old enough to see what was going on. I think Daddy knew it too, but he was a kind of man who'd never bring things into the open if he could help it, so it went on and on. Every man who ever came to our house was fair game for her. Even Mr. Brush, I think." She began to stroke his chest again. "So you mustn't feel badly. Lord, she must have thought you were the answer to a matron's prayer! You, you beautiful thing! And Serena was always hard to resist."

"I didn't resist much," he said. "I would have raped easy, as they say. But we were interrupted. Providence. Looking after the foolish and the randy."

"Why should you have turned her down?" Flavia said reasonably. "You're a man—God, what a man you are! And Serena's a handsome, well-kept woman. What did she do? Want to be consoled as the unhappy wife of a man who didn't love or understand her?"

"Something like that."

Suddenly he gathered her into his arms and began to laugh. It was a huge and happy laugh and it filled the room. The girl, crushed against him in his arms, drew her head back and smiled at him in bewilderment. "What," she asked him, "is so terribly funny?"

"I am, my darling," he said through his laughter. "I am! Madame, you have allowed yourself to be seduced by the dumbest biped in all of God's grand, green, gooey Creation!"

His laughter went on until she looked alarmed. "Please, Jud, what is it? What's the matter?"

He stopped long enough to kiss her many times, quickly, and said, "Nothing's the matter. Not now." Releasing her, he sat up in the bed, got his packet of Baltos from the bed table, and lighted one for each of them. Through a cloud of smoke, he said, "I mean it. I am the dumbest. All along I've been swearing up and down that your father must have had honest reasons for doing whatever he did that was crooked."

"I know," she said seriously. "I guess you and I are the only people in the world who think so."

"Sure," he said. "But with all my evangelical carrying-on, I didn't think it through clearly. I believe I can explain everything he did, but the most important thing of all, the thing he did that nobody saw, that he didn't *have* to do crookedly, I've just been *assuming* he did crookedly. I've been making a liar out of myself."

"Please, Jud," she said again. "What are you talking about? What do you mean?"

"I mean, my lovely Flavia," he said happily, "that I know where the plates are, must be."

"Well, good," she said, puzzled. "But what difference does that make?"

He turned to her. "Listen," he said. "If your father was acting honestly, then certain things have to follow. It has to follow that he made himself appear to be short of money so that Brush and your mother would consider him as a mark. I can't prove that, but I'll bet when they probate his will they'll find he hid a good deal of dough in various places, the way you can do in Switzerland. He also had to let your mother blackmail him into working for Brush. Between you and your mother, I think I can make a case for his having done that."

"Why?" she asked. "How? I don't understand."

"Serena accused him of having been your lover," Van Horn said easily. "She really thought he had been. From what you told me a minute ago, he knew perfectly well he hadn't."

The girl looked at him in blank amazement. Then she buried her face in her hands and said, "Serena did that? That's what she thought had happened that night? God, how vicious she is!"

"Was," Van Horn said. "Serena's pretty well shot at the moment. I think she's learned about the expense of spirit in a waste of shame. But we can talk about her later. What I'm trying to tell you is that I think it can be proved that your father deliberately got himself mixed up with Brush and Soloviev and the rest of them. For us. For the people I work for." He grinned wryly. "Now, if all this is true, what would he have done with the plates as soon as he got hold of them? To get hold of them, he had to doublecross everybody at once, and it'd be hard to imagine a more suicidal thing to do. Naturally he got rid of the plates immediately. And here we come to my spectacular display of stupidity. Because at this point I thought exactly what the others thought, the others who assumed he was crooked. I thought he'd arranged to send them where he could pick them up later. If he'd done that, having left us in the dark about where he sent them, he had to be crooked. If he wasn't crooked he would have told us where we could find them. He didn't tell us or leave a single hint. It has at last occurred to me why he didn't."

"Why didn't he?" she asked. "Stop being deliberately mysterious."

"Just a careful build-up, my girl," he said. "I want the shock of my revelation to obscure the fact that I should have thought of this three days ago."

She hit him on the chest with her fist in exasperation. "Go on!" she said. "Stop teasing me!"

He seized her fist and kissed it. "He didn't let us know where he sent the plates because he sent them to us. My guess is that right about now those two plates are in Paris in the possession of a colossally difficult character by the name of David Black."

"Your boss?"

"My boss. Whose men love him."

"Well, then," she said, stretching magnificently, "everything's going to be all right, isn't it?"

"Everything but the reception I'm going to get." He started out of bed. "A fine auto-da-fé that ought to be."

She caught his arm. "Where are you going?"

"To face the music, of course," he said. "Up betimes and down among my workmen and all that." But he didn't go farther.

She drew him back beside her. "Ah, no you don't. Plenty of music right here. Mr. Black can wait."

"A good thought," he said. "So he can." He sighed in resignation as he collected her to him. "Oh, well. And so to bed."

An hour later they were sitting, fully dressed, eating a monstrous late breakfast when the door to the sitting room opened quietly to disclose two large men in black overcoats and shapeless hats. They, guns in hand, covered Van Horn as the remains of Kirill Soloviev walked gingerly between them into the room. He was almost invisible under bandages and a sling, but his voice was the same, light and cultivated. He said, "Now, my dear, how *charming!* But you *have* put us to a great *deal* of trouble."

Van Horn, on his feet but tensely helpless, turned to the girl, who had not uttered a sound, and said, "Flavia, I'm sorry."

CHAPTER TWENTY-ONE

lack had just finished his lunch and was elegantly sipping coffee in his study. The room was, unlike the apartment's drawing room, meant for comfort, and it expressed its tenant thoroughly. The desk was imitation *Directoire,* but good imitation. The two hunting scenes on the walls were undistinguished, but the huge novelty silver key with the number "21" instead of teeth was really a gift corkscrew and bottle-opener and jigger from "21" in New York. The cup Black was drinking from was delicate and translucent and worth more than anything else in the room. The green leather Chesterfield he was sitting on was unabashed modern.

"Want some coffee?" he asked Van Horn, who stood somberly in the middle of the room.

Van Horn said, "No, thanks," and moved to lean back against the desk. He dug out his cigarettes and offered one to Black.

"Do you buy them crumpled that way," Black asked idly, refusing Van Horn's offer with a disdainful shake of his head, "or is crumpling them part of your charm?" He put down his cup and smiled. "You might as well start now. I'm going to enjoy listening to you justify yourself. Don't make me wait."

"You sent me to meet Trimble and get his report," Van Horn said around his cigarette. "You wanted the report by Wednesday morning. It's now Friday afternoon. Five men are dead that were alive Tuesday morning. But I have the report." He stopped.

"That won't do at all," Black said querulously. "I want the whole yarn." He smiled again. "You seem to forget you started this errand in trouble. You're in worse trouble now. Shoot. Straight."

"I'm in a hurry," Van Horn growled.

Black laughed harshly. "No, you're not, Van Horn. No, you're not." He waved his demitasse spoon. "Tell it all and make it good."

Suddenly Van Horn grinned humorously back at him. "All right," he said. "Cast your mind back to the year 1944, here, in Paris, in August."

Black's face went flinty. "Don't get fresh," he said. "You haven't got enough credit to get fresh."

Van Horn shook his head impatiently, "Just listen, then fire me at your leisure. In 1944 this city was freed by an Allied force spearheaded by Leclerc and the Free French. The Germans left a rear guard and the citizens blew their tops when they realized the end of the occupation had arrived. There was a lot of pretty dirty street-fighting. They've got little plaques all over town marking the spots where young hotheads with antique guns or just sling-shots got cut down by Germans."

"Get on with it," Black said. "I can read."

"There was also a lot of the usual looting during the uproar. Two of the places where the fighting was sharpest and the confusion was greatest, according to eye-witness accounts in the Swiss papers, were around the Banque de France and the Hotel des Monnaies. Somebody got into them. And the bank is where the money comes from, or Willie Sutton was a liar."

"You *are* on edge, aren't you? Real cocky. Go on."

"Well, so those plates are real. There were a set of fives and a set of tens. And what a nice prospect they must have presented!"

"All right," Black said. "So somebody was potentially rich. So what?"

Van Horn went on, "I can't prove much of this. Not yet But in 1948 the French raided a press in Antibes and caught the plates for the fives. Your buddies at the Ministry can tell you if those

were real. The government withdrew all fives and tens from circulation and the stolen plates for the tens went to earth. After
the fives and tens were reissued a few years ago, the people with
the tens went to work again. They had to work outside of France.
They found a paper manufacturer in Milan and an engraver in
Turin and an Englishman in Geneva, and they began to move.
The Englishman was a man named Brush who is just a crook for
hire. But he has some style and he recruited a bored and spoiled
Italian-American woman who felt her husband didn't pro-
vide enough dough. But he was an American. The woman was
induced to force her husband by a kind of blackmail into doing
the outfit's running. He used his passport to smuggle the inks
and paper, and finally the plates themselves, into Switzerland,
where the Englishman had a villa with a roomy cellar and no
objection to acting as front man and thus being a set-up for a
frame if anything went wrong."

"The American was Trimble, I suppose," Black said. "Your
old sidekick. The man you admired so much."

"Yes."

Black looked at him steadily. "And you're trying to tell me he
nobly allowed himself to be used as a common smuggler in order
to expose this counterfeiting gang."

"Yes."

"Why? Why'd he bother? Why didn't he just call the cops?"

"Lots of reasons. Until the plates were available, police
action would simply have sent the counterfeiters underground
again until the next time. Also, he didn't have time to set things
up so that he could blow the whistle without involving himself in a way he couldn't clear. He was as interested in keeping
himself clear as anybody would be. Also, he wanted not to be
killed, which he would have been within an hour if he'd tried
asking for some law. He was no martyr, just a good man. He
died, in the end, but I don't think he liked dying, if you see what
I mean."

"Any other reasons?" Black asked, still looking at him with no expression in his watery blue eyes.

"Yes. The people behind the counterfeiters were too big and too political."

Black let his breath out in a long "Ahhhh..." He dug out his cigarette case and one of his kitchen matches and blew a long streamer of smoke at the ceiling. "Go on," he said. "I want to hear you try to get yourself off the hook with this." His voice grew unctuous. "You weren't just swashing and buckling around acting like a jerk over there, you were really tracking down a political master plan of some kind. Go on."

Van Horn flushed and grunted with impatience. "That's right. I found Trimble shot and his report, if any, gone. But he'd been searched for something a hell of a lot bigger than a report, unless he'd taken to writing it on folio bond. I retraced his steps and found a card-carrier named Monselice, an engraver. I went a step further back and found a guy named Zerho who'd hired himself out to the Party in 1948. I went further and found a blush-pink friend of Mrs. Trimble whose husband is a paper manufacturer. Later I learned how big and complex and all-knowing the counterfeiters are. I saw how much the plates were worth in terms of human life. I learned by accident that the *Surveillance du Territoire* instead of the *Sûreté* was interested. That was odd. And finally I tumbled to the fact that the plates must be real. You might clear me up on that guess. They are real, aren't they?"

"Yes," Black grunted. "They're real."

"I felt they must be to command so high a price and if the Party was using them. I found Party members and sympathizers cropping up wherever I looked. Also I found no distribution set-up at all. They didn't need one because they already had one."

"Tell me about that. That sounds interesting." But Black did not look interested. He looked merely glum.

Van Horn stubbed out his cigarette in an ash tray from the Colony. "All they had to do was print a great mass of the queer using real paper, real inks, and real numbers already in circulation. Now how many card-carrying Party members are there in this country? A million? Hell, say its only half a million, it's still plenty. Give each of them two million francs in ten-thousand-franc notes. Tell them they have a week or ten days to spend it all. But they have to spend it on consumer goods only, on food and clothes and refrigerators and television sets and electric coffee grinders and wallpaper and cigars and booze and kitchen utensils. In a week or ten days the innocent middle class all over the country has been flooded with notes the banks have to redeem at first, because they're real as real, but that the Government can't honor without going handsomely bust. About a trillion francs' worth bust. A couple of billion dollars. It's a delicious idea. Time a move like that right—say when the strong man is sick or out of the country—and you could start anything from simple panic to a revolution. And the Party could only stand to gain."

Van Horn stopped and dug out another Balto and lighted it. Black said, "Very pretty. And Trimble fell into all this and played it cool, like they say, and was with us all the way?"

"Yes."

"Just how do you figure that?"

Van Horn snorted. "Because he sent you the plates. They're here, aren't they? Came in a package from Turin. *You* remember."

Black gestured elegantly toward the desk with his cigarette. "Yes," he said. "They're there, on the desk behind you."

Van Horn pulled Trimble's notebook out of his pocket and tossed it onto the coffee table. "Mission accomplished," he said. "Faithful old Dog Tray. A good retriever."

"Huzzah for old Dog Tray," Black said, leafing through the book. "It seems to be the veritable bacon. You expecting maybe a medal?" He stopped leafing and began to examine the notebook more closely.

Van Horn turned to the desk behind him, saying, "The Englishman, Brush, got hold of it when he killed Trimble." On the desk, among a collection of bestsellers and luridly covered paperbacks lay a copy of Fox's *Book of Martyrs,* huge and heavy and old, but not old enough to be of any real value. An English nineteenth century reproduction. It suited the room. Van Horn said, as he picked it up, "He must have taken the notebook simply because it was in cipher and looked potentially valuable."

"He may even have deciphered some of it, if he had any experience," Black put in. "It's pretty simple stuff."

Van Horn opened the top cover of the great book in his hands. It was almost an inch thick. The inside of the top edge had been cleanly slit. "Brush had experience," he said. "He was with M.I.6 during the war. Anyway, he made no mistake about me. Soloviev, the Party bigshot who's in charge of the operation, thought I was just a poor Government flunky who'd fallen over something juicy and was out to make a crooked buck. But not Mr. Brush. He sent a friend to give me the notebook, feeling sure once I had it he'd be rid of me."

While he spoke Van Horn carefully worked his big fingers into the slit in the book's cover and drew out the steel plate that was inside. The plate was beautifully engraved, a work of art in itself. He slid it back inside, checked to see that the other plate was inside the back cover, closed the book, put it under his left arm, and turned to face Black. "I've asked myself a few times how he knew he could get rid of me so easily. He's no dunce."

"Well," said Black, snapping the notebook shut, "now it's a matter for the cops, and I have a lot of reading material on my hands." He gazed blandly up at Van Horn. "And you still have a lot of explaining to do."

"I told you I was in a hurry," Van Horn said, gazing back as blandly. "You see, they have the girl. Flavia Trimble."

Black's gaze did not alter, but there was a moment of dead silence between the two men. At last he said, "You're crazy."

"Maybe," Van Horn said. "They caught up with us in a place about an hour from here. I wasn't careless, but it's hard to escape their intelligence network in this country. They've got at least half a million willing informers here. Anyway, they barged in on the girl and me, and I had to make a deal with them. They sent me to get the plates. I'm to call when I've got them. They'll let me speak to the girl, and Soloviev will tell me where to meet them to make the exchange. Any interference at all and the girl dies. I've seen them work. They aren't kidding."

Black said, "The girl's already dead, ten to one, and they're laying for you outside."

Van Horn shook his head. "No. They agreed not to follow me here and nobody did. I left the car I came in on the outskirts of town and took the Métro here. In the Métro, nobody could have picked me up. I'm in the clear for the moment. I'm going to try to get the jump on them when I leave here, but it's a very long shot." He stood away from the desk and his big right hand hung loose and dangerous. "I'll take whatever's coming to me if and when I get back. Right now all I know is they have the girl, they won't release her without the plates, and I have the plates under my arm. You going to try to stop me?"

Black did not look at the hand that hung inches from his jaw. He said, "Of course not. In fact, I'll help you."

Again there was a moment of silence between them. Van Horn's face was quite blank. He said finally, "I don't get it."

Black's voice went throaty with earnestness and sincerity. "It's real simple," he said. "You got to rescue that girl. Naturally. You can't do it without the plates. So naturally you have to take the plates with you. And there's no reason why our—uh—facilities shouldn't be put at your disposal. After all, we're human, you know. Same as you."

Van Horn looked baffled. He shook his head. He frowned. He started to speak, stopped, then began again. "No," he said. "This can't really be happening. What was in that coffee?"

Black went on, sweetly reasonable, "It's not right that you should have to go up against these people all alone like this. We can work out an arrangement."

Van Horn pulled himself together and said, "I don't under-stand you. But I can't let anybody help me. I've got to go it alone. Though I suppose I ought to thank you for the offer and for letting me have the plates." He had the look of a man who was breathing in a bad smell he couldn't identify.

"Not at all," Black said, with a languid wave of his hand. "You have to do what you have to do. Very well. If we can't help you, you go ahead, and good luck to you."

Van Horn began to pace in the small area between the desk and the coffee table. "This is crazy, and I don't believe it, but, whatever's behind what you're doing, thanks." He turned, almost pleading, toward Black. "Even with these plates, you know, Soloviev's outfit is in bad trouble. They're in France to begin with, and you know how to trap them here. I burned down their printing plant in Switzerland and they'll never be able to start up again over there. A couple of their best men are dead and Soloviev himself is half dead. The plates won't do them much good as things stand now."

Black smiled indulgently. "Please, boy. You don't need to jus-tify yourself. I understand absolutely. I'm getting to know you, boy."

Van Horn went on pleading. "If I can pass a miracle and make this thing work out right, you'll have something to hand the French that they ought to be very grateful for. You'll even have bested M.I.6."

Black looked less languid. "How's that?"

Van Horn told him briefly of his encounters with Sean Butler.

Black shook his head. "Rings no bells. I never heard of him. And M.I.6 here hasn't mentioned any special missions or this here Nigel Brush. But then, why in hell would they?"

Van Horn said, "Well, I better go while you're still out of your head this way. I'll need a gun."

"Take mine, boy. Take mine. It's in the desk drawer."

Van Horn found a big .38 automatic in the drawer and pocketed it after checking its load. Turning back to Black, he said, "You won't try to have me tailed, or interfere?"

"You've asked me not to, boy. Don't you trust me?" The look on Black's long, handsome face was that of a man who has just learned that his only son has turned against him.

"Well," said Van Horn, "maybe someday I'll figure you out. This is the fishiest thing that's happened yet, but I haven't time to go into it. So long."

"So long, boy," Black said, rising. "And be careful."

"God!" Van Horn said. "I can't stand any more of this." He bolted out the door.

CHAPTER TWENTY-TWO

H e caught the Métro at the Place de l'Alma and no one followed him. At the Châtelet stop he spent five minutes
walking swiftly from one transfer point to another in that teeming maze, then caught a train for the Porte d'Orléans. No one
could have traced him through the Châtelet. He was in the clear.
Fifteen minutes later he was in the Delahaye, away from the sea
of afternoon Paris traffic, on the road to Rambouillet. Five miles
from the cut-off to Montfort-l'Amaury he stopped at a roadside
restaurant that looked forlorn at this season, its terrace tables
grimy and uncovered, its greenery bare. Inside, the hard-faced
proprietress was alone behind the zinc. He approached her with
gallantry and money, and the combination worked, as usual.
She was, after all, willing to help him perpetrate a little pleas-
antry on some friends. If Monsieur was willing to pay decently
for such foolishness, she had no objection. Playing the part of a
long-distance operator with great skill and just the right amount
of bruskness and irritable confusion, she put in a "person-to-
person" call to Monsieur Soloviev at the Auberge de la Moutière.
Paris, she said, was calling. As Van Horn had warned her would
be the case, Monsieur Soloviev was not at the inn, but he had
left a number in Millemont, fifteen miles to the west, where he
could be reached. The woman called the number, argued with
somebody for a moment, got Soloviev on the phone and said,
"Quittez-pas, Monsieur. Alors, parlez, Paris," and she handed the
receiver to Van Horn.

He winked at her and made a great deal of noise with the phone, rattling it against the edge of the zinc. Then he said, "Hello. Soloviev?"

"Ah, Mr. Van Horn," the cultivated voice said tinnily in his ear. "You were successful?"

"Yes," Van Horn said. "It took longer than I thought it would."

"No trouble, I hope?"

"A little, but nothing you need to worry about. Let me talk to Miss Trimble."

"What sort of trouble?" Soloviev asked, losing his pleasant tone somewhat.

"Do you think what I just did was easy?" Van Horn said angrily. "For God's sake, man, I've just committed a kind of suicide. Now put Miss Trimble on the phone."

"Of course, of course," Soloviev said.

There was a pause, then Flavia's voice said, "Oh, Jud, don't do this thing! Don't let them—"

Van Horn cut in, "Are you all right, Flavia? Are you all right?"

"Yes, yes," she said. "No one has touched me. But please, Jud, don't think about me. Don't do this thing."

"It's done, my darling," Van Horn told her almost gaily. "Anyway, I couldn't not do it. Now let me talk to Soloviev again."

Soloviev said, "You see? Miss Trimble is quite well, though perhaps not happy. Now listen carefully and you will be able to resume your idyl in a very short time. You will come here."

"No," Van Horn said. "I will not come there. Do you take me for so great a fool as that? Neutral ground, Soloviev. Neutral ground."

The cultivated voice acquired an edge. "You can hardly expect us to agree to a point you select."

"Let's avoid a stalemate," Van Horn said. "Name a place. I'll come there. We both know I could give the directions to the police. We also both know that if I do the girl will be killed. On the other hand if you try to trap me I'll see to it you get no plates. Name a place."

There was a pause at the other end. The proprietress was looking at Van Horn with a flat, childlike stare of curiosity. He made a face at her. She looked away.

At last Soloviev's voice said, "Do you know the forest of Rambouillet?" and a look of satanic triumph spread over Van Horn's face.

His voice carefully even, Van Horn said, "Not well, but I know where it is."

"Of course you do. You will find your way to Dampierre. You will take the little road from Dampierre to St. Rémyles-Chevreuse. At a distance of three kilometers from Dampierre, you will find a very modest road that leads north. You will see an abandoned farmhouse a short way up this road. You will sound your horn four times outside the gate to this farmhouse. You will alight from your car unarmed and with the package. You will bear in mind that at the slightest sign of trickery, Miss Trimble will die, unpleasantly. Please do not strive to be clever. Is that clear?"

"All right," Van Horn said. "It's clear. But I'm smack in the middle of Paris. Give me time to get there. Don't get nervous if I'm a little late. I'll make it as fast as I can, but I don't want to risk being followed. It may take time."

"Very sound, Mr. Van Horn. We shall be as patient as we reasonably can."

"You better be," Van Horn said, with all the menace he could muster. "And you'd better be ready to deliver Miss Trimble in mint condition."

"Very humorously put, sir. We shall be ready."

"Let me talk to her again."

In a moment Flavia said, "Jud, this isn't right."

"Listen, darling," Van Horn said. "Go very carefully. Don't panic and don't worry any more than you have to. Your life's worth a lot more than these two steel plates. Don't fret if I'm a little late. Take your time. I have to come to you all the way from Paris. Do just as you're told. They know if anything happens to you they get no plates. They won't hurt you."

"All right, Jud," she said. She sounded tense but in control. "Be careful, please."

"So long," he said, and they hung up.

At the zinc, the proprietress said, *"Alors, ça a réussi?"*

"Magnificently!" Van Horn said jubilantly, thrusting another thousand francs at her. "It may turn out to be the best practical joke I ever played. They think I'm in Paris. Now I can beat them to our rendezvous and prepare an innocent surprise for them. Marvelous, *hein?*"

It took him twelve minutes to cover the fourteen miles from the roadside inn to Dampierre, and another four minutes to reach the little road that headed north. He pulled the Delahaye off the road a quarter of a mile beyond the farmhouse and got out with Black's gun in his hand and the big book under his arm.

Behind its wall the farmhouse looked absolutely desolate and empty, its windows blank, its interior shutters closed and fastened, no sign of life about it. Van Horn approached it as though it might at any instant explode in his face. He vaulted over the wall and paused, waiting, watching the house. But there was no one there. The drift of dirt and leaves on the doorsteps and windowsills was undisturbed. No one had entered it in weeks.

He circled the place completely before he found a window with a loose, half-rotten lock and forced it gently open, then as gently forced the shutter inside until its latch popped. He climbed inside and carefully closed the window and shutter behind him. Then he struck a match and looked around. On the sill of the window next to the one he had come through he found a stub of candle and lighted it. His breathing, rapid from tension, sounded loud in the lifeless air of the place.

There were only four rooms in the house and no loft. What little furniture there was had been amply chewed by mice; there was a frantic scurrying on all sides of him, outside the range of the candle's light, whenever he moved. Next to the big, cold fireplace that dominated the principal room, he found a lopsided bookcase containing the remains of a couple of dozen "Série Noire" thrillers, a Larousse, and an assortment of empty tobacco tins, moldy pipes, stubs of pencils, more candles, and two damp match boxes. He set the *Book of Martyrs* carefully in the midst of this, and blew over it gently a handful of dust and ashes from the fireplace.

For a couple of minutes then he merely stood in the middle of the room and looked slowly around. The front door was opposite the fireplace, beside which was the door to the big farm kitchen beyond. In the wall opposite the window he had climbed through was the low door to the two bedrooms beyond. A man standing with his back to the fireplace commanded the entire room, part of the kitchen, the front door and the door to the bedrooms.

On the smoke-blackened mantel were two cheap green pottery candlesticks and an imitation ormolu clock that had given up at ten past three on some long-gone day. Its face was partly obscured by mold. In the inch or two of space between its back and the chimney, Van Horn carefully propped Black's automatic, butt up, the safety off. He took a long look around the room. He had left no visible imprint anywhere. Wetting his fingers with saliva, he carefully snuffed out the candle so that it did not smoke. There was a slight odor in the room, under the heavy stench of mold and mildew, from the match he had lighted, but it was very faint. He let himself quickly out the front door.

Outside, all was quiet. He ran to the Delahaye, turned it around and headed it back toward Dampierre. Half a mile away from the farmhouse he pulled off and hid the big car as best he could in the naked brush and second-growth trees, twenty yards north of the road. Then he once again turned toward the farmhouse on foot, keeping well away from the road. A hundred yards from the farmhouse he found a clump of alders on a rise from which he could see the farmyard, the front of the house and, on his right, the intersection. He crouched in the chill of late afternoon. It was thirty-five minutes since he had hung up on Soloviev.

A farm truck passed on its way to Dampierre from St. Rémy-les-Chevreuse. Minutes dragged by. A 1927 Renault chugged by in marvelous antiquity on the way to St. Rémy. Then suddenly there was a dusty black Citroën turning up the little road to the farmhouse. It stopped and a man in a shapeless hat got out from behind the wheel and he and his colleague, each holding a gun, circled the house, then unlocked the front door and entered. In a moment, one of them came back outside and started gathering brush and windfalls for firewood. He went back inside. The other man came out, got into the Citroën and drove off toward Dampierre. Ten minutes went by. Smoke came out of the farmhouse chimney. More traffic passed on the road to Dampierre. Van Horn shivered and waited.

Two Citroëns appeared. The first drove straight into the farmyard, disgorged the man Van Horn had seen take it away and then a third man, this one tall and thin and without an overcoat or hat.

The second car paused at the intersection. A fourth man got out and found a hiding-place for himself behind the shrubbery that edged the road. The car drove on and turned into the farmyard. The thin, hatless man spoke to the driver, then went out the gate, closing it after him, and loped off up the road a short way and disappeared over a rise. The driver of the second car helped Soloviev to climb painfully from the back seat Then Flavia Trimble got out of the car and she and the two men went into the house. The driver of the first car went around the house to the rear.

Soloviev and the girl and five able-bodied men carefully scattered. Van Horn waited ten more minutes. Nothing happened.

He sighed and crabbed his way out of the alders and went back to the Delahaye.

Driving again to the farmhouse, Van Horn was careful to seem hesitant at the intersection, careful not to notice the man lying on his belly behind the hedge. He pulled the car up to the gate, honked four times, and got out. Dark was falling.

The gate swung partly open and a voice called, *"Viens. Laisses la voiture."*

His hands swinging free, Van Horn walked through the gate. One of the men with shapeless hats searched him thoroughly, then gestured with his gun toward the farmhouse. The front door stood open. Van Horn walked over and went through the door and the man closed it behind him.

The room was not as he had left it, but he did not let his eyes go too quickly to the bookcase and the mantel. Half a dozen candles had been lighted and two chairs had been pulled to the hearth where a fire was fitfully burning. The place smelt decently of woodsmoke now. Soloviev and Flavia sat in the chairs, Flavia half turned to look at Van Horn, but Soloviev facing the fire. The driver of the second car stood with his back to the wall between the two windows on the left. The big revolver in his hand was trained carefully on the middle of Van Horn.

Flavia said, "Oh, Jud, what have you done!"

"What had to be done," he said, smiling at her. He walked around to stand in front of Soloviev with his back to the fire. "I'm glad to see she is all right," he said.

"The package, Mr. Van Horn," Soloviev said faintly. He was huddled deep in the rickety chair, paler than ever. "Where is the package?"

"You didn't really expect me to bring it in here with me, did you?" Van Horn asked brightly. "That would have been clever. Then all you'd have had to do was kill Miss Trimble and me and go away. How stupid do you think I am?"

Soloviev seemed to be summoning the last shreds of his stamina. He sat a little straighter in his chair, but his voice was fainter than ever. "Where is the package?"

From the farmyard came the sound of the Delahaye being pulled in and parked. The gate clanged shut.

"Listen, Soloviev," Van Horn said. "I'm an outlaw now. I became an outlaw the instant I stole the plates. Being an outlaw, I don't find Miss Trimble's life a high enough price for the merchandise I have to sell. I want money, too. Lots of it. In cash. *Real* money, I might add."

Flavia Trimble gasped and said, "Jud, what—"

The front door opened and the man who had opened the gate for Van Horn came in, saying, *"Rien dans la voiture. Rien du tout."* He took a position with his back to the door, and he, too, kept his gun trained on Van Horn.

"How much money?" Soloviev asked.

"Jud, please!" Flavia said. "Don't do this!"

"About fifty thousand dollars," Van Horn said. "In cash. American currency. Small bills. The usual thing." He managed to extract his Baltos from his pocket without being shot, stuck one in his mouth and said in French to the two men with guns, "Don't be nervous. I need a light." He turned his back on them and lighted the cigarette at one of the candles on the mantel. Black's gun still lay behind the clock where he had put it.

Soloviev obviously was able to speak only with the greatest physical effort. His voice was scarcely more than a whisper. He said, "How very tiresome you are, my dear. You have no bargaining power at all. Truly you don't. For while you may have the plates, we have you and the girl. There is no question of your courage, of course. We know your mettle. But there is Miss Trimble. My men are strong, and they have, I am afraid, no delicacy of feeling whatever. They have many hungers men are heir to. I have only to liberate them from—"

Van Horn laughed. "Do you really think that will make me blench to the teeth and agree to anything? You know damned well you'd have to kill me before anybody could touch the girl. You had your chance to harm her while I was gone. Now I'm here. If any of your chums goes near her somebody's going to have to kill me. Then you get no plates, ever. So let's stop talking claptrap. Send somebody for the money. Fifty grand." He laughed again. "Fifty grand! Listen to me! I haven't been an outlaw two hours and I'm already talking like the late Mr. Zerho."

Flavia suddenly spoke. "Jud, what has happened to you? You mustn't do this." She seemed stunned and puzzled and at the same time half angry.

Van Horn beamed at her. "Man cannot live on love and self-righteousness alone, darling. We've got to have the means to move."

Soloviev said, "And if I refuse?"

Van Horn turned to him in exasperation. "Wake up, Soloviev! Can't you see what's happened? This is a Mexican stand-off. We can sit here dickering for days on end. Or you can make a move toward Miss Trimble that ends this whole deal and leaves you where you were the day before yesterday. Or you can simply send for the money, pay me, get the plates, and go off about your business. Send for the money and let's get this over with. I hate the stink of heliotrope."

Silence fell. Soloviev closed his eyes. Flavia Trimble turned her face away from Van Horn and stared wretchedly into the kitchen. Without opening his eyes Soloviev asked, "If I have the money brought here, how long shall I have to wait for the package?"

"Not long," Van Horn said. "Not long at all." He grinned. "Come on, man. Resign yourself. The Party can spare fifty thousand. To make a couple of billion."

Another silence fell. The two men against the walls stood motionless. If they had understood a word of what had been said they gave no sign. Their guns did not waver. They did not even appear to breathe or blink. Flavia Trimble punctured the silence with a long sigh of great sadness, and Van Horn glanced toward her quickly, his face betrayed into a look of real concern. Then his mask of indifference returned and he lounged against the mantel again.

At last Soloviev gently inserted his good hand into his jacket and drew out a notecase and a gold pencil. "You will have to assist me, my dear," he said to Van Horn.

"My pleasure," Van Horn said and squatted beside him to hold the little notecase pad steady on Soloviev's knee. Soloviev carefully penciled a note, then said, "Franco." The man by the front door moved to him and Van Horn backed away. Soloviev gave the man the note, folded, and muttered instructions to him. The man nodded and moved to the front door and went out. Soloviev said, "He will return within two hours. Then, my dear, we shall have an end to this."

"Suits me," Van -Horn said amiably. Outside a car started up and the gate to the barnyard creaked open. Van Horn said in French, "I would like to be sure he really leaves. Don't shoot me. I am going to look out the window."

Soloviev nodded to the man by the window and he stood aside as Van Horn walked over and opened the shutters and leaned close to the rippled, clouded glass. One of the Citroëns was pulling out of the barnyard. There was one man in it. Van Horn watched it as it moved to the intersection. It paused there while the driver spoke to the man behind the hedge, then it sped off toward Dampierre. Van Horn watched it out of sight in the gathering darkness. He was drawing back into the room and reaching for the shutters to close them again when he glanced toward the clump of alders on the rise a hundred yards distant where he had waited earlier. There was a vague flicker of movement there, hardly more than a shadow. Then, as Van Horn was closing the shutters, a small, slight figure without an overcoat drifted out of the clump of alders and moved off to Van Horn's right, crouching low.

Van Horn fastened the shutters and turned back into the room. "All right," he said. "Nothing to do now but wait." He returned to his position in front of the mantel and looked down at Flavia. "Honey," he said, and when she had raised her eyes to his, "try to trust me. A little while longer."

"I—I just don't understand," she said.

"Don't bother to try," he told her seriously. "Only trust me."

"All right, Jud," she said.

Soloviev sniggered feebly. "Terribly touching," he said. "It almost makes one wish one weren't *de la troisième*—" Two shots sounded outside, one a heavy roar, the second, a flat crack. In the little candlelit room a great many things seemed to happen at once. Soloviev rasped an order in French to the man by the window who moved to Flavia and seized her arm. At the same time Van Horn snaked Black's gun out from behind the clock and threw down on the man holding Flavia, saying loudly, "Drop the gun and get away from her!" The man seemed to hesitate, then moved back and tossed his gun aside. Van Horn said, "Flavia, get into the next room, block the door with whatever you can find and lie down on the floor. *Move!*"

The girl fled. Soloviev cried out, "Martin!" There was movement in the kitchen and the man stationed at the rear of the house came in, his gun in his hand. Van Horn whirled to his left and shot the man in the throat. The man pitched forward on his face, dead on the instant. But Van Horn's moment of command was gone. The man he had ordered away from Flavia, in the instant of Van Horn's turning, had scooped his discarded gun from the floor and now flung himself on Van Horn's back. For a few seconds they stood locked, Van Horn's gun hand pinned to his side. Then, as Van Horn braced himself to break free, the man suddenly released him and brought his gun down on the back of Van Horn's head.

The little period of compressed time, confusion, violence and noise was abruptly cut short as Van Horn, stunned, dropped Black's gun and fell heavily to the floor. The gun skidded under a chair. Time now became elongated and ponderous. The man who had struck Van Horn knelt on his back. He doubled Van Horn's arms up high behind his his back and held them there with one hand while with the other he put the muzzle of his gun against the base of Van Horn's skull.

Soloviev unsteadily inched his way to his feet and managed with slow care to get his tiny pistol into his good hand. The blood of the corpse in the kitchen doorway spread richly over the floor. The room was resonant with the heavy breathing of the three living men in it.

The front door opened and the tall thin man entered, gun in band, half-dragging the small, slight figure of Sean Butler, who staggered at his side. Butler's arms hung loose and his face was entirely obscured by blood. The tall thin man surveyed the room and muttered, *"Ah, pauvre Martin!"* when he saw the corpse in the kitchen door. He flung Butler across one of the spavined chairs, and said to Soloviev, *"Ce crapule a tué Prosper. Vous voulez que je le tue?"* Butler lay on the chair where he fell. He looked dead already.

Soloviev said, *"Non. C'est possible qu'il peut être utile."*

Soloviev turned to look down at Van Horn, who lay without struggle under the weight of the man on his back, looking painfully ungainly with his arms pinned high behind him. His eyes were open; his face was blank.

Soloviev said, "You chose to be clever, Mr. Van Horn. You and your friend here. And that is too bad. You secreted a weapon in this room before we arrived here. You must also have secreted the package here. Now your choice is very simple. You and your friend are doomed, of course. We know that you would gladly die before giving us satisfaction, and consequently I shall not attempt to make inducements. But we are short of time now.

There has been too much noise and activity here. So this is your choice: Tell me where the package is and I shall release the young lady. Otherwise I send my man into the next room to take what delight he can in Miss Trimble while you watch. It should be an easy choice, my dear."

Van Horn looked toward Butler and said, "Let the girl go, first." Butler's face was still invisible under its coat of blood but he was breathing evenly. His head hung awkwardly sideways, over the chair arm, facing Van Horn.

Soloviev said, "Nonsense. You would then merely face death contentedly. No. This is once you must accept my word. First the package, then the girl goes free." He nodded to the tall thin man, who stepped to the door the girl had left through. "Otherwise ... "

Van Horn continued to stare at Butler and appeared to be thinking. Then, as he watched, the red mask that was Butler's face cracked perceptibly. One bright blue eye opened very slightly, and very slightly but definitely it winked at Van Horn.

Van Horn looked at Soloviev and said, "I'm no *voyeur*. The plates are in the big book on the shelf there."

Soloviev turned and stepped to the bookcase. He laid his pistol on the top shelf to handle the cumbersome *Book of Martyrs*. He lifted it and laid it beside the pistol and opened the top cover. He found the first plate in the inside of the cover and began to finger it out of the binding. The eyes of the tall thin man were on Soloviev. The man on Van Horn's back twisted himself slightly to watch. "Ah," Soloviev said. "That's better."

At that instant Van Horn shouted, "Now!" and shook himself like a whip, rolling in a half somersault on his left shoulder, throwing the man on his back toward Soloviev. The man, as he was thrown, fired his gun. The bullet took off the lobe of Van Horn's left ear. Once more time became compressed, mad with action, full of noise. Soloviev tried to put down the book and retrieve his pistol, but the man Van Horn had thrown tumbled into him and he was knocked hard against the bookcase. He yelped with pain. The tall thin man strode toward the tumbling group by the bookcase, but as he passed Butler's chair Butler uncoiled and flung himself like a projectile, hitting the tall man in a ludicrous kind of body block and they both crashed to the floor. The room now came to seem full of arms and legs and guns and thuds and grunts and gasps. Van Horn, once released from his man, threw himself sideways to grope for the gun of the man he had shot earlier. The weapon was sticky with blood. He swung it toward the man he had thrown and fired, too fast. The bullet hit the *Book of Martyrs,* where Soloviev had set it down. Soloviev and the man who had tumbled into him were by now disentangled. The man, rolling, fired at Van Horn, but he too was rushed and the bullet went wide, smashing a window on the other side of the room. Van Horn fired a second shot, more carefully, and this one took its target full in the chest as the man was in the act of squeezing off another round. He was dead when he fired, his bullet striking the floor in front of him. Sitting as he was, with his back against the bookcase, he didn't fall but went on sitting, in an attitude of relaxation, his eyes open and a look of mild concentration on his face. During all of this, Butler and the tall thin man were thrashing noisily about near the bedroom door.

Soloviev had his little pistol in hand now. He fired twice at Van Horn from a distance of seven feet. The first shot missed, the second struck Van Horn in the left shoulder, causing Van Horn's third shot to go wild. Soloviev pulled the trigger again and the little gun, far too small to be reliable, jammed. Soloviev cursed in a piercing falsetto, hurled the little gun at Van Horn, missed him, and burst into tears. Van Horn swung to his right as the tall thin man pulled away from Butler, who now lay dead or stunned on the floor. Van Horn emptied his gun at the tall man. For a moment the bullets appeared to have had no effect, although the man did not raise his own gun or do anything, in fact, but stand like a pole, facing Van Horn. Then, like a pole, he crashed straight over backward, not collapsing in sections but falling all of a piece on top of Butler.

Time slowed again. Soloviev leaned sobbing against the bookcase. The air was thick with the stink of smokeless powder. Van Horn, on his hands and knees, blood soaking the left side of his body and dripping viscously from his ear, began to retch. Under the body of the tall thin man, Butler groaned and said, "Really, this is too much by half. Dear oh dear oh dear." He emitted a high whinny of laughter.

Van Horn began to suck great breaths into his lungs, and gradually the retching subsided.

Soloviev made no move to carry the action any further. He did not, however, stop sobbing. Tears streaked the makeup on his narrow face.

Butler was having difficulty struggling free of his burden. "Come now," he was saying. "I refuse to survive the war only to be smothered by a casualty. Really, this is too much! Much too much!"

Favoring his left side, Van Horn managed to rise precariously to his feet. He surveyed the field, his face stony and very white. Then he drew one more great breath into him and walked heavily through the room like some monstrous housekeeper, picking up guns. There were seven in all: the three belonging to the men he had killed, his own, Soloviev's useless toy, and two others he found in the tall man's clothes, apparently taken from Butler. He put all but his own on the mantel. Then he stepped to the tall man and pulled him off Butler. Butler slowly got to his feet.

He and Van Horn stood swaying and regarded one another. They were fantastically gory, particularly Butler who had been liberally bled on by the tall man. Butler's sanguine countenance split in a smile. Against the sticky redness, his eyes and teeth were more brilliant than ever. "Never lack for fun, do we, you and I?" he said. "We've only to get together, it seems, and we find ourselves with any amount to do. Bloody but unbowed, what?"

Staggering slightly, he made his way to the bookcase. Nudging Soloviev idly to one side, he picked up *The Book of Martyrs.* "Bit of a hole in this, but the *objets d'art* seem intact. Jolly good." He tucked the book under one arm and with his free hand began to swab blood from his face with a big handkerchief he took from his trouser pocket. He stepped toward the mantel, saying, "We better get a move on, you and I. Wouldn't do to be here when the *gendarmerie* comes galloping up, late as usual, to see what all the din and gaiety's been about, now would it? Four dead men and a weeping pansy to explain would be a touch thick, eh?"

Van Horn finally spoke. He said, "Don't bother." He had to clear his throat before he could get the words out clearly.

Butler stopped and turned, saying, "What say?" Then his eyes opened wide as he found himself staring at the muzzle of Black's automatic as Van Horn held it steadily pointed at the little man's chest. "Here, now," he said in a reproachful tone. "What's this?"

"Don't move," Van Horn said with a sigh. "I've killed three men in the past five minutes. I don't enjoy the pastime. But I'm willing to go on if I have to. Don't move." Without turning his head, he shouted, "You can come out now, darling, the battle's over!"

Butler frowned and went on wiping his face, but he moved no nearer the mantel. In the next room, where the girl had fled, furniture was scraped across the floor. The door opened and Flavia Trimble, very pale, stepped into the room.

At sight of Van Horn's blood-soaked state she cried out, "Jud! What's—" Then she saw his gun pointing and followed its direction and she saw the little man, who had finished a poor job of cleaning his face by now, and she said, after a moment's pause, "Hello, Nigel."

And Nigel Brush laughed his high whinny of laughter and said, "Ah, well, then. I expect that's that. Hello, Flavia, dear."

CHAPTER TWENTY-THREE

Once more Black and Van Horn confronted one another across the parquet of Black's salon. Once more the autumn sunlight poured through the tall windows. But this time Black was wearing a violent foulard dressing gown over an open shirt, ascot and flannel bags, for it was Sunday morning and he was the very model of a modern minor diplomat at his ease. His black slippers gleamed brighter than the parquet.

Van Horn was dressed much as he had been the previous Tuesday except that the left side of his head was covered by a large white bandage and his left arm was in a sling inside his old Alligator.

Flavia Trimble sat rather primly on one of the room's unyielding tapestried chairs, her gloved hands folded in her lap, her eyes apprehensively fixed on Black, who was saying, "How'd he give himself away? A smart man like Brush?"

Van Horn said, "Well, as Sean Butler of M.I.6 he puzzled me in several ways. Too many guns, for one thing, and he used them far too freely. Back in the chalet, he was going to polish off Soloviev until I talked him out of it. That sort of thing is hardly characteristic of our British friends.

"But mainly I think it was the business of Zerho turning up so aptly with Trimble's notebook. I'd only told Butler that the notebook was all I was interested in. Yet somehow Brush knew it too, and was sure he could get rid of me by giving it to me. Very fishy." Van Horn paused and shrugged. "Then, of course, there was that laugh."

"Laugh?" Black asked. "What laugh?"

"Why, a kind of silly, whinnying guffaw that sounds very English for some reason. Flavia and I heard it by the train in Bardonecchia. I heard it again when I interrupted Brush in Flavia's hotel room in Turin. I heard it last as Butler was trying to get out from under a corpse in that farmhouse on Friday. Brush had always been around, I knew that, and he'd always been a jump ahead of me. It seemed impossible that I hadn't seen him. Easiest explanation was that I had. As Sean Butler. When I saw him slipping up to the farmhouse on Friday I got Flavia out of the room, knowing that if my hunch was right Flavia would recognize him and he might kill her out of hand to stop her identifying him. There was the chance someone else would give him away, but having seen him at work I didn't doubt for a moment he could handle any number of Soloviev's men and Soloviev too. If he was to be any use to me he had to believe I still thought he was Sean Butler. After the battle I made sure he was unarmed and let nature take its course. He's quite a guy."

Black smiled brightly at Flavia Trimble. "All very neat and logical, isn't it, Miss Trimble?" The smile disappeared and he turned back to Van Horn. "What would you have done if Brush hadn't turned up to give you backing? What would you have done?"

Van Horn reddened slightly and frowned. For a moment he fingered the bandage on his ear gingerly and looked at the floor. Then he said softly, "There was only one thing I could do. I'd got rid of one of their men by having him sent for money. I meant to hold out for their letting Flavia take the Delahaye and drive away. Then I was going to go for your gun and run the string out as far as I could."

Flavia spoke at last She said, shocked, "Oh, Jud!"

Black looked at her fondly again. "Such bravery, eh?" he said. "Such sacrifice! It's like in one of those novels by what's-his-name, Dickens—real noble." He laughed.

Van Horn's frown grew darker. He said, "I had a good chance. They had no idea I had a weapon near me. They were being watchful but not really too alert. And we were at very close quarters, which is always a help in that kind of a pitched battle, as it proved to be when the fight did start. I had a good chance." He looked up at Black stonily and added, "Anyway, I had the plates hidden in the room in case they were needed. I knew they were worthless, so I could have given them to Soloviev if I'd been forced to. They were one last diversion left to me."

Black's face had assumed its look of outraged innocence. "What do you mean, worthless? You know damned well they're real."

Van Horn grinned at him. "Sure they are," he said. "But I know damned well you'd never have let me take them if they really were worth anything." Awkwardly he got a Balto out of his pocket. Flavia rose and came to him and lighted it for him. He smiled at her and said, "This is the redoubtable David Black, darling. He's as sentimental and awash with the milk of human kindness as any other headsman. When I came here to take the plates by force, in order to buy you back from Soloviev, you would have cried real tears to hear him sympathize with our predicament. He insisted I take the plates and play the whole thing my way. He offered any help he could give, but he didn't insist when I told him I didn't want help. Oh, it was the most touching performance I ever saw. I worried about it all the way back to the country."

Black, fiddling with his cigarette case and one of his big kitchen matches, looked more hurt than ever. "Miss Trimble, I ask you! I'm a sympathetic man. One of my boys comes to me with a situation like the one you were in, how can I do anything but sympathize? Like I said at the time, those plates weren't worth sacrificing a good young American life for. I only did what any decent man would do under the circumstances. Now hé twists it all to make me out some kind of a beast. I ask you!" Black turned away, not actually biting his lip, but with the same air of controlling hot tears.

Flavia Trimble looked completely baffled and said to Van Horn, "Jud, what are you talking about?"

Van Horn put his good arm around her and said, "Darling, I have been in trouble with my superiors for some time because I can't seem to take the deadly attitude toward people that they like their employees to take. I was by way of being fired. The people in Washington sent me over here to work for the toughest man in the whole lash-up, who is David Black. He was told to straighten me out or get rid of me. He started by trying to humiliate me by sending me on the kind of errand new boys are sent on. I was sent like any messenger to meet your father and pick up his report. I went. Then the errand turned out to be something bigger so they recalled me. But my replacement was killed before he could take over and I carried on as best I could. I managed to get back here with what I'd been sent for and I even seemed to have unraveled something rather big. Everything was fine. But then, bango! I went all soft again. I had let you be taken by the other side, and instead of shrugging you off and letting it go at that, as the proper code of behavior dictates I should, I proposed to bail you out at the possible expense of the plates your father died to get hold of. I came here fully expecting to have to fight my way loose. I knew Black would certainly kill me before he'd let me foul things up. Instead I got a fatherly pat on the shoulder, and I got the plates. There could be only one explanation. The plates were worthless. If I lost them and you were killed, perhaps I'd learn my lesson—that having human feelings is the worst weakness of all. On the other hand, if I lost the plates and was killed myself, nothing would be lost but an agent who'd pretty well shown he was valueless. It was a nice scheme. Either I came out a sadder but wiser man, hardened by losing you, or I wouldn't come out at all and *tant pis.* Thanks to Brush I got away with the whole works—you and the plates and Soloviev and Brush and my own life. It must be galling our host here pretty badly. Now he'll have to find another way to rehabilitate me. Or he'll have to fire me." He subsided. Black was still turned away, his shoulders slumped.

The girl shook her head. "I can't believe it."

Van Horn said, "Ask him."

The girl turned to Black and asked, "Is it true?" She looked very stern, her dark eyes hotly accusing. "Is it true, Mr. Black?"

Black turned back and held out his elegant hands in a gesture of supplication. "Please," he said, "keep in mind I'd never met you. What I'd of done if I had known you as I do now, I can't say. But—" He shrugged and dug in his dressing-gown pocket and drew out a banknote and held it toward the girl. She took it from him and she and Van Horn examined it. It was a ten-thousand-franc note on the Banque de France, very beautifully done as always, but not much larger than a dollar bill. Van Horn laughed. The girl grew red and looked back at Black as though she had never seen anything like him before.

Black said airily, "The French had given up. They knew those plates were loose, and they knew that as long as they were loose they were always a bad threat. The economy of this country has been a pretty delicate thing. It costs a lot of money to change money, if you see what I mean. So they put off issuing these new little bills as long as they could. But then there were some rumors about a new bunch that were working in Italy and Switzerland and had the plates. So the French finally moved. All the big old tens will be gradually withdrawn starting in about ten days." He sighed and looked sorrowful. "Miss Trimble, I don't expect you to understand. This is a hard world, and Van Horn and I are in the hardest work there is in it. I had my duty and I did it. I had to try to teach Van Horn his duty. You don't suppose I liked doing it, do you? Why, my men are like sons to me! But it had to be done, so I did it." He hung his head and stared miserably at the floor. "I hope you won't hold it against me. I'd hate that."

Van Horn choked slightly, apparently on his cigarette.

Flavia Trimble's look of revulsion softened and she chewed at her lip.

Black went on sadly, "Somebody has to do this work. Somebody has to protect our country's interests. Van Horn and I have the privilege of doing it." He raised his handsome head and gazed with stunning sincerity at the girl. "And remember this— Van Horn is one of our finest men. We like him and we want him and we need him. I'd of been doing him a great wrong if I hadn't put him to this test. I'm only glad he came out of it okay and you did too. I hope you'll forgive me."

The girl said, "I don't know. It seems wrong. There's something wrong. But I won't hold it against you."

Black smiled tremulously and said, "Ah, thank you for that, my dear!" He stepped to her and wrung her hand. "If I had a daughter I'd want her to be like you. You're an admirable young lady and you make me very happy."

"Oh, boy!" Van Horn said at last. "Let's get out of here, Flavia." He bowed to Black. "If you'll excuse us, sir."

Black waved a hand. "Sure, sure. You young people run along. Enjoy your youth. But just remember one other thing, Miss Trimble." He had her hand in both of his now and was looking deeply into her eyes. "I'm always here to help you. Your father was one of us and it's a great sadness to me to have lost him. I'd like to think that you'll turn to me now in your times of need. I'll be ready to help you any way I can." He released her. "Now go along and have a fine time."

Van Horn steered the girl to the door as fast as he could without actually pushing her. She said over her shoulder, "Good-by, Mr. Black. And—uh—thank you."

Out in Black's foyer she said, "Jud, this is all crazy. Everything is turned upside down."

He bent and kissed her lightly. "Don't worry about it. You have just been treated to a performance by a real master. You must expect to be overwhelmed."

Black's voice came from the salon behind them, calling, "Van Horn! One last thing, please!"

Van Horn sighed. "Well, we almost made it," he said. He left the girl and went back into the salon and closed the door.

Black was lounging by one of the tall windows. He didn't look at Van Horn. "I'll see you in my office at nine in the morning, so don't oversleep."

"All right," Van Horn said. He turned to leave, but at the door Black's voice stopped him again.

"And Van Horn," he said.

"Yes?"

"Take care of yourself, boy."

"Oh, for God's sake!" Van Horn said and went out the door. Black's laughter followed him out. Van Horn got the girl and they left. As the heavy door swung shut behind them, Black's laughter still sounded inside.

Out on the sunny street by the Seine, the girl took a deep breath and leaned against Van Horn. "I don't suppose I'll ever really understand," she said. "But I feel very glad about everything anyway."

Van Horn kissed her and said, "I'll explain it all someday. God knows, we've got world enough and time."